The Potter's Story

The Potter's Story

A NOVEL

A Journey of Unexpected Turns,
Second Chances, and the Power of Purpose

ISOEBELLA LUCAS

MSRUBIA

The Potter's Story

First Edition

ISBN: 978-621-06-2164-8

Published by Isoebella Lucas

hello@isoebellalucas.com

www.isoebellalucas.com/contact-the-author

To stay connected: www.isoebellalucas.com/letters

Printed in the United States by Amazon KDP

This version was prepared specifically for Amazon distribution.

For my father, who knew me well.

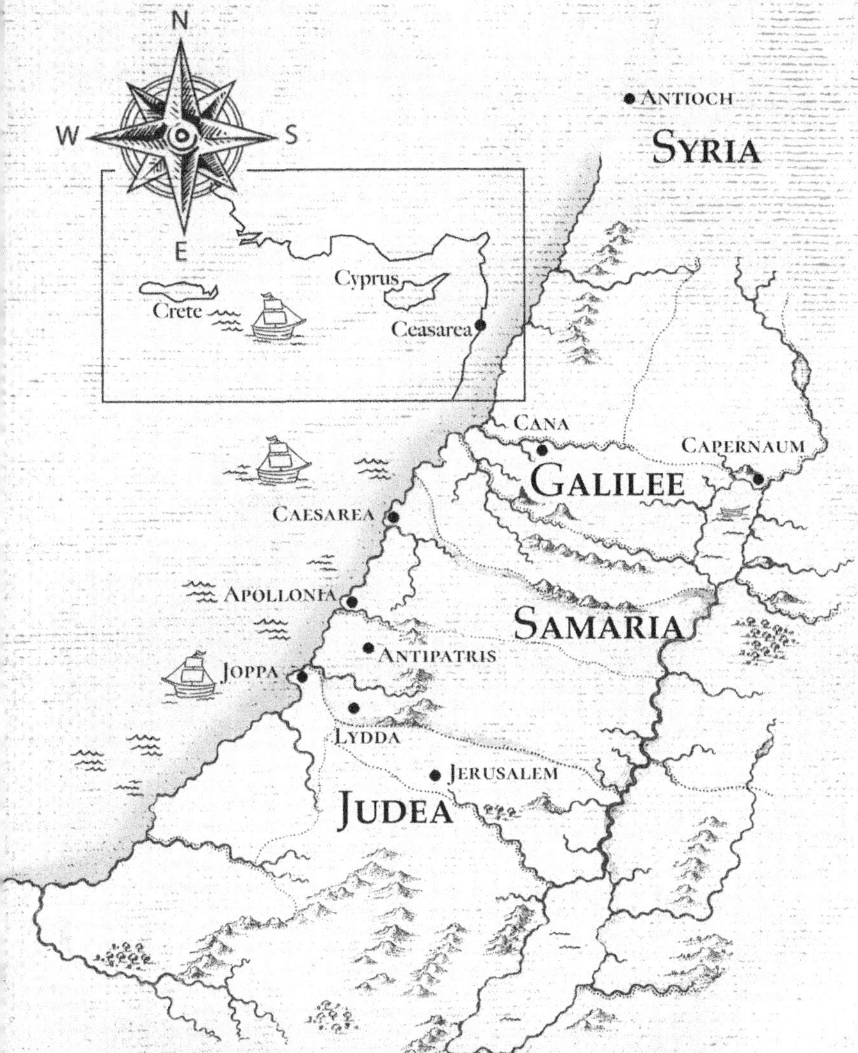

Judea-Galilee Map

CONTENTS

Preface xi

1. Bowstring 1
2. Caesarea 11
3. Truth 22
4. Blue 37
5. Janus 48
6. Dan 62
7. Samir 74
8. Joseph 86
9. Cana 94
10. Caravanserais 107
11. Journal Entry 1 116
12. Trust 121
13. Journal Entry 2 137
14. Journal Entry 3 143
15. Family 146
16. Jerusalem 160
17. Travelers 175
18. Journal Entry 4 182
19. The Unexpected 185
20. Mercy 203
21. Transformation 211
22. Treasure 224
23. Journal Entry 5 234
24. Beginnings 237
25. Tyche of Antioch 248
26. Amos 255

About the Author 261
Production Notes 263

PREFACE

There comes a time when leaving is no longer the answer. When the buried past begins to resurface, not as a weight, but as a call that can no longer be ignored.

Years have passed since he walked away, carving out a new identity far from the place that once defined him. Yet no distance can erase the unfinished work left behind. Some journeys are not about escape but about return, not about leaving something behind, but about seeing it with new eyes.

The road back is never as simple as retracing one's footsteps. It is a reckoning, a confrontation with truths long buried beneath silence and time. Certain burdens linger, waiting to be acknowledged, while other legacies demand a response, no matter how far one has gone.

In a land restless with uncertainty, where decisions carry unseen consequences, his return is not merely the crossing of seas. It is a collision of past and present, the forging of something unknown, something meant to endure.

Life is a dance between divine purpose and human choice, where every decision not only shapes everything that follows but reveals its purpose in its own time.

The journey forward is rarely simple and often demands a willingness to make extraordinary choices.

1

BOWSTRING

WITH EACH ARROW RELEASED, JONATHAN SENT A PRAYER ACROSS THE sea, not for accuracy, but for redemption. With eyes closed and the bowstring drawn to his cheek, he shot his arrows at a mark he did not care to see.

He had perfected this ritual over six years of exile.

Every arrow carried the weight of a runaway son's regret and the desperate hope for forgiveness from a father who might never grant it. The bow in his hands wasn't merely wood and string; it was the bridge he constructed between the boy who fled and the man who yearned to return home.

He opened his eyes just as the arrow embedded itself directly in the center of the mark. With a sigh, Jonathan strode toward the target, the weight of his dream lingering in his consciousness, uninvited. He couldn't shake off last night's dream about his father. He had dreamed of him for several months, but last night's dream felt different and more urgent.

As in previous dreams, he couldn't recall what the dream was about, but it left him with a lingering sense of fear.

He chuckled softly. *I am pretty familiar with fear, especially when it comes to Father.* He shook his head at the thought of his famous father, the stern man who demanded perfection in everything and everyone.

Jonathan reached the mark and, for a few seconds, stared at the arrow stuck in the center of the mark. He pulled it free with a single, firm tug and began his walk back to the shooting line. His intention had never been about hitting the mark, but only about the balance of the bow he had created.

With his eyes closed, he could focus on and feel the bow's arms much better as they bent from the draw. He needed to feel every movement in his bow. Closing his eyes helped him visualize how every part of his bow responded to his draw. He would feel his back and arm muscles adjust and move automatically for each shot.

Archers called it muscle memory; his arms and back had it, but he was not an archer. He was a bowyer, a proud bow maker who crafted bespoke bows for Crete's high society and the top Roman military officials assigned to the island, a fact he believed his father would have difficulty accepting.

He made bows that were magnificent to the eye and deadly in capable hands. Nothing amazed him more than a cut of wood that could bend without shattering into pieces. It was almost magical, he thought. *How can something so beautiful be so lethal at the same time?*

He reached the shooting line and stood ready to draw again.

Staring at the mark, he stretched the bowstring as far as it would go and felt the wood resist. He closed his eyes, took a deep breath, and released his pull. He opened his eyes just in time to see that it was another direct hit, but something didn't feel right.

He checked the bowstring to ensure the tension was sufficient. He hoped his last-minute change to the brace height would improve the bow's performance and accuracy. *It was working, but something didn't feel right, and he couldn't explain why.*

He felt helpless, and his anger began to rise.

The last few pieces assigned to him would go to the top commanders of the Roman army. They all had to be perfect. With several bows still to complete before his journey, each delay chipped away at his patience. His jaw clenched.

The wind unraveled a few strands of his hair, brushing against his cheek like an uninvited whisper. He shoved them away, irritation simmering. It was precisely why he had grown his hair to mid-length so that he could tie it all back, but it still wouldn't stay in place.

His life was a constant struggle for control and order, like his hair. Making bows was the only space where he found both, where anything out of place could be identified and corrected. Control and order, however, had been lost in bowmaking these last few days and had become as chaotic as the rest of his life.

He placed and gripped the bow between his legs, pulled a leather string from one of his pockets, and tied his long hair back in one quick, effortless motion. He winced as his eyes watered from feeling his scalp and forehead stretch.

The cool gust of sea wind threatened to loosen the leather string that bound his hair in a ponytail once more. The wind balanced the heat of the sun. In many ways, the weather in Crete felt like home, though the pine trees dotting the landscape reminded him he was still on foreign soil.

Lost in thought, Jonathan failed to notice the sidelong glances from passing women. His hastily tied-back wavy hair framed his striking features: deep blue eyes, prominent cheekbones, and lips that hinted at a smile that never quite appeared. Instead, his face settled into his father's famous scowl.

Returning his attention to the bow, he started with the upper notch. He remembered the tension he had felt as he pulled the string moments ago. Something didn't feel right. His fingers traced the curve of the wood, seeking the telltale signs that only a bowyer would recognize.

As he examined the notch, a firm clap landed on his shoulder. He turned, startled.

"That was a perfect shot, Jonathan," said one of the Roman archers who had just arrived at the archery range. The archer couldn't believe his luck that he had chanced upon one of Greece's most sought-after bowyers! Jonathan was hardly seen in the island's watering holes or joining any of the parties thrown by the officers. He kept to himself.

Upon recognizing the renowned bowyer, the archer's eyes widened with unmistakable awe and respect. *Is he younger than I am? This is the young man the Sagittarii talk about in the barracks, saying he's so gifted that he must be Diana's own.*

"Is that one of the new bows they'll be giving us soon?" the Roman asked with the practiced casualness of a soldier accustomed to coveting superior equipment.

"Not this one," the young bowyer answered, adeptly masking his disappointment that he wouldn't have the entire archery range at this early hour. "This bow is for one of your commanders." Jonathan turned to face the archer and asked, "But could you help me? Would you mind shooting an arrow so I can closely observe the bow as you aim?"

Startled by the request, the bowman grinned and eagerly nodded, saying, "I'd be glad to." He reached for the bow Jonathan held in his hand, staring at it with delight, a smile slowly spreading across his face.

"This is a beautiful bow!" he remarked, his calloused archer's fingers feeling the smooth yew wood. "It's incredibly light as well!"

Jonathan smiled at the compliment his work received as he stepped back to observe the shot. The Roman stepped into the shooting line, pulled an arrow from his quiver, and aimed at the target.

The young bowyer closely observed the upper notch and the bend of the upper limb as the archer drew the string. There it was: the uneven tension that twisted the bow when pulled. The upper limb was weaker than the lower limb!

Jonathan clenched his jaw. He had felt that subtle twist moments ago but failed to recognize its cause. Dreams about his father and his impending journey home clouded his judgment and disrupted the focus he prized above all else.

"This unit needs another adjustment," Jonathan whispered, relieved to have identified the problem yet angry that he had not seen it sooner.

The bowman released his arrow and hit the target. "The bow feels amazing! It's perfect!"

Jonathan half-smiled as he extended his hand. "Not yet, but it will be after a few adjustments. I appreciate your help."

"It has a flaw?" The *Sagittarii's* brow furrowed. "But it responded perfectly to my draw."

"It needs correcting. It will be perfect afterward." Jonathan took the bow with a nod of gratitude. Jonathan turned toward the studio, noting the sidelong glances from the two women who had just passed him.

His tanned, well-toned physique, ideal for an archer, had led to frequent misidentification, which he didn't mind. The only aspect of his appearance that made him self-conscious was his blue eyes, a color rarely seen in the region. Rather than explain their origin, he'd look down and immerse himself in mastering his craft: bowmaking.

His father's relentless pursuit of mastery had never been spoken aloud. Yet, Jonathan had always felt its weight, an expectation he could not ignore, for he had two fathers who viewed mastery in different ways.

His real father was a perfectionist, expecting mastery, demanding excellence, and accepting nothing less. Every effort was measured, and every flaw was noted.

The other, the man Jonathan considered his second father, was different. His father's childhood friend and lifelong assistant had been a steady presence in his life. He praised where the other would have criticized, found victory in the smallest steps, and believed that growth mattered more than perfection.

Jonathan had long sensed his father's unspoken challenge, a demand for mastery that felt impossible to meet. But from his second father, he had learned something else... a different kind of mastery, one built on encouragement, not on expectations.

Jonathan smiled at the thought of these two distinctly different men who had raised him, one demanding perfection, the other providing the guidance and affection his father was too busy to give. The memory of that nurturing presence intensified his longing for home, despite his fear of facing his father's judgment.

Jonathan stepped into the bowyer's studio, the scent of resin thick in the air. Two apprentices glanced up, offering silent nods of respect. He returned the gesture, his thoughts already elsewhere. The sharp tang of resin and the earthy scent of wood shavings wrapped around him, a grounding force in an existence otherwise shifting like the tide.

Jonathan remembered being the first to arrive at the workshop six years ago when he started his apprenticeship under Andreas. He wanted to be the first apprentice to choose from the wood supplies for the day. Since no one knew when fresh supplies would be delivered, he made it a point to be the first person to arrive and open the studio to receive the wood delivery if it came.

Jonathan couldn't help but stare at the wood pieces and see what each could become. He saw beyond the rough, uneven wood and found the beauty of a bow hidden in each one.

Perhaps this, too, was what his father felt for clay.

He knocked as he entered Andreas's room. "Good morning, Master," Jonathan greeted.

Andreas looked up, nodded at Jonathan, and asked, "Have you found what's wrong?"

"Yes, I did. Uneven tiller," Jonathan replied.

Andreas nodded. "Did you feel it?" he asked.

"Yes, but it became more apparent when I saw how the upper limb subtly twisted when fired by an archer. The movement was slight, but it did not escape my attention," Jonathan answered.

Andreas smiled. "The wood speaks softly. *Only those who listen closely will hear its secrets,*" he said. "You will learn to trust your instincts more as you progress. You will rely on visual confirmation less and less as you advance to a particular stage in your mastery. You said you felt the bow twist, yet could not identify the problem?" Andreas asked, looking at the young man who had suddenly cast down his eyes.

"My mind wandered off," Jonathan admitted, his eyes still downcast. Jonathan found it hard to admit to his teacher that he had not been as focused lately. His impending trip home had disrupted his concentration and significantly affected his work. Jonathan was sure this had not escaped Andreas, even though his teacher had not asked why.

Andreas looked at Jonathan, concern in his eyes, but decided not to press the young man further. He knew Jonathan had not been sleeping well lately. "Now, tell me, how will you address the uneven tiller?" Andreas asked, trying to make his voice sound as if he were teaching new apprentices.

"I will double-check the alignment of the bowstring because it is the easiest and fastest thing I can do. If the problem isn't there, I will check the tension next.

"I hope the problem is with the tension because if it isn't, the only remaining things to check are the limbs and the glue. Those two would be a pain to correct or adjust." Jonathan held up the beautiful bow. "If it's the limbs or the glue, then I'd have to admit that this is an imperfect bow," he said humbly, lowering his eyes.

Andreas smiled at his protégé, the most gifted bowyer he had ever met. He nodded to Jonathan, saying, "Then you have your work cut out for you today. Let's hope it all lies on the string so you won't have to check the limbs and the glue."

Jonathan nodded to Andreas and returned to his workstation. With a few more pieces to finish, he would finally be home.

Andreas looked at the young man who had just left his workshop. He knew the boy he had met six years ago had a gift with wood, but never realized how gifted the boy was until he bent his first bow. Andreas was sure that Jonathan would ascend to the rank of Master Bowyer in his own right, and the thought filled him with bittersweet pride, knowing he might not be there to witness it.

Andreas lowered his sketching tool and walked toward the chair facing a window. He sat down and stared at the open yard, illuminated by the sun's morning light against a beautiful ocean vista.

Andreas doubted he would ever find another apprentice as gifted and devoted as Jonathan. He wished, in a quiet, unspoken way, that the boy had been his own. Jonathan had brought him immense joy and pride, and Andreas suspected that another person felt the same way about him.

Marcus, Crete's *tribunus* and the Roman responsible for the garrison's daily operations, was also fond of the young, unassuming lad. Marcus viewed Andreas's most promising protégé as a valuable asset to the Roman Empire.

Marcus introduced Jonathan's bows to Crete's most influential families, who couldn't get enough of the young man's beautiful creations.

Andreas exhaled, the weight of Jonathan's departure settling deep within him, an unshakable certainty that their time together was coming to an end.

He remembered the day a young boy, no older than twelve, came knocking at his studio, asking to be taken on as an apprentice. The boy said he loved bows and had traveled for days to find him.

Amused, Andreas listened to the lad's incredible story of how he had left his home and boarded a ship as a stowaway. The lad spoke Greek fluently, with an accent he couldn't identify. He said he was ready to be a bowyer.

Andreas handed the boy a long piece of wood and a carving tool. He gave him three hours to shape the wood into a distinguishable bow, and the lad had impressed him ever since.

Long before Jonathan revealed the truth to Andreas that he had fled Judea for a craft his father had intended for him, he had already earned Andreas's respect. Yet mastery alone could not free him from his father's shadow, leaving him to wonder, at times to question, whether his craft was truly his own or a quiet rebellion.

Passionate and brave at such a young age, Andreas thought. And now, six years later, that passion was taking Jonathan away from Crete.

A few weeks ago, Jonathan visited his studio to tell him that he was ready to return home and seek his father's forgiveness and blessing. Andreas felt unprepared to lose his most prized student, yet he knew the protégé must leave to become a master.

Many would miss Jonathan.

Andreas closed his eyes, offering silent gratitude to the father who had unknowingly shared his son. Perhaps, in time, the man would realize the depth of what he had given.

2

CAESAREA

Jonathan shook his head, a gesture of uncertainty that cost him his carefully established order. The leather string securing his hair slipped, and a cold sea breeze scattered black tendrils across his face like uncontrollable thoughts. His jaw tightened with familiar frustration. Even his appearance defied his discipline, a reminder of why he'd fled to the precision of bowmaking years ago. With practiced movements, he retrieved a fresh leather string and restored his messy ponytail, temporarily imposing order on at least one small aspect of his life.

Bathed in the sun's fading light, Jonathan presented a lonely figure on the ship's deck.

He drew his cloak tight, letting his fingers reach for a small, shiny pin that glinted as it caught the sun's fading rays. He gazed out at the horizon, trying to catch a glimpse of the outline of the place he had left six years ago. He sighed. By the time the ship sailed into port, it would be dark. He wouldn't know whether the city had changed since he left. *Will it be just as I remember it?*

The more pressing question was: Will the two most important people in my life recognize me if I reveal myself to them?

Earlier in the day, he had glanced at his reflection on the water's surface. Anyone who had known him six years ago would have had a hard time recognizing him, except for his eyes. His deep blue eyes, unusual in this part of the world, remained unchanged, the only feature that still connected him to his past. The person returning from Crete had nothing in common with the boy who left Caesarea, save for that one unmistakable inheritance from his father.

"Master, please don't lean too far from the rail!" a crew member shouted to Jonathan, interrupting his train of thought. "The captain warns of treacherous waters approaching land," the sailor added, his weathered face creased with the concern of a man who has seen the sea claim many careless passengers.

The waters had grown choppy, and the ship began to roll back and forth. The deck timbers groaned in protest as the vessel pitched and rolled. Some men rushed to tighten the sail ropes, as if trying to control an angry bull. Jonathan had experienced a similar feeling when he left Caesarea; he had felt caged in.

A massive wave crashed against the ship's bow, sending Jonathan reeling and crates tumbling across the deck. Saltwater spray stung his eyes as crew members rushed to secure the precious cargo. Through the haze, Judea came into view on the horizon.

The sight of Judea looming before him stirred conflicting emotions. Part of him yearned to return to Crete. He had been traveling for nearly nine days, and not a day had passed without him considering returning to the island and spending a few more years under Andreas's tutelage.

The other half of him, however, felt excited to return home, where his father's name was known and respected.

Jonathan heaved a deep sigh as he paused near the foremast. *Is it excitement? Apprehension? Trepidation?* He couldn't quite put his finger on what he was feeling.

Would he be welcomed, or had the years and distance been enough to sever the remaining ties that bound him to the two people he loved most?

"Judea, ahead!" shouted a crew member, his voice carrying the practiced projection of a man accustomed to being heard over crashing waves and whipping winds.

Jonathan started to pace. His heart raced, pounding so fiercely that the crashing waves seemed to echo its rhythm. He drew a breath, steadying himself. But the question remained, unyielding, relentless. *Would Father ever forgive me?*

Jonathan closed his eyes and grasped the nearest handrail. Another wave rocked the ship, followed by a gust of wind that threatened to loosen the leather string binding his hair in a ponytail.

The thought of meeting his father brought back the one emotion he believed he would never feel again: terror. Jonathan had never been close to his father, whose silence had always seemed as impenetrable as kiln-fired clay. *My father could never understand how difficult it was for me to live in his shadow, carve my own path, and find success. I've returned to prove to him that it is possible, that I've escaped his shadow and made a name for myself.*

Jonathan's bows were popular among Crete's influential families and high-ranking Roman army officers. They all commissioned him for custom bows. *Will this be enough for Father? Will this pin persuade him?*

Jonathan's hand lightly brushed the pin Marcus had given him, tucked under his cloak.

Marcus had summoned Jonathan to his office a day before leaving for Judea. He handed Jonathan a letter to deliver to a friend named

Janus, a *praefectus* in Judea. Marcus sealed and signed the letter with his sigil.

He also attached a silver disc mounted on a pin to Jonathan's cloak. The disc featured the image of an eagle with wings spread wide, clutching a bundle of thunderbolts.

Marcus explained that the disc marked him as a Roman envoy. Citizens of the Empire must offer the disc bearer all the assistance he needs. "I hope this speeds up your journey and gives you all the support you require in your travels," Marcus added.

A crying seagull overhead jolted Jonathan from his thoughts of Crete and the people who had made the past six years of his life memorable. The bird's plaintive call seemed to echo his uncertainty, caught between sea and shore, belonging fully to neither.

The ship rocked violently, and the crew rushed to tighten the ropes and secure the cargo. The ship's sudden movements, however, were nothing compared to the inner turmoil Jonathan was experiencing.

He would ask nothing from his father except forgiveness for running away and his blessing to start his trade. He had earned enough coins in Crete to start his studio, so his father had no choice but to finally see him as a man and a master of his chosen craft.

He had prepared a speech and committed it to memory.

Jonathan

"Father, forgive me for running away.
I had to pursue a calling
beyond your shadow.
I had to be my own man..."

Night had fallen when Jonathan's ship docked at Caesarea's harbor. The familiar scents of fish, tar, and spices from the port transported him momentarily back to his childhood. The journey through familiar yet strange streets had been a blur of anticipation and dread, along torch-lit pathways he barely recognized. The distant calls of tired night vendors hawking the last of their wares filled the air, and the weight of anticipation grew heavier with each step toward the familiar doorway of a courtyard as lush as he remembered. The scent of the docks that had comforted him when he arrived faded quickly at the door.

Now, the carefully rehearsed words remained unsaid as Jonathan found himself seated in his father's studio chair, the scent of clay long gone from a room that looked so empty it appeared abandoned.

Nothing had prepared him for what awaited, for the words that would shatter everything.

"Your father *died* more than a year ago."

The words struck Jonathan like a blow. The meaning behind the urgent dreams that had haunted his sleep in Crete became devastatingly clear. Those nightmares weren't calls to reconcile. They were echoes of a farewell he'd never had the chance to give.

His father had been reaching for him across the divide of death, and Jonathan had arrived too late to respond.

Time seemed to stop. The room tilted around him as his mind struggled to process what Dan had just said. *This can't be real.* His father, the man whose forgiveness he had crossed seas to seek, was gone.

"No," Jonathan whispered. His fingers found the back of a chair and gripped it until his knuckles turned white. The solid wood beneath his hands was the only thing anchoring him to reality as the floor seemed to shift beneath his feet.

Dan's weathered face crumpled with shared grief as he watched the young man he had helped raise succumb to the weight of the news.

The pain in his surrogate father's eyes confirmed what his heart refused to accept.

"He *can't* be..." Jonathan's voice cracked, the words barely escaping his throat. His eyes searched Dan's face desperately, silently begging for a retraction, a mistake, anything but this finality. But Dan only returned his gaze with quiet sorrow, offering no denial, no alternative truth.

The forgiveness Jonathan had traveled to find now lay beyond his reach forever.

Dan, his father's lifelong friend and assistant who had raised him as his own, looked at Jonathan helplessly, leaning on an unfamiliar young man for support.

"I found him sitting in the chair you are now gripping, with his head bowed," Dan said, pointing at his father's studio chair that Jonathan was clutching. "I thought he was just asleep; he looked asleep," Dan said. His voice carried the gentle cadence that had once soothed Jonathan's childhood fears, attempting now to soften an unbearable truth.

Jonathan felt disoriented.

He looked around. He was in his father's pottery studio, where Dan quietly led him to break the news. Everything looked familiar yet felt different. The scent of clay that had perpetually filled this space was faint now, almost a memory rather than a presence. The usually pleasant dust motes that danced in shafts of light, even from lamps, seemed ghostly now. Something vital was gone.

The studio looked empty. The worktables were scrubbed clean, and the tools were aligned with unnatural precision. No half-formed vessels waited under damp cloths; no clay scraps clung to the worn stone floor. Everything was so tidy that it appeared desolate, like a shrine rather than a workshop. Jonathan's father had not been in this room for a long time. *Father wouldn't have been able to stand being away from this sacred space for too long unless... Caesarea's pottery artisan was dead.*

The thought hit Jonathan like a blow to the chest. His knees buckled, and he slid into the chair, taking a deep breath to steady himself.

Jonathan had envisioned three scenarios for his return, but this was never one of them. He would have preferred to face his father's famous silence and penetrating gaze rather than this permanent absence. A deep ache settled in his chest, daring him to lose control and cry out.

His gaze fell upon the old potter's wheel at the heart of his father's pottery studio, less than an arm's length away. He felt his jaw clench. The wheel's stillness seemed unnatural, like a bow permanently strung but never drawn. Older than he was, it had given birth to hundreds of clay works. Now, it sat silent, waiting for hands that would never return.

He fought the urge to overturn the wheel and crash it to the ground. Jonathan hated that battered thing. It had robbed him of his father's time, demanding all of it and leaving none for anything or anyone else.

He grew up competing with that spinning tyrant for his father's attention and always lost.

It creaked when his father worked, as if mocking him for never being able to pull that gaze away.

Jonathan closed his eyes and breathed deeply, trying to regain some control. He consciously unclenched his fists and placed his shaking hands on his father's worktable, trying to summon his last memory of him before he ran away. But no memories came to mind.

Jonathan had silently hoped he and his father could make up for lost time upon his return from Crete. There would be no making up for lost time now. Jonathan would never have time with his father the way his father had had time with that wheel.

His father was dead. The wheel had won.

Jonathan opened his eyes to look directly at Dan, his last remaining family member. Dan appeared frail, a stark contrast to his strength throughout Jonathan's childhood. Everyone knew Dan as his father's pottery assistant, but to Jonathan, he was a true family member, the man who had been present at every critical moment his father had chosen to miss.

When he first arrived, Dan welcomed him with a smile that contradicted the sadness in his eyes. Jonathan felt confused but strode forward in two giant steps to envelop Dan's frail frame in a tight, warm hug.

Dan had seemed caught off guard but returned the embrace, uttering softly, "Welcome home, Jonathan. I have some sad news."

Then Dan quietly led him through the familiar hallways to his father's studio, where he now sat trying to make sense of a world that had been turned upside down.

"Jonathan?" Dan's voice broke through the fog of memory, pulling him back to the bleak studio bereft of his father's presence.

Jonathan shook his head, trying to clear the thoughts that flooded his mind.

"Are you well?" Dan asked.

Jonathan took a deep breath. "I'm fine, Dan. I will be fine. This room just brought back a flood of memories. And please stop calling me Jonathan. You've always called me Nathan." It was a familiar comfort, that shortening of his name that only Dan had ever used.

"Your father is gone. You are now the master of this house, not a son. It is only proper to call you by your full name," Dan politely replied.

"It may be proper for others, but not for you. To you, I was and still am Nathan." Jonathan saw a hint of a smile on Dan's face when he insisted on being called Nathan.

Dan, whose graying hair framed a weathered face, nodded to Jonathan and said, "Forgive me for being remiss. Nathan, this is Jacob, our new pottery apprentice. He joined us a few months before your father died."

Jonathan nodded to the young man standing beside Dan in acknowledgment.

"Caesarea's best families paid tribute to your father. It was touching to hear the public praise heaped upon him," Dan added, lightly touching the pottery wheel between them.

Jonathan fought the urge to tell Dan that his father's work was his father's life, and no one, including him, was ever as important. To his father, his work came first. Nothing came second. This studio was his father's throne room. This was where the rich and the mighty came to buy his father's works or beg him to accept their commissions for a piece or two of pottery with the famous fish sigil. Now, his father was dead.

For Caesarea's rich and powerful, there would be no more pottery to buy.

For Jonathan, there would be no forgiveness, no absolution.

Jonathan stared at the abandoned potter's wheel, the symbol of his father's life's work. He had spent six years mastering a different craft, defining himself through wood and string rather than clay. Now fate had placed his father's legacy before him, silent, waiting. A craft he had fled from. A burden he might no longer have the choice to resist.

Jonathan ran his fingers along the edge of the potter's wheel, feeling its smooth surface, which was so different from the rough-grained wood he had grown accustomed to shaping. *His bows bent without breaking. His father's clay resisted fire without shattering. Their crafts were as different as they were: one yielded and the other endured.*

"I am so happy you're home," Jonathan heard Dan say, his voice triggering memories that rushed unbidden into his mind. "There are so many things I need to tell you. I never thought I'd live to see the day you returned," Dan continued softly. "But you must be tired. We can talk tomorrow. Your room was always ready for your return."

Dan's eyes reflected the concern that had always made Jonathan feel cared for. Jacob gently guided Dan out of the room, leaving Jonathan alone with the pottery wheel, the object that had always commanded his father's attention.

For Caesarea, Amos, the Master of Clay, was gone.

For Jonathan, everything he had dreamed of, planned for, and hoped for had died with him.

Jonathan stifled his sobs until Dan's footsteps faded, then finally let his grief flow freely. The tears that fell to the dusty floor left small dark marks, each a prayer for forgiveness that would never be heard.

3

TRUTH

THOUGH HIS BODY ACHED FROM DAYS OF TRAVEL, SLEEP ELUDED Jonathan as he stood in his childhood bedroom. The tears he had shed alone in his father's studio had left him hollow, yet he was still unable to rest. The space around him existed in a perfect, preserved state, as if time had frozen when he fled. Every familiar object remained precisely where he had left it six years ago, down to the smallest detail.

The painful irony wasn't lost on him: while his room remained unchanged, he had undergone a complete transformation. The boy who once occupied this space was replaced by a man who now felt like a stranger in his home. Even his father's studio stood as a monument to the past, untouched by the years that had reshaped Jonathan's entire being.

Caesarea's high and mighty visited his father in that studio. Jonathan sometimes felt like he was living in a fishbowl, closely observed by everyone. Jonathan felt that everyone who paid homage to his father expected him to follow in his father's footsteps. Everyone looked at him expectantly when the conversation turned to who would be Caesarea's next pottery artisan.

The pressure to be his father's successor was stifling. He felt no one had given him a voice or choice in the matter.

Jonathan grew up like any other boy, except for two things: first, he received special tutoring in reading and writing Aramaic and Greek, languages his father insisted were necessary for their trade to flourish. Second, he started learning about his father's craft before he could even walk.

His father never discussed Jonathan's mother. The only thing he knew about her was that he had inherited the color of her eyes. Blue.

Jonathan was introduced to his father's pottery wheel at an early age. It was fun at first. He loved playing with the clay, throwing it around at his father's workers, who dodged the flying pieces and laughed with him. He was covered in clay from head to toe, having a great time in the studio. Dan would scoop him up and take him out as soon as his father arrived to begin work. But as he grew older, the happy days of throwing clay gave way to frustration and fear during pottery lessons.

The pottery wheel demanded coordination that Jonathan never mastered. His feet struggled to find the rhythm needed at the bottom wheel, while his hands failed to coax the clay into shape at the top. His father's intense gaze only worsened his performance, transforming every lesson into a nightmare. The wheezing, screeching sound *(woo-ik, woo-ik)* seemed to mock him, exposing the unbridgeable gap between father and son.

Jonathan sat abruptly on his bed and ran his fingers through his tangled hair. Six years later, the sound the pottery wheel made when it spun still haunted him. Jonathan's creations, which always collapsed into misshapen lumps, were all quietly whisked away by Dan before his father could see the extent of his failure. That cursed wheel had been the physical embodiment of everything he couldn't be, everything that drove him away.

Jonathan shook himself from these bitter memories and walked to his window, where the peaceful moonlit courtyard starkly contrasted with his inner turmoil. He breathed in the cold night air, feeling the pain that had driven him to flee. The scent of night-blooming lilies drifted up from the courtyard, impossibly the same as on the night he left. While everything outside looked serene under the moon's golden light, his thoughts remained chaotic.

The tranquility of the night did nothing to quiet his mind. His father's voice echoed in his thoughts, as clear as if he were standing beside him, instructing new workers: "You must control the potter's wheel with your feet, keeping it at the right speed. This coordination between your feet and your hands is crucial; any mistake could ruin the piece."

Dan, however, took the time to carefully explain to Jonathan why his work could not hold its shape.

"You have to find the middle ground where strength and gentleness meet, and bring your clay to that balance. It is only at that point that it will understand what you want to do and hold its shape. You have to guide it to shape it. Forcing it will only cause it to collapse. It has to find the strength to hold its shape. Read the clay! You must check the clay's moisture, texture, and feel when you touch it. You must be familiar with it to understand and anticipate its behavior. The clay is not the tool, Nathan; you are."

Jonathan smiled at the memory of Dan painstakingly explaining to a frustrated twelve-year-old why his pottery pieces couldn't hold their shape.

Try as he might, Jonathan couldn't mold the clay. His work wouldn't hold its form. His feet lacked the rhythm needed to master the pottery wheel. His hands lacked the skill to read and coax the clay into shape. Neither did he have the patience that the craft required. *Why couldn't everyone see that he didn't have the skill for clay?*

Clay was too unpredictable and demanding for him. Pottery required hand-foot coordination, which he didn't have. The slightest mistake ruined his work, making him feel like a failure. Jonathan found solace in wood.

He was fascinated by bending wood without breaking it, finding it magical how a well-crafted bow could influence an arrow's speed and precision.

How can wood turn into such a beautiful, powerful weapon?

He realized his passion lay in wood when one of his playmates showed off a bow and arrow set given to him by an uncle. The bow took his breath away.

In his mind's eye, he could picture himself making beautiful and powerful bows, just as his father made pottery.

He sneaked away and wandered into the woodcarvers' alley to watch them work. He observed how they bent wood and became familiar with their tools.

He followed Roman soldiers who carried bows and arrows, bombarding them with questions about their craft, how their bows were made, and how they worked. He discovered that Roman archers were called *Sagittarii*, and the various titles appended to their class depended upon their rank and position. The soldiers often looked surprised and amused when he addressed them in Greek, granting him permission to examine their bows closely and even touch them.

He was relentless in his pursuit, asking soldiers and anyone knowledgeable about wood where to find the best bowyers. "Crete," most of them said. Jonathan whispered the word like a prayer: "Crete."

Jonathan became a regular visitor to the woodcrafters' alley. He sat among them, his eyes fascinated as they carved and shaped the wood. Jonathan eagerly assisted the carvers and often asked them to let him try under their guidance. He wished his pottery lessons were just as enjoyable.

Pottery lessons with Dan had been tolerable. The coming lessons with his father were something else entirely. The thought of Amos beside him at the wheel, watching, judging, was more than he could bear. The weight of expectation pressed against his chest, tightening with every breath. And so, the panic attacks began.

He started practicing at the pottery wheel when everyone was asleep. His apprehension affected how he handled the clay. He fought the clay, hands shaking, breath uneven. It wouldn't hold, wouldn't listen. Frustration boiled over, his fingers tightening before he could stop himself. The lump of clay flew, striking the finished piece beside him. It shattered with a sickening crack. Shards scattered across the floor.

Then silence.

Then footsteps.

He had broken what was likely worth a fortune. He had woken up the house. And he had reached the point of no return.

After the scolding and cleanup that left Jonathan angry, frustrated, and alone, he decided it was time for everyone to stop hoping he could master pottery. *Enough! He was off to Crete!*

He scribbled a note.

He grabbed a bag, stuffed it with a few clothes, retrieved his savings from a drawer, and quietly tiptoed into his father's studio. He left his note on his father's pottery wheel, where he knew it would not be missed. He left the house, running toward the port where ships bound for Crete were moored. He felt free.

He had left, knowing it would break his father's heart. Had vowed to make amends. Had pictured it: the conversation, the moment, the words that would finally pass between them. But today wasn't that day. That day would never come. Forgiveness lay beyond his reach, sealed beneath the weight of time and silence.

Jonathan finally drifted into a listless sleep, remembering the words he had written to his father the night he left.

> Dearest Father, I know you have always known I do not have what it takes to follow in your footsteps, even though I feign interest and do my best to ensure your legacy and make you happy.
>
> I know in your heart that you will agree that a legacy does not mean owning a craft one will never master, nor spending the rest of one's life feigning love for it.
>
> Pottery is your chosen craft, Father; it is not mine.
>
> Allow me to discover my trade and establish a legacy where I can bring honor to your name as your son. - Jonathan

THE MORNING LIGHT FILTERED THROUGH THE STUDIO WINDOWS, casting long shadows across the empty pottery wheel that had once been the center of his father's world and the bane of Jonathan's existence. He stood motionless in the doorway, his hand resting on the worn wooden frame.

He hadn't planned to come here, had intended to avoid it entirely, yet found himself drawn back to this sanctuary not by choice but by something more profound, a pull he couldn't explain. His feet had carried him here of their own accord, as if following a path worn into his soul.

Jonathan stood at the heart of his father's domain.

He could feel the void left by his father's absence, the commanding presence that once filled the room. Once alive with constant motion, the center of the studio now sat silent. Its stillness felt like an accusation. He could sense the longing of the wooden tools arranged with painful precision in their containers, waiting for the hand of their creator who would never touch them again. Everything was deathly still.

He felt sadness and regret. *His father was truly gone.*

The room sighed, longing for its master.

Lost in the hollow space between memory and reality, Jonathan failed to notice Dan enter the studio, with Jacob following close behind. The slight shuffle of sandals against stone finally broke his reverie.

Dan's weathered presence brought a flicker of comfort, a reminder that Jonathan still had one person who felt like family. The older man moved with the deliberate care of someone who understood the weight of silences. Dan nodded in silent greeting as he took a seat opposite Jonathan. Jacob quietly slipped away, his apprentice's intuition sensing the fragile moment unfolding between the two men.

"How was my father when I left?" Jonathan asked Dan. His fingers traced a crack in the wooden workbench, following its path like a river across a map.

Dan took a deep breath, settled into his chair, and looked intently at the boy he had helped raise. Something in Dan's expression suggested he was measuring how much of the boy he'd known remained in the young man before him.

"He was lost. We both were. Our lives stopped," Dan answered in a tone that suggested he remembered every single day since Jonathan left. His words came slowly and deliberately.

"What do you mean by 'stopped'?" Jonathan asked.

"Work stopped. The pottery stopped. Everything stopped. Our lives revolved around finding you and bringing you home."

Jonathan could hear the sadness and frustration in Dan's voice. He felt a deep ache in his chest, realizing the pain and suffering he had caused to the two people he loved the most. He was aware that while he could ask for forgiveness from the man before him, he would never be able to seek forgiveness from his father.

"I was young and foolish. I only saw the need to cut away from something that was forced on me," Jonathan admitted, his voice heavy with regret.

"Sometimes what we think is being forced upon us is only being offered," Dan said gently. He paused, letting the words settle. "Like clay that resists the potter's touch until it learns the hands mean no harm."

Dan paused. Jonathan silently absorbed everything his second father was trying to tell him. He felt his chest struck by a deep, penetrating pain he couldn't understand.

"I'm genuinely sorry that you felt forced into something you had no passion for. It was never our intention to do so. The only thing that truly mattered to us was securing your future and ensuring you never needed or wanted anything." Dan's voice quivered with emotion. After a lengthy silence, he whispered, "Where have you been, Nathan?" Dan asked. "Where did you go?"

"Crete," Jonathan said in a whisper. "I went to Crete to seek a master bowyer and learn from him."

Dan was surprised; he had never expected Jonathan to travel across the sea. The thought of Jonathan traveling to Crete alone at such a young age filled Dan with both pride and concern for the boy's remarkable bravery. Questions flickered across Dan's weathered features as he studied Jonathan. Jonathan understood that his surrogate father needed to hear about where he had been and what he had done.

Jonathan spoke about his apprenticeship in Crete, the people he met and worked with, and the places he visited. He told Dan about his six years of training, including Andreas and Marcus, as well as the people who deeply appreciated everything he had created. He shared everything he had learned and experienced, except for the haunting dreams about his father that had grown more intense these last few months.

He then discussed bowmaking and everything he found fascinating about it.

Jonathan hoped Dan could see what he found so beautiful about bowmaking.

Jonathan explained to Dan how making bows was as challenging as forming clay. "There's no required footwork as in pottery, but there's the same focus on form, balance, and detail. In pottery, you mold clay to shape it, while in bowmaking, you cut wood to give it form. It's the same," Jonathan said, trying to get Dan to agree.

Dan remained silent longer than Jonathan found comfortable. Dan then shook his head slightly in response. "No, Nathan, they're not the same," Dan said, his voice gentle but firm. "In bowmaking, you cut off the parts you think you don't need. A wrong cut or a miscalculation renders the entire piece unusable. You can't magically bring back what you discarded, correct?" Dan asked.

Jonathan nodded, suddenly seeing the parallel that Dan was drawing.

"If a form doesn't hold in pottery, we collapse the clay and begin again. Pottery gives us the space to learn from our mistakes. In pottery, the only true failure is giving up. Passion for your craft can only sustain you so far," Dan said. He leaned forward, his eyes searching Jonathan's. "Your father pursued his passion with single-minded focus, discarding everything that didn't fit his vision, including time with you. Such ruthless focus is unusual for those in pottery, where patience and discernment are key. When you left, he learned what couldn't be reclaimed once lost. That's when purpose found him."

Jonathan was quiet. He knew his second father was trying to tell him something beyond the obvious lesson about persistence. Jonathan had given up and run away.

Jonathan broke the long silence following Dan's response and spoke slowly, his tone thoughtful and measured.

"I see the form waiting inside each piece of wood, as you see potential in clay. How I cut each piece of wood determines what it will become. If I cut correctly, the vision comes to fruition. If I cut wrongly, I destroy what could have been," Jonathan explained to his second father.

"This is why I came back, despite choosing a different trade than what my father wanted for me. I wanted you both to guide me because I intend to bring my visions to life. I need guidance to grow my trade, achieve success like my father, and be wise with what I cut away so I don't destroy what could have been. But I've come home too late. I've lost one father," Jonathan whispered.

Dan looked intently at Jonathan and asked, "This vision you see, this dream you chase, why do you chase it?"

"I want to follow in my father's footsteps, to excel in my craft and become renowned, respected, and successful. I'm just following my father's path, Dan," Jonathan answered. "He mastered his craft and has done well. I have chosen mine now, and I hope my future will be just as bright."

"This future, the kind your father had, do you think it will be fulfilling for you?" Dan asked tentatively. "Do you believe it will make you happy?"

Jonathan paused. "You are asking tough questions, Dan. Now, I'm confused. Why are we discussing this?"

"I'm sorry if I'm confusing you, Nathan, but aren't the things you are pursuing the things you think will bring you happiness?" Dan knew he was asking tough questions, but he wanted to know where Jonathan's heart was. He wanted to be sure that Jonathan would understand what he was about to reveal.

"You ran away because you thought being a bowmaker would make you happy, did you not?" Dan asked.

Jonathan sighed deeply, closed his eyes, and then covered his face with his hands.

"I like bowmaking, Dan. I truly do," he said. "Will making bows make me happy for my entire life? That question never crossed my mind. I honestly don't know."

Jonathan questioned everything he was so certain of before arriving in Caesarea. Dan's questions prompted him to think about the future when he had only considered the present. His six-year plan had ended the day he arrived home. He needed to rethink everything.

"You would know much better than I do, for you've been with my father long before I was born," Jonathan whispered. "Tell me, Dan, was my father a happy man, immersed in his craft?" Jonathan's eyes were fixed on Dan, desperate for answers that might help him understand his own path.

"I watched your father struggle after you left," Dan said softly. "For months, his pottery wheel sat untouched. One day, I found him working again but seemingly driven by something new and greater. His hands shaped clay not for wealthy patrons, but to bring to vision what he felt for you."

Dan's eyes met Jonathan's. "That's when I realized what had

changed in him. I recall him saying something that prompted me to reassess what my life was about."

"I've spent my life following my passion when I should have been living for my purpose. Passion is what we chase, but it is purpose that defines us."

Dan leaned forward. "They're different paths, Nathan, often leading in opposite directions. Your father realized that mastery of his craft meant little without the purpose that gave it meaning."

Jonathan felt confused. What was the difference between passion and purpose? And what did either have to do with choosing the right path? Growing up, he learned that he had to choose and master a craft to earn a living, build a reputation, and achieve success. He saw his father do this well and followed in his father's footsteps, even if he had chosen a different craft. *Now, Dan was telling him that his father had made a mistake by following his passion.*

The room fell silent. Dan slowly stood up, walked to one of the work cabinets, and retrieved something covered with a cloth.

"Your father made this for you," Dan said, placing the covered object in front of him.

Jonathan removed the cloth. The object caught the morning light, its glazed surface gleaming softly. It was an intricately designed clay box with deeply etched patterns that gleamed as light struck it like a well-polished bow. The clay box depicted father and son figures in a loving embrace, surrounded by pottery vessels, flowers, and ferns. The piece was tinted with hues of blue and green and glazed to a fine sheen.

"He did this?" Jonathan couldn't take his eyes off the breathtaking pottery piece before him. "It looks so different from everything he has ever made!" His hands hovered over the box, almost afraid to touch something so delicate yet so profound.

"The change I spoke of wasn't limited to his heart, Jonathan," Dan said. "It transformed his work as well."

Jonathan had trouble imagining his father creating something so tender. The style was so different that he struggled to connect this magnificent piece to his father, even though Amos's other work was equally beautiful.

The gold color had made his father's pottery pieces stand out from the work of other artisans. His father's creations embodied wealth, abundance, and power, never the ordinary. Because of this, Romans and Caesarea's wealthiest families coveted his father's pieces, each bearing the famous fish sigil.

The pottery piece before him lacked any trace of gold. This design radiated not power or wealth, but warmth and joy, a father's deep love for his son. Yet, it was truly stunning!

Jonathan recognized the same care for the tiniest details that his father was famous for. He traced the coloring and glazing techniques he knew were his father's. They were all there.

It was unmistakably his father's work, yet completely different.

"Can you see it?" Dan said. "Can you see how it looks so different, yet still carries traces of the father you knew in every detail?"

Jonathan marveled at the box his father had created for him. His fingers slowly traced the prominently designed father-son figure on it. *The clay felt alive beneath his touch, warm despite the coolness of the room.* "Father," Jonathan whispered. *What happened?* he wondered. *What changed you? What changed your craft?*

As Jonathan gently lifted the intricate lid of the pottery box, letters caught his eye.

The letters were Aramaic. He looked underneath the lid and saw the word "truth."

"Have you seen this, Dan? Have you seen the letters?" he asked excitedly, pointing under the lid.

"Your father started adding Aramaic words to his last few pieces."

"But I thought you said his pottery stopped when I ran away?"

"It did, for nearly two years, until..."

"Until what?" Jonathan asked.

"Look inside the box," Dan said gently.

Jonathan's heart raced as he carefully set aside the lid, his movement as delicate as when testing a new bowstring. As Jonathan lifted the box lid, he found a small, leather-bound journal rolled into a scroll with leather thongs, its soft brown cover worn at the edges from handling. It fit perfectly inside the small clay box.

"Your father started journaling, hoping that one day you would be able to read his thoughts and understand, in his own words, that he had always loved you," Dan said.

Jonathan's hands trembled as he stared at the journal. The parchment pages carried a hint of his father's scent, along with the smell of clay dust and ink. His fingers shook as he gently lifted the journal from the clay box. He released the leather thong that held the journal in its scroll form. The journal opened to reveal pages of parchment, cut and stitched with remarkable precision. Each page bore the same delicate marks at the edges that characterized his father's pottery.

Across the cover, Jonathan noticed a subtle fish symbol pressed into the leather, nearly invisible unless caught in the right light. *He ran his fingers over the leather, feeling every crease where his father's hands had rested.*

"He wrote for me," Jonathan whispered. *I will still hear my father speaking to me.*

Jonathan's heart raced, and his eyes filled with tears. He stared at the journal containing everything his father would want to say to him, everything Jonathan thought he had lost by coming home too late.

The weight of it in his hands felt like both a burden and a gift.

Jonathan's heart ached as he took a deep breath, afraid to look at Dan and lose control.

Truth

It was an intricately designed clay box with deeply etched patterns that gleamed as light struck it like a well-polished bow. The clay box depicted father and son figures in a loving embrace, surrounded by pottery vessels, flowers, and ferns. The piece was tinted with hues of blue and green and glazed to a fine sheen.

4

BLUE

"What was my mother like?" Jonathan remembered asking Dan this exact question one late afternoon in the courtyard while they worked on a commissioned pottery piece that Dan was painting.

"You knew her, right? What was she like?" Jonathan tentatively asked his second father.

Dan slowly lowered his painting tool and looked earnestly into the blue eyes that seemed as deep and mysterious as the sea. "I didn't get to meet her, Nathan, remember? Only your father did," he confessed with a strange look in his eyes.

"But he must have told you something about her..." the young boy begged, holding tightly to the arm of the man he felt closer to than the man who called him "son."

Dan touched the boy's grip and quietly said, "You know your father doesn't want to talk about things that break his heart, right, Nathan? We never talk about them at all." The old man looked at the boy, whose heart must have broken a thousand times, for never knowing anything about his mother.

Jonathan lowered his gaze and heaved a deep sigh of resignation. At such a young age, the boy had finally come to terms with the realization that he would never know. No one would ever tell him, least of all his father.

Dan looked at the young boy he had claimed as his own in his heart. Nathan's heart is breaking, and so is mine, Dan thought. Make that three hearts breaking... Dan said to himself after a brief moment. Amos's heart has never stopped hurting since he first held Nathan. It heals at night and breaks again at first light.

Dan picked up his painting tool and looked at the young boy beside him. "Pass me a different shade of blue, Nathan," Dan said, trying to put a bit of lilt in his voice. "Let's see if your chosen shade of blue can bring something special to this piece."

Jonathan let out a sigh, pulling back to the present. He still vividly remembered that exchange from more than a decade ago, when he was young but already conscious of how others looked at him when they saw his eyes.

Jonathan shifted his gaze inside his room. It didn't feel like his anymore; it felt like someone else's. However, the courtyard still felt like home. He gazed back at the garden below his window.

The question he asked Dan that day had never faded from his memory. It played repeatedly in his dreams and sometimes in his waking hours, whenever he caught sight of his reflection in a mirror, his blue eyes gazing back at him.

Blue.

He looked forward to this homecoming when his father would finally see him as a man and share everything he had never told Jonathan about the woman who gave birth to him. Like the forgiveness and blessing he had hoped to receive, the truth about his mother had died with his father.

Until he saw the clay box his father had left him.

It bore one word, truth, etched into the clay with the same deliberate precision his father brought to everything he created.

Jonathan lightly traced his fingers over the beautiful father-and-son clay design his father had made. This is his father's work. Jonathan is one of three people who could clearly distinguish between the works of his two fathers. Dan has his style, and Amos has his. Amos himself made the design on the clay box. It must have taken a considerable amount of time to complete this piece. Everything was intricately and lovingly detailed and colored.

He lifted the lid again and looked at the word etched beneath—"truth" in Aramaic. Inside lay a journal rolled into a tight scroll. Dan said his father had written everything he wanted to tell him before he passed away.

Jonathan placed the lid back. He stood up from the chair in his bedroom, overlooking his father's beautiful courtyard below, and carefully carried the box out.

Jonathan found himself once more in his father's studio, seated in his father's chair. He placed the box on top of the work table and quietly stared at it. It was an arm's length away from where his father made it, his father's pottery wheel.

He found it ironic that, since his return, his feet had led him twice to the room he had tried to escape from by running away six years ago.

Growing up, his father's studio was the last place he wanted to be, and it was also the last place anyone who knew him would find him.

Here, he felt insignificant next to an object his father worked with daily, his pottery wheel. By experience, Jonathan knew that being less valuable than a flat stone could destroy a young boy's self-worth. It took him six years to forget the hurt the wheel had caused.

Now, he was back within an arm's length without being forced by anyone.

Jonathan exhaled slowly, eyes falling on his father's wheel. It had outlived its master. For years, he had hated it for what it took, for what it demanded. But now, the anger was gone. All that remained was silence. It would never spin again.

He had to start reading his father's journal. He needed to understand his father better than he had before he ran away. However, his mind kept shifting to his conversation with Dan that morning.

Dan asked him tough questions, giving him more to think about than the answers he sought.

Jonathan wanted his father to see how successful he had become and how close he was to mastering his craft. Jonathan had planned to prove his father wrong, but how could he prove it to someone no longer around? The better question was, w*hy did he want to prove it?*

Jonathan had always believed that following one's passion would bring happiness. His father did. And Jonathan had always assumed his father was happy. Who wouldn't be with the coins he earned and the ardent patrons who coveted every pottery piece he made? It made his father famous, wealthy, and powerful.

But Dan said his father wasn't happy until a few months before he passed away.

What made his father happy? The question lingered in Jonathan's mind. Dan said it was purpose, not passion. *Purpose?*

Jonathan hoped his father's journal would hold the answers he sought.

For all his years in Crete, Jonathan had planned for this homecoming: to learn his craft, seek forgiveness, establish a trade, and achieve success. It was that simple until he discovered his father was gone. Now, looking earnestly at his plans, which had been carefully constructed and meticulously pursued, he felt lost.

Stripped of his father's presence, his plans seemed hollow. *Passion, yes. But purpose? If success meant nothing without proving Father wrong, then I was doomed.*

Dan had numerous questions about happiness and whether he believed his life plan would ultimately make him happy. If Dan had asked him yesterday, he would have quickly answered, "Yes." But today, he was no longer sure. Jonathan's whole plan depended on proving that he was right and receiving his father's forgiveness and blessing.

Lost in these thoughts, Jonathan almost didn't hear the voice calling from the courtyard.

"Jon!" A loud voice startled him back to the present.

"Jo-na-than!" the voice bellowed again, demanding attention.

Jonathan rose from his chair and placed the clay box containing his father's journal on one of the empty shelves. As soon as he turned around, he found himself locked in by two strong arms that squeezed the breath out of him.

The man who had rushed into the studio was now squeezing the air out of him. His thick black hair, cut short, framed a young, friendly face that seemed used to grinning. His sun-tanned skin revealed him to be a man who spent hours outdoors. The strong arms around Jonathan lifted him off his feet like he weighed nothing. The grinning man said, "I knew you'd be back!" Someone saw you at the port last night and rushed to tell me this morning. I had to come and see if it was true!" exclaimed the young man. "You're home!"

Jonathan looked into the bright hazel eyes that looked back at him with warmth and friendship.

"Benjamin?!"

Jonathan laughed upon recognizing his old, trusted friend.

He looked nothing like the chubby, round-faced boy Jonathan remembered six years ago. Jonathan recognized his old friend by Benjamin's bright hazel eyes. Benjamin's eyes had always been warm and genuine and remained unchanged.

The two young men sized each other up, patted each other on the shoulders, and laughed even harder about how they had each changed but remained recognizably the same.

"Where have you been? What happened to you?" Benjamin asked, his eyes full of concern.

"I sailed to Crete," Jonathan said. He told Benjamin about his apprenticeship under Andreas and the training he received to become a bowyer. When he finished, there was silence.

"You made bows for the *Romans*?" Benjamin asked. Jonathan detected a note of surprise in his voice.

"I made bows in Crete, Benjamin," Jonathan said. "Hunters, government officials, and even some Roman commanders bought my bows." He paused. "Why do you ask?"

"I've been traveling with my father on trade routes across Galilee and Judea, which has been valuable training in the family business," Benjamin explained, naturally falling into the measured tone he used when assessing goods. "The investment has paid off in knowledge, far more valuable than the weight of *shekels*. I've witnessed changes we never accounted for growing up in Caesarea, Jonathan. The market outside these walls has shifted." He leaned forward, as if sharing insider information. "I can't speak for conditions in Crete, but things are becoming *unsettled in Galilee."*

Jonathan was silent as he listened to Benjamin.

"Various groups in our community that were quietly at war with each other when you left are now openly fighting," Benjamin continued, his voice dropping to the hushed tone of marketplace gossip. The familiar scent of olive oil lamps flickered around them, casting dancing shadows across his troubled face. "Everyone claims that what they follow is the 'real truth'! Everyone!" He struck the table with his merchant's calculating finger. "How many truths can there be? How many gods?" The words hung in the air, mingling with the distant sounds of evening prayers drifting through the open window.

Jonathan was taken aback. The word "truth" seemed to echo around him, from the inscription on his father's box, in Dan's voice discussing purpose versus passion, and now from Benjamin's lips. *What was this truth that everyone sought, but none could agree on?*

"We are now a confused people, and with the Romans expanding their influence throughout our lands, things are changing," Benjamin added.

"More people are questioning Roman rule. I find myself wondering too. They present themselves as allies, but their actions sometimes suggest otherwise. Some of our people have begun to resist, while others, struggling with heavy taxes, have turned to questionable means of survival. We seem to be losing our way," Benjamin said, his brow furrowed.

"The Scribes and the Chief Priests argue about everything related to worship, while the Council tries to maintain peace and good relations with the Romans. I worry about what might happen if these tensions continue to grow," Jonathan's friend said with a furrowed brow.

"You sound suspicious of Roman intentions," Jonathan quietly observed.

"I witnessed a Roman punishment while traveling, Jonathan. A crucifixion." Benjamin lowered his voice. "It changes how you see things. It makes you question what we're told about Roman justice." Benjamin's gaze dropped to the floor.

Jonathan sensed the concern, or maybe fear, in his friend's eyes.

The room was deathly silent for a while.

In Crete, Jonathan hadn't witnessed such Roman violence. To him, the Romans had been patrons who commissioned his finest bows and appreciated his craftsmanship. Marcus, in particular, had been a respectable man and benefactor whose support had opened many doors.

Jonathan felt the stark contrast between his experiences with the Romans and Benjamin's bitter account. The years spent away from Caesarea had given them very different perspectives. *Perhaps my position as an artisan in Crete shielded me from the harsher realities that Benjamin encountered in Galilee.*

Has Crete changed the way I look at the Empire? Or has it shown me a different face of Rome that Benjamin has never seen?

Sensing the tension, Jonathan shifted the topic. "But you look good, my friend. I'm happy everything is going well for you!" Jonathan said.

Benjamin shook off the anger and dread, then smiled broadly at his long-lost friend.

"I am! I now run one of my father's trading businesses. I trade in olive wood and limestone for building. The trading part is easy to learn, but sourcing and moving the products require much hard work, and I think I'm getting the hang of it," Benjamin laughed, showing off his strong arms.

Jonathan noticed how much Benjamin had changed. Though Jonathan was two years older, Benjamin was now taller and more muscular. He looked like he had moved a lot of wood and stone under the sun. There was no trace of the old, chubby Benjamin. He looked healthy and happy.

Happy? Jonathan mused.

"And I'm betrothed!" Benjamin announced with excitement. "My father arranged my marriage! She's beautiful, Jonathan! I can't wait for you to meet Priscilla." His face lit up at the mention of his bride's name.

Jonathan hugged Benjamin.

"Congratulations, my friend. I'm truly happy for you!"

They both laughed.

"And Caleb is married too! He has a son!" Benjamin added.

Caleb? Jonathan suddenly remembered Caleb. They grew up together, all three of them. They had adventures and misadventures and were like brothers in mischief. They were never far apart from one another.

Caleb was different from Benjamin. Caleb was the quiet one who listened to Jonathan's complaints about the pottery wheel. Benjamin was the one who always pushed him to go out and play. With Caleb and Benjamin, Jonathan had a great childhood. The two were opposites, and Jonathan was the one in the middle who held them together.

"Where is Caleb?" Jonathan asked.

"He lives in Cana now. His family moved there a few months after you left. My father told me they started trading wine exclusively and decided that living in Cana would help their business. I haven't seen him since, but our fathers often meet on their trade routes, and that's how we stay in touch.

"My father told me a few days ago that he would be meeting Caleb's father in Joppa for the Maritime Trade Fair, which starts in three days. He asked if I wanted to come along since Caleb would be there. I said yes! It's been so long since I've seen Caleb! And now you're here! You have to join my father and me on the trip! We have to see Caleb!"

There was much to discuss. They had much to catch up on. Benjamin shared stories of his travels and dealings with his most prominent clients, the Chief Priests and Council members. He also updated Jonathan on all the developments happening in Judea and parts of Galilee. Then, they planned their trip to Joppa to surprise Caleb.

Benjamin

"I witnessed a Roman punishment while traveling, Jonathan. A crucifixion.
It changes how you see things.
It makes you question what we're told about Roman justice."

By the time Jonathan went to bed that night, he felt exhausted. So much had happened since his return.

His father had changed. Amos had left a journal for Jonathan to read.

Dan looked sick.

His childhood friend was wary of the Romans, saying Galilee had changed. Had Judea changed, too? Benjamin didn't say. And here he was with a new skill and a plan that would never have his father's blessing.

I have to start reading the journal.

He was unsure whether he meant this as a reminder or as reassurance that there was nothing to fear in his father's words.

Jonathan didn't sleep well that night either.

5

JANUS

The courtyard was awash in golden sunlight as Jonathan settled beside Dan after breakfast. Lost in his work, Dan moved his brush across the pottery piece, his concentration so intense he wasn't aware of Jonathan until their shoulders nearly touched.

"You're up with the birds today," Dan remarked, glancing up to see Jonathan about to loosen the leather straps that secured the bow across his back.

When Jonathan set the bow on the table between them, Dan's hands froze mid-stroke. The morning light captured the bow's curves and polished surface, showcasing its intricate craftsmanship. "That is extraordinary," Dan breathed, his voice brimming with genuine admiration. His eyes met Jonathan's with childlike eagerness. "May I hold it?"

Jonathan smiled as he carefully placed the weapon in Dan's outstretched hands, watching his surrogate father's face light up with appreciation. Coming from a master craftsman whose work was revered throughout Caesarea, such spontaneous praise felt like an incredible blessing with which to begin the day.

Dan ran his fingers along the length of the bow. "The wood is perfectly curved!" he complimented. "The wood and bone feel as smooth as silk. What a lovely finish! This must have taken you days to complete!" He looked at Jonathan as he continued to trace his fingers over the carvings on the bow.

"The detailing is exquisite!" Dan exclaimed. He was impressed by Jonathan's work, and his eyes showed pride in the young man he viewed as his son.

"It took longer than I anticipated. The wood was rare and costly. I measured three times before each cut," Jonathan admitted to Dan. "I made it as a gift for my father."

Dan believed Amos would be thrilled to receive such a gift. He could envision Amos proudly displaying the bow in the house, admiring it for days, and telling every visitor that his son had made it! As he smiled and became lost in thought, Dan heard Jonathan speak, breaking the temporary silence between them.

"I'm going to the garrison today to meet with a *praefectus*," Jonathan said.

"*Praefectus*?" Dan asked as he placed the bow on the table.

"Janus," replied Jonathan.

Dan closed his eyes and pondered for a moment. Opening his eyes, he said, "He's the *Praefectus Castrorum*, Nathan. His office is next to the *Procurator's*. I've heard he's a kind and honorable man," Dan added, looking at Jonathan.

"Have you met him?" Jonathan inquired.

"I met him several times with your father," Dan nodded. "Why are you meeting with him?"

Jonathan drew the letter marked with Marcus's seal from his belt and set it beside Dan's brushes on the table. "A *tribunus* in Crete asked me to deliver this to him," Jonathan explained.

"These Roman officials are very busy people, Nathan. You might have difficulty securing an audience with them," Dan said, his brow furrowing slightly.

Jonathan reached inside his cloak with a confident smile. "I also have this," he said, revealing the pin Marcus had tucked into his garment when he departed from Crete.

Dan's eyes widened. He had seen similar pins and understood their significance. "That pin will open doors for you and provide all the assistance you need in any Roman office. You must have impressed the person who gave it to you. It is rarely given to non-Romans and is often awarded to Roman emissaries for their valuable service to the Empire," Dan explained as he looked more closely at Jonathan.

"Marcus is my patron," the young bowyer explained. "He's the *tribunus* of the garrison in Crete. He introduced my bows to the noble families of the island, who pay a high price for them."

"Did you provide bows to the Roman army in Crete?" Dan interrupted, his fingers still on the pottery piece in front of him.

Jonathan noticed the sudden tension in Dan's posture. "Benjamin asked me the same thing," he said, meeting his surrogate father's gaze. "Why do you ask?"

Dan's eyes dropped to his work. "It's likely because Benjamin and I have witnessed the effects of bows and other weapons in the hands of Roman soldiers," he replied quietly, each word heavy with meaning.

Jonathan shifted uncomfortably, feeling the space between them widen. After a moment of silence, he leaned forward. "Marcus once told me that a knife is a knife. It serves as a weapon for defense and attack," he said carefully. "A knife maker, a craftsman, brings to life the beauty he perceives in the metal and wood. His work concludes when he completes the piece."

He sought Dan's eyes again. "*We are craftsmen,* Dan. We create. That's what we do. How the world sees and applies what we create is their choice. Ours is a response to the call of our craft."

Dan's weathered hands resumed their work, but his expression remained troubled. "Is that how your master explained bowmaking to you?" he asked softly.

Jonathan replied with silence. *I struggle to reconcile my observations of the Roman army in Crete with what Benjamin and Dan say about them in Judea and Galilee.*

The morning air grew heavy between them as both men held their tongues, each fearing to wound the other with words that couldn't be taken back. A scattered pile of pottery tools and brushes sat between them, quietly echoing what Jonathan had turned away from, the tools still binding them in ways neither could name.

He searched Dan's expression, wondering if the words would come, if Dan would speak what Jonathan feared to name, the very thing Benjamin had discussed with such passion. Dan didn't. *Perhaps some bridges are best crossed another day.*

As Jonathan closely observed Dan, now outdoors under the morning sun, it became evident that his surrogate father was not only pale but also frail. Dan had lost a significant amount of weight, far too much, and Jonathan felt alarmed.

"Please try to finish the piece early," Jonathan told Dan. "I'd like you to rest today. I'll see you later tonight if I make it back for supper," he added as he stood up to strap the bow to his back, preparing to leave.

Dan nodded and returned to his work.

The streets of Caesarea were just as Jonathan remembered, always alive with activity. Some hurried about their business, weaving through crowds. In contrast, others strolled lazily, admiring vibrant cloths, earthenware, oils, spices, incense, and perfumes from across the Empire: a heady assault on the senses.

Immersed in the familiar colors, scents, and sounds of his childhood city, Jonathan smiled. Everything was exactly as he had remembered it from Crete. He was home.

He still knew his way around. Except for a few new stalls, most buildings remained unchanged on streets he knew like the back of his hand. But entering a Roman office without his father or Dan would be a first. As a boy, he would beg to accompany them on deliveries, amazed by the wonders inside the garrison.

Jonathan grew up speaking and writing Greek. His father insisted that he learn Greek, as it was the only means of communicating with the Romans. Amos said it was the language of trade. Consequently, he became fluent in Greek, which greatly benefited him during his time learning the art of bowmaking in Crete.

Fluency in Greek would be crucial now that he must learn to interact with the Romans in Judea without his father or Dan beside him.

Jonathan made sure his pin was visible and securely tucked into his cloak. He adjusted the straps of the bow slung over his shoulder. Jonathan had only his bow and refrained from bringing arrows to avoid looking dangerous. He was entering a garrison after all.

A quick word and the sight of his pin made his entry effortless. The guards let him pass through.

The courtyard sprawled beneath the unforgiving midday sun, its limestone pavers radiating heat. As in Crete, rows of spears stood in perfect formation against sun-baked walls, their metal tips catching light like stars. Wooden stocks and iron-tipped weapons were piled high, with the distinctive clatter of metal against metal punctuating the air. Soldiers in leather cuirasses moved with practiced efficiency as they took inventory. The familiar scent of rust-preventing oil mingled with sweat and dust, the unmistakable aroma of Roman military precision.

The scent transported him to Crete… and Marcus.

Jonathan's eyes were drawn to the tethered horses. *Magnificent creatures,* he thought. He always found horses to be beautiful and graceful. He made a mental note to visit the stables after he had delivered the letter to the *praefectus*.

Jonathan presented himself at the entrance of the most imposing door down the corridor. He stated his purpose and was told to wait.

It wasn't long before he was ushered in and told to take a seat. He had yet to take stock of the unique items he saw in the room, including the map that hung prominently on the wall, when an imposing figure emerged from an adjacent room and stood at the table before him.

The man before him was imposing, just like Marcus. *This must be Janus,* Jonathan thought. They both had an air of authority that could move hundreds of men with a wave of a hand. Marcus had a muscular frame and moved slowly, as if always in deep thought. This man before him was leaner but half a foot taller. His movements were spare yet fast and deliberate; hence, Jonathan was surprised to see him standing there without noticing his entry into the room. Like Marcus, the man facing Jonathan had piercing, dark gray eyes that conveyed a serious demeanor.

Jonathan bowed, introduced himself, and handed the letter to Janus. Jonathan remained standing while Janus checked the seal, opened the letter, and read its contents.

"I met Andreas during my deployment in Crete," Janus stated, his words efficient and measured like a military report. "I served alongside Marcus, and both men proved their worth and reliability." He folded the letter with precise motions and assessed Jonathan with the appraising glance of a commander evaluating a recruit.

"You've earned high commendation from respected men. They've recommended you to be a supplier of bows to this garrison."

Jonathan was stunned. He hadn't been aware that the letter he carried was a recommendation for his work!

"*Dominus Praefectus*," Jonathan said, surprise evident, "I didn't know the letter I carried contained an endorsement. I was just instructed to deliver it to you. I arrived in Caesarea the day before to be with my father, Amos, after finishing my apprenticeship in Crete."

"You're the son of the pottery artisan?" Janus asked, his face unable to mask his surprise.

"I am *Dominus Praefectus*. Amos is my father. It saddens me that I was not with him when he died," Jonathan said.

"I'm surprised you're into bowmaking," Janus said, studying Jonathan more closely now. "I have two of your father's beautiful pieces. My wife demanded two at whatever cost and adores both pieces I selected and purchased for her."

Jonathan smiled at the familiar praise, a bittersweet warmth spreading through his chest. Throughout his childhood, he had witnessed Judea's elite compete for his father's work, willing to pay double or triple to claim a piece before their rivals. And here was Janus, whose wife had secured not one, but two of these treasures.

"If you're as skilled in bowmaking as your father was in pottery," Janus continued, leaning forward with newfound interest, "I can understand why Andreas and Marcus were *impressed*. May I?" Janus gestured at the bow peeking over Jonathan's shoulder.

Jonathan released the straps that secured the bow on his back and carefully handed it to Janus for inspection.

Janus closely inspected Jonathan's bow, his eyes noting every detail. He thought the weight, the balance, and the careful joining of materials must have taken this lad weeks of patient labor. He ran his thumb along the limb, feeling the wood respond to even that slight pressure.

He was surprised to recognize the distinctive grain of yew, a wood not found in Crete. It was rare and prized for its strength, flexibility, and durability. The smooth surface reflected the afternoon light, revealing subtle color variations that only appeared in wood that had been meticulously prepared and shaped.

"How did you manage to source the yew?" Janus asked.

"I purchased it from a trader whom Andreas knew well. It was priced highly, for it was straight and long," Jonathan answered curtly.

Janus ran his calloused fingers over the bow, his touch detecting the subtle variations in texture. The upper and lower sections of the handle riser were made of bone, not just any bone, but one polished to a luster that caught light like still water. His fingertips traced the intricate fish-scale patterns carved with a jeweler's precision. A knowing smile crossed his lips, the rare expression softening his typically stern demeanor. *This design was surely a homage to the young man's father, whose fish sigil had marked the finest pottery in Caesarea.*

The shelf was smooth as river stone, offering perfect balance against the arrow's spine, while the grip, also fashioned from bone, continued the scale pattern that would prevent slipping even in the sweat of battle. Where the bow required flexibility, it was wrapped perfectly in sinew that felt alive under his touch. Leather thongs, oiled to a suppleness that would resist rain and sun, provided ideal handling.

As he turned the bow in his hands, Janus quietly marveled at the craftsmanship, his admiration evident in his eyes. The bow's finish spoke of countless hours of patient work. The wood seemed to warm to his touch, responding as if it recognized a skilled archer's hands.

The nocks were made of bone, resembling rolling waves with a fishtail at the end; cool and smooth against his fingertips, yet unyielding where they needed to be strongest.

The upper and lower limbs curved with the grace of a dancer, their elegantly balanced arcs promising both power and control. Sinew inlaid for reinforcement caught the light differently than the wood, creating a visual harmony that matched the bow's perfect balance in his hands.

Standing tall, Janus held the bow before him, gauging its length. He drew the string, imagining the release of an arrow. *Light, flexible, and powerful. Flawless. He would give as many denarii as it took to own such a weapon.*

Janus looked at Jonathan with newfound respect. *This lad was a master bowyer, a young one, but an artisan in his own right. Truly, Andreas's successor. "In a few years, men will pay dearly for bows crafted by his hands. Janus would pay dearly for one now.*

Standing at arm's length from one of the most powerful men in Caesarea, Jonathan closely observed how Janus handled his bow.

When Janus mentioned meeting Andreas in Crete, Jonathan suspected that Janus practiced archery. *Only fellow archers sought out the Master of Bows.* How Janus handled and inspected the bow confirmed Jonathan's suspicions that Janus was part of the *Sagittarii*, perhaps one of Rome's best.

"If I had not met you, I would say this is Andreas's work. It's beautiful, and it's perfect," Janus complimented.

"I made the bow as a gift for my father."

"Your father would have treasured this," Janus replied, running his hand over the carved grip once more before handing the bow back to Jonathan.

"Are you interested in supplying bows to this garrison?" Janus asked.

"*Dominus Praefectus,* I'm honored by your offer," Jonathan replied, his bowyer's sense of quality and precision evident in his careful response. "Though I've learned much from Andreas, I would need to establish a proper workshop, select and season the right woods, and train apprentices who understand every step to create consistently high-quality bows at the scale the army requires."

"I hope you can do this soon. Good bowyers are hard to find in Judea. We have a small contingent of archers. Our bows come from Syria, and the delivery time is longer than we'd like," Janus explained.

"If you're not ready to supply us, would you consider commissions? Some officers and I would gladly pay for a bespoke bow from you," Janus continued as he smiled at the young man.

"You honor me, *Dominus Praefectus*. Thank you for the offer. May I have a few days to think about it? I have just arrived from Crete and must settle my father's affairs. I need some time before planning anything for myself, including accepting commissions," Jonathan answered.

"I see why Andreas and Marcus speak so highly of you, Jonathan. You conduct yourself well. You make your father proud," Janus said with a smile.

"Yes, please think about it. I'd love to hear about Marcus and Andreas. I've learned a lot from your teacher in Crete. Unfortunately, I have some urgent matters today and won't be able to spend more time talking. Please visit again," Janus said, extending the invitation to the young man.

"I will," Jonathan answered and bowed as Janus left the room, followed by two armed soldiers who stood patiently waiting by the door from which he had entered.

Jonathan left the *Praefectus Castrorum's* office, wishing his father were alive to share in his success. He couldn't believe the letter he carried was a recommendation to supply bows to Caesarea's archers! Marcus, his benefactor, had introduced him, a bowyer who had just started his trade! Marcus's gesture was completely unexpected and deeply appreciated. Jonathan vowed to return to Crete and thank Andreas and Marcus for their support.

Would Father, if he were alive, celebrate my good fortune? Would he be proud of my work? Would he cheer for me as I build my workshop and train my team?

He had dreamed about this when he was in Crete! For six years, he had dreamed of starting his trade and building it as successfully as his father had built his own.

Jonathan was so deep in thought, remembering all the plans he had made while in Crete (from building his studio to connecting with all the known suppliers of wood, leather, and sinew), that he took a wrong turn and ended up behind the offices instead of in the front, where he had entered.

Jonathan found himself in an unfamiliar section of the garrison. After wandering through identical corridors, he stopped, momentarily disoriented by the unfamiliar surroundings.

The passageway opened suddenly into a vast space where rows of majestic horses stood, their coats gleaming as stable hands groomed them. The scent of hay and horsehair filled the air, a sharp contrast to the official quarters' polished stone and rich leather. Among them, a beautiful brown mare caught his eye, her intelligent gaze locking onto his. She stepped forward confidently, her harness swinging loosely around her neck.

The mare's gentle brown eyes enthralled Jonathan. *They're stunning!*

Jonathan held out his hand as the mare came within reach, when suddenly he heard a shout. A stablehand was shouting, pointing at a black stallion charging at Jonathan.

Jonathan stood frozen, watching the powerful animal rise on its hind legs before him. The stallion's muscles rippled beneath its gleaming black coat, its nostrils flaring wide with aggression and releasing plumes of hot breath that Jonathan could feel against his face.

He was so transfixed by the creature's grace and raw power—like a force of nature embodied in flesh and bone—that he closed his eyes. The thundering of his own heart matched the rhythm of the approaching hooves as he waited for the inevitable impact.

Then, he felt a hand pull him away.

Jonathan was flung onto a pile of crates. He hit his head against something hard before falling to the ground. He glanced at the man who had saved him, the man who had taken his place under the stallion's hooves and been buried under its weight.

Pandemonium erupted. Men rushed out from various parts of the stable to control the stallion and calm the panicked horses. Jonathan lost consciousness.

Jonathan woke with sharp pain in his head, shoulder, and back. He remembered falling with the bow on his back. The bow's wood dug painfully into his skin. He was sure his skin had broken, and the open wound would require some tending.

Jonathan slowly opened his eyes. He was still in the stables, and Janus was beside the man who was bandaging Jonathan's head. Janus saw Jonathan's eyes open and asked, "Are you all right?"

Jonathan nodded as he attempted to prop himself up against some crates. He saw a man lying near him, unconscious. The man who had just finished bandaging Jonathan's head was now attending to the man who had saved Jonathan's life.

"My stallion attacked you," Janus said to Jonathan. Jonathan's head throbbed.

"You came too close to my stallion's mare, Jonathan. Your scent was unfamiliar. My stallion considered you a threat, so he charged," Janus explained.

"Only a few can go near the horses behind my office—mostly grooms and select riders. This is where we keep the highly strung horses that require special attention. The ones you saw on your way in, in front of my building, are more approachable than the ones here," Janus explained.

"I apologize, *Praefectus*. I didn't mean to frighten your horses or cause a commotion. I got lost on my way out," Jonathan explained.

"I was told my slave, Samir, saved you from being trampled," Janus said, glancing at the unconscious man lying an arm's length away from Jonathan. "Samir takes care of all my horses, including the stallion that attacked you."

Jonathan caught a glimpse of Samir's bruised back. The man who had bandaged Jonathan finished bandaging Samir's shoulder and walked toward Janus. He whispered something to the *Praefectus*, bowed, and left.

"My physician says you're both all right. Samir will take some days to mend. He has a broken bone and needs to heal," Janus said. "Please take Samir to his quarters so he can rest," he instructed his men.

Then he turned to Jonathan. "My men will escort you home. It would be best if you rest as well, Jonathan. It's been quite a day for you and Samir. I must go now, but I look forward to your visiting again," Janus said, leaving the courtyard with his soldiers.

Janus

"You came too close to my stallion's mare, Jonathan. Your scent was unfamiliar. My stallion considered you a threat, so he charged."

6

DAN

JACOB APPEARED AT DAN'S DOORWAY AS SOON AS DAN'S FEET touched the floor. His timing was so precise that Dan often wondered if the young man possessed some gift beyond ordinary senses. *This kind of intuition is valuable and aids a potter in determining when the clay has reached the perfect consistency.* It was as if the boy could sense the subtle shift in the household's rhythm when Dan awoke. Dan smiled as Jacob warmly greeted him.

With a full day ahead, Dan moved with purpose. He inspected Jonathan's breakfast preparations, attended to the studio's finances, and then settled into his cherished spot in the courtyard where morning light fell perfectly upon his work. Here, brush in hand, he could lose himself in the delicate art of pottery painting.

Jacob seated Dan comfortably with a hot drink beside him before he left.

This corner of the courtyard held fond memories for Dan. The morning sun warmed the worn stone bench just as it had for decades, with the scent of Amos's lilies lingering in the air. They would sit here and talk for hours when one needed the other's advice, the stone beneath their fingers growing smoother each year.

Even after Amos's death, Dan felt at peace here. He could still hear his friend's voice, that distinctive timbre caught between gruffness and tenderness, offering wisdom when needed. The wind through olive branches sometimes carried the faint echo of his laughter.

Dan never truly spoke to Amos, but the silence between thoughts somehow brought answers. In this corner, Amos was always near... just a breath, just a memory away. He reached out in thought, and Amos met him there, speaking through silence.

You should have seen our boy yesterday. He came home with Roman soldiers, his head bandaged and his arms bruised! I almost had a heart attack, Dan thought, chuckling.

In his mind, Dan could hear Amos laughing, too. It had been a long time since he had heard that laugh.

A heart attack? Dear friend, you can't join me yet. Jonathan needs you. He's young and has a lot to learn. You must remain healthy and strong for Jonathan, Dan imagined Amos saying.

Dan nodded, feeling the weight of Amos's words. He missed his friend, who had always been the anchor in his life. Amos's vision and wisdom propelled them to financial success, and his passion for their craft elevated their skills to heights he never imagined they would attain. Amos was Dan's friend, brother, and family.

A smile tugged at his lips, remembering when he'd first met Amos, a brash young boy who declared, without shame, that he would become the most successful pottery artisan in Galilee. Dan was just a local potter's assistant then, watching Amos's family fall on hard times and admiring how tirelessly the young man worked to support them through his craft.

Those early years had forged a bond between them that transcended mere friendship. As Dan's brush moved over the pottery, he could trace the journey of their lives together, how they had leaned on each other during the tough times and celebrated each small victory as if it were a triumph. His eyes glazed as the memories washed over him.

It had been a challenging yet rewarding life, despite its hardships. Dan wouldn't trade a single moment of it for all the wealth in Judea.

"Good morning, Dan," Jonathan said as he walked into the courtyard and sat beside him.

As his eyes settled on Jonathan, Dan marveled at how life had surprised him. After losing his family and spending years as an orphaned servant just trying to stay off the streets, he'd never imagined he would find a family again, let alone one not of his blood.

Jonathan had removed the big bandage from his head, leaving just a smaller one over a cut he had sustained. "How are you feeling?" Dan asked.

"I'm much better today," Jonathan said. "A good night's sleep was all I needed."

"That's good to hear," Dan said with a smile. "I could use some help."

"Help?" Jonathan asked curiously.

"With your old friend, the pottery wheel," Dan said, trying to keep a straight face but failing.

Jonathan pretended to be horrified. "You can't be serious! I escaped that wheel six years ago! I won't go back!" he laughed. Their laughter filled the sunlit courtyard, making the house feel warm and alive again.

"Please tell me you're joking, Dan! Pottery?" Jonathan repeated in protest, sounding like a kid again.

"I'm old, Nathan," Dan said, using Jonathan's childhood name with a gentle smile. Jonathan felt the familiar pang of obligation that always came when Dan used that name.

Dan leaned forward, his weathered hands clasped together. "I want to make a water vessel, a gift for an old friend. My feet can't dance around the wheel like they used to." His eyes twinkled with fond memory. "But I can guide you, just like before. You can make a mess until we get it right."

He remembered the times he and Dan worked on the wheel, often ending with him flinging clay in frustration. Dan had always been on his side, baptizing the wheel as *"Jonathan's Tormentor."*

Jonathan tried to protest but couldn't help smiling. "I've forgotten everything, Dan. I honestly don't remember how."

"There are some things you never forget," Dan said, sipping his drink and closing his eyes.

Today is the day, Dan thought. He had waited six years for this moment. *Watch me, Amos,* he thought. *This is how we should have done it.*

Dan took another sip of his now-cold drink, his eyes looking forward to the familiar curves of the pottery wheel before him again. Jonathan would sit at the wheel today. After six years, he would place his hands upon the clay again. Dan could almost hear Amos's laughter, soft and knowing. He will be watching.

DAN WATCHED AS JONATHAN EXAMINED THE LUMP OF CLAY ON TOP OF the old pottery wheel they had secretly dubbed *"The Tormentor."* Dan remembered how, before leaving Caesarea, Jonathan had promised he wouldn't let the creaky wheel mock him again. Yet here he was, already looking threatened just by sitting before his father's pottery wheel.

"Your father isn't here, Jonathan," Dan said gently. "He's not watching over your shoulder."

Jonathan gave a small smile but kept his eyes on the clay. "I know, Dan. I'm just trying to figure out how I feel. Do I want Father to see me fail so I can blame him for my inability with clay? Or do I want to fail without his presence so I can finally realize I am to blame for not trying harder?"

Dan stayed quiet, resisting the urge to reach out. The young man before him looked utterly adrift, like a boy folding in on himself.

Breaking the silence, Dan said, "Jonathan, when you're at the pottery wheel, you're in control. You decide how fast or slow it spins. It's just a tool, like your bowery tools. They help you create. They don't control you or make decisions on your behalf."

His eyes met Dan's, haunted and aching. He looked like the same little boy Dan had once comforted years ago after a failed pottery attempt. Jonathan had looked lost then, and he still looked lost now.

"There was so much pressure, Dan." Jonathan's voice cracked as he stared at his hands. "Everyone expected me to be as great as my father. What if I can't be, even if I give it my best?"

"Expectations?" Dan moved closer, resting his hand lightly on Jonathan's shoulder. His voice softened to the tone he'd used when Jonathan was a child with skinned knees. "Nathan, neither your father nor I planned on anything regarding your future trade. We taught you pottery so you'd understand the craft that *provides* for our family, its rhythms and demands." He gestured to the wheel between them. *"That knowledge was a gift, not a burden."*

Dan gently turned Jonathan's face toward himself, meeting the young man's eyes with a steady, compassionate gaze. "You were never bound to follow in our footsteps. The choice has always been yours to make. We simply wanted you to understand the trade that sustains us."

Dan watched Jonathan's face as the truth settled slowly and relentlessly. It didn't strike like lightning; it seeped in, filling the spaces Jonathan had tried to leave empty. *Amos had never forced him into anything. There had been no plan to run from. No expectation to escape. He had fled a shadow of his own making. And because of it, his father had died without him by his side.*

The realization dealt a heavy blow to Jonathan's chest.

He exhaled, but the breath only deepened the ache. Heavy. Unrelenting. His fingers curled around the wheel, not gripping, but clinging... like a man lost at sea with no land in sight.

Breath came shallow, uneven. His chest hurt. Remorse pounded heavily on his chest, but he willed himself to stay still.

Then came his father's voice, not spoken, but waiting.

Truth.

The dam broke, not with a roar, but with a slow, aching surrender. A quiet, painful wail, small at first, then breaking through, spilling over, unstoppable.

Dan turned and quietly stepped out of the room, leaving Jonathan alone with the truth that had waited six years to be heard.

Dan

"We taught you pottery so you'd understand the craft that provides for our family, its rhythms and demands. That knowledge was a gift, not a burden."

THE SUN HAD CLIMBED TO ITS ZENITH WHEN DAN RETURNED TO THE studio. He found Jonathan sitting straight-backed before the wheel, a newfound determination in his posture. Dan had already prepared the clay just as he used to for Amos, clean and smooth, ready for Jonathan to shape.

He sat before the wheel, lighter though not healed, but quieter inside. His eyes were brighter; the tension around them had been replaced by a clarity that spoke of some internal resolution. His face was calm, and the muscles relaxed into what Dan recognized as the perfect state for making pottery.

He spun the wheel, and the familiar sound of wood against wood filled the studio. His feet began dancing to a rhythm only he could feel, the subtle press and release creating a hypnotic cadence that seemed to rise from the floor.

The clay centered with a soft squelching sound as his moistened hands guided it to the wheel's heart.

Jonathan was lost in its rhythm, his breathing synchronizing with each revolution.

He began kneading the clay with firm, measured movements, his fingertips registering every granule and air pocket. The earthy scent rose to meet him, damp and primal, the same smell that had filled this studio for years. The clay yielded to his touch, cool and responsive, neither too firm nor too soft.

Dan observed, pleased that Jonathan remembered to "read" the clay with all his senses. The slight resistance against the heel of the hand, the lightest touch as fingers pressed into the surface, even the subtle change in color as it absorbed moisture from his skin, all these told stories to those who knew how to listen.

Dan had constantly reminded Jonathan that a good potter knew when the clay was too dry and needed water, and that the material itself would speak if given the chance.

Jonathan cupped the clay, his thumb pressing gently to find its center. He then gently pulled the clay upward while maintaining a steady rhythm with his feet and applying the right amount of pressure with his hands.

Pulling and guiding the clay was where Jonathan usually struggled and failed.

Dan watched Jonathan's concentrated expression, recognizing that the young man remembered his lessons, not to force the clay but to guide it... that shaping clay is a process, not a moment. Dan could almost see Jonathan hearing Amos's voice in his head, telling him to find the form hiding behind the lump of clay and guide it to its new shape.

Jonathan's feet continued their movement as his hands guided the clay in a dance, celebrating the new form taking shape. He checked the thickness of the jar's walls, ensuring there was enough clay for Dan's planned engraving. He added water when needed and let it dry when it became too soft. He was in rhythm, never losing a beat.

He felt the clay move as his fingers gently guided it. He knew that forcing the clay into the desired shape would weaken it when it was time to hold its form, which was why all his previous clay work had failed. *Dan was right.* He needed to read the clay and respond to it.

Jonathan cupped his hands to round out the shape and to feel if the clay was ready.

He smoothed the base and shaped the sides. His fingers gently pinched and curled the lip of the jar. He smiled, half in disbelief, as the jar's lip curled gently. It looked as if it were smiling back. He cupped his hands around the base to strengthen it. He closed his eyes, knowing, without doubt, that his father would have been watching... not in criticism, not in judgment, but in quiet pride.

The Tormentor slowly crawled to a stop, and Jonathan stared in awe at the simple jar he had formed.

"It's finished," Jonathan whispered, his voice barely audible over the slowing creak of the wheel. "Only the handles remain..." His hands hovered above his creation, almost afraid to touch it again, as if the jar might dissolve back into formless clay under his fingers.

Dan nodded, a craftsman's understanding in his eyes. He knew when to let the moment breathe before speaking. "Your process was perfect," he said finally. "What made it different this time?" he asked, looking at the young man, hoping to make him ponder what had happened rather than simply telling him the answer.

Jonathan thought for a moment. "I wasn't trying to impress my father," Jonathan said, his voice so soft it was almost lost in the stillness of the studio.

"I wasn't trying to prove anything, Dan. I was doing it in his memory."

Dan felt a lump in his throat, a physical manifestation of emotion so powerful it momentarily robbed him of speech. Jonathan's simple truth bridged years of misunderstanding in an instant.

Jonathan couldn't have said it better. In those few words, he had captured everything Dan had tried to teach him about pottery, as well as life itself.

"Let it sit for a while," Dan said, his eyes glazed over. "I'll do the handles myself and start engraving them in a few hours." Dan stepped away, quickly and quietly, before the tears betrayed him.

Jonathan couldn't have expressed it better, Dan thought. Amos would have been so proud to hear those words. Dan's chest ached with the weight of love unspoken, of years stretched too far, too wide. If only they had seen each other, one last time.

~

THE AFTERNOON LIGHT SLANTED THROUGH THE WINDOWS, CASTING amber stripes across the studio's worn floor. Dust particles floated lazily in the golden beams, occasionally glinting like tiny stars. Dan worked on the jar, his hands creased with age and stained with decades of clay. He moved with practiced precision, each finger knowing precisely where to press and pull.

The familiar, earthy and primal scent of damp clay filled the space between them. He sat in reverent silence, watching Dan's hands coax the handles into place, as if the clay remembered those weathered fingers.

Under Dan's guidance, the simple vessel transformed into something that would carry more than water, holding their shared history made tangible in earth and fire.

After attaching the handles, Dan began preparing his design on the vessel. Dan's design closely resembled the clay box Jonathan's father had made for him, though Jonathan noticed the subtle differences between Dan's work and Amos's.

"Everything is so different from how we used to design our pottery," Jonathan said. "Why did we change?"

"We're not making pottery to sell anymore," Dan explained. "We're creating pieces for ourselves, telling our story. Some people won't understand, but a few will."

"I would buy this piece," Jonathan said, looking at the jar.

"This one is for Levi," Dan explained, his voice taking on the gentle cadence he always used when sharing wisdom. "I'll engrave 'Teach' at the bottom."

"Like 'Truth'?" Jonathan asked, remembering the word engraved on his father's piece for him.

"Yes, like 'Truth,'" Dan nodded, his weathered hands moving deliberately over the jar's surface.

Dan's fingers paused on the clay as he asked, "Have you started reading your father's journal yet?"

"I haven't," Jonathan answered, his voice barely audible.

Dan set down his carving tool and raised his eyebrows, the unspoken question hanging between them.

Jonathan cast his gaze downward, his fingers tracing the edge of the work table. "The last few days have been overwhelming, Dan," he finally admitted. "I want to read it, but I'm scared of what my father wrote." His voice caught on the words.

Dan reached across and placed his weathered hand over Jonathan's. He felt the young man's fingers trembling beneath his own. "Your father wasn't perfect, Nathan," he said gently. "He made decisions with the best intentions. When you read the journal, do so with an open mind and a forgiving heart."

Jonathan's shoulders tensed, then relaxed as he absorbed the words.

"Have you read it, Dan?" Jonathan asked.

"Only the one chapter your father shared with me," Dan answered. "Your father did not write the journal for me, so it is not for me to read," he added.

"I'm going on a trip the day after tomorrow, Dan. I will join Benjamin and his father on their caravan to meet Caleb at the Joppa Trade Fair," Jonathan said. "It will be great to reconnect with my friends and have space to think about recent events and how they've affected the plans I made before returning home," Jonathan added.

"I plan to read my father's journal while traveling," Jonathan said. "Benjamin said that we would be back in a week, so can we have a long talk when I return?"

Dan nodded, understanding the inner journey Jonathan was about to undertake, and silently hoped that Jonathan was ready to face the truth from which he and Amos had shielded him.

7

SAMIR

JONATHAN SLIPPED AWAY BEFORE FIRST LIGHT, LEAVING ONLY A hurried message with Jacob about visiting the *Praefectus Castrorum's* stables. His mind needed room to breathe.

The awakening streets of Caesarea offered comfort as he walked, vendors arranging their wares, the city stirring in soft morning light.

His feet carried him to the harbor, where he had disembarked from Crete a few days earlier. Ships lined the docks, their crews unloading goods as merchants gathered to claim their treasures.

He paused. *Confident then. Adrift now.* The realization settled over him as he stood watching the trade unfold, the hum of voices rising into the morning air.

I fled to escape a predetermined future, only to discover that Father had never set one for me.

Dan's words from the day before lingered.

Father only wanted me to understand the family's trade. Nothing more.

Had he misread everything? Yesterday, the clay had told him something unexpected. His hands had remembered the material, moved with it naturally, as if shaping vessels had never truly left him.

Perhaps the urgency to master pottery, to prove myself, led me to overlook my skill.

His fingers curled slightly as he remembered the feeling of clay beneath them.

I had the skill, after all. I was just in a hurry to master it.

A worn bench sat empty, overlooking the harbor. Jonathan lowered himself onto it, watching commerce unfold—the rhythmic creak of pulleys hoisting cargo, the sharp staccato of merchants haggling in various dialects, the cries of seabirds slicing through the salt-laced air.

Stillness settled over him as the weight of this newfound truth took hold. The morning sun climbed higher, casting elongated shadows. His past and future stretched before him, untouched, like fresh clay awaiting its shape.

Around him, the pulse of labor continued. Seabirds dove for scraps, their piercing calls punctuating the laughter and shouts of men unloading goods at the pier. A thin film of salt spray clung to his skin as he struggled to make sense of his shifting reality.

A commotion snapped him back to the present. A Roman soldier had seized an amphora from the goods unloaded off a nearby ship, a tall clay vessel with twin handles, meant for storing wine, oil, or grain. Ordinary, practical, unremarkable.

Except when crafted by an artisan like his father.

Amos' pieces were something else entirely, breathtaking in form, flawless in finish, sought after by Caesarea's affluent families, traded for bags of *shekels* at prices that turned simple clay into wealth.

Jonathan watched as the soldier shoved away a harbor worker who tried to reclaim it, sending the man crashing into a fruit crate. Wood splintered, spilling its contents onto the dusty ground. The soldier strode off, laughing, the amphora tucked carelessly under his arm, while everyone around pretended not to see.

Other workers at the harbor rushed to help the fallen man gather the scattered fruit. The incident happened so quickly that Jonathan, who was a few meters away, didn't have time to see the soldier's features. He was shocked that such a thing could happen openly in broad daylight, and no one seemed outraged. *Are people so used to it? Why isn't anyone indignant?*

Jonathan hurried over to the group of men collecting the scattered fruit. No one looked surprised or angry, as if it were just an ordinary incident.

He picked up a few pomegranates rolling near him and placed them in the crate with the rest that the others had gathered. He looked at the man who had confronted the soldier. The man's lip was bleeding, and his face was swollen with bruises. He appeared more defeated than angry.

"That soldier always looks for wine when assigned to this pier," the man muttered bitterly. "He takes an amphora each time, claiming it's his tax! My employer will be displeased. I hope he doesn't deduct it from my wages—it will cost me several days' worth of pay. Beware of him! Get your goods off the pier quickly!"

Jonathan nodded at the man, placed a comforting hand on his shoulder, and walked away. He couldn't believe what he had just witnessed, having never seen anything like it in his life in Crete. *Was it just him? Why isn't anyone in the crowd surprised?*

Is this why Benjamin and Dan seem wary of Roman soldiers? Jonathan shook his head. *Benjamin was right. It's not just Galilee; Judea is changing as well. It's seething underneath the surface. In time, it will boil over.*

Jonathan turned away from the docks, his mind troubled by what he'd witnessed. The Roman soldier's casual theft and the worker's resigned acceptance gnawed at him. This was the reality Benjamin had warned him about, so different from his experience in Crete, where Romans had been patrons, not oppressors. The contrast between memory and present reality, between Crete and Judea, left him unbalanced and prompted him to question what else he might have misunderstood.

As he began the familiar walk toward the *Praefectus Castrorum's* office, the unexpected aroma of freshly baked goods wafted toward him. The mingled scents of warm bread and sea salt momentarily transported him to a simpler time.

He remembered running these same streets as a boy, clutching a bag of bread while Caleb and Benjamin chased behind him, all three laughing as they raced to get the best pastries before they cooled. Those memories belonged to a different Caesarea, one without the harsh realities he was now witnessing as an adult.

The boyhood friends racing after treats seemed worlds apart from the men they'd become: one a bowyer returned from exile, the others merchants in their fathers' trades. None of them were children anymore.

Lost in this thread of memory and doubt, Jonathan let his feet carry him forward of their own accord. When he finally looked up, he found himself standing in the courtyard of the *Castrorum* office, the morning already half gone.

The courtyard was empty as he headed straight for the back stables to see Samir, the man who had saved him from being trampled by the stallion.

When he asked where he could find Samir, a stable boy pointed him to a door near a corner where a handful of men were grooming horses. Jonathan knocked and heard a voice inviting him to come in.

The cramped room held little more than a weathered table, its grain exposed from years of use, and a low cot with roughly hewn legs. A single oil lamp cast meager light, its flame reflecting in a dull metal holder. The sparse space revealed care in how the few possessions were precisely arranged despite their poor quality.

Jonathan paused at the threshold, taking in the scene. Samir was sitting on the cot, his back turned to the door as a stable boy bandaged his shoulder.

Jonathan couldn't help but notice the maze of old scars covering Samir's back, pale silver lines crisscrossing the skin like a cruel map of past suffering. The fresh injuries from the stallion's rampage stood out in stark contrast: angry, purple bruising that spread like spilled wine across his shoulder blades, with two deep cuts that were beginning to heal, their edges puckered and faintly glazed with healing salve, which filled the room with the sharp scent of herbs. *That looks painful,* Jonathan thought, recognizing the same careful stitching he had used to repair torn leather on bows.

When he saw Jonathan, the boy stopped bandaging Samir, set down the bandage, and left the room. Samir turned around, his expression shifting from pain to practiced neutrality as he recognized his visitor.

"Master," Samir said, straightening despite the obvious discomfort it caused him. "What can I do for you?" The deference in his voice contrasted sharply with the courage he had shown when saving Jonathan's life.

"Hello, Samir," Jonathan greeted. "I'm Jonathan. I came to thank you for saving me the other day and to check in on how you're doing. May I?" Jonathan pointed to the only chair in the room. Samir nodded, and Jonathan sat opposite him.

"How are you, Samir?" Jonathan asked.

"The one that attacked you was Master Janus's stallion, Master Jonathan. He is called Black Lightning. He has a few scratches on his leg from the incident. Nothing serious. A stablehand had just finished grooming Black Lightning. His mate is named Diana's Favor. She's the mare that approached you. Her hooves have just been trimmed. Diana's Favor is ready for my inspection," Samir replied as if reporting to someone who wanted an update on the horses rather than on his condition.

"It's good that the horses are fine today," Jonathan said. "What about you?" Jonathan asked again.

"I will be up and about, back to my normal duties in a day or two," Samir responded, his voice finding strength when speaking of his charges. "The horses will start looking for me if I'm away much longer. Black Lightning will paw at his stall floor. He always does when anxious. The mare will toss her head and refuse her grain. They can sense my presence even from inside the stables, you see, and will wonder why I haven't come." His words flowed more naturally when describing the animals than when speaking of himself.

Jonathan realized that everything was and would always be about horses for Samir. He seemed to forget his pain when he discussed horses, becoming animated and happy, like a craftsman discussing his latest work.

"I've instructed the grooms to inform me once they finish with Master Janus's horses. I need to check their work to ensure Master Janus is satisfied," Samir added. "Do you own a horse, Master Jonathan?"

"Sadly, I don't, Samir," Jonathan said. "I was in Crete for six years and always admired them. I was allowed to ride a few, and I haven't forgotten how it felt, how rare and exhilarating it was to move with such power and grace."

"Crete," Samir said. "I've heard stories of a different kind of horse the Romans ride there. They say the Romans got them from the far north. They're big and muscular but shorter than the horses here. Their coats are denser, and their chests are wider. Is this true?" Samir looked at Jonathan.

"They're called Illyrian horses, Samir. And yes, it's true," Jonathan said.

"Illyrian horses are shorter but more muscular than Black Lightning's breed," Jonathan explained, warming to the subject. "They have thicker necks and broader chests, which makes them suitable for long marches and heavy work. They're perfect for Crete's rough terrain." He smiled at the memory. "I was allowed to ride a few while there."

Jonathan leaned forward slightly. "Illyrian horses are rare in Judea and Galilee. They wouldn't thrive in our climate, but I saw one on the ship I took from Crete."

Samir's eyes widened, and for the first time since Jonathan had entered, genuine excitement transformed his face. "You did? Is the horse here in Caesarea?" he asked, momentarily forgetting his injuries.

"I don't know if the horse is still here in Caesarea, but I saw it on the ship," Jonathan said. "I assume whoever owns it is a Roman official. If it's not still here, the horse might have been taken to other garrisons. We can ask around. Have you been to other garrisons or stables outside of Caesarea, Samir?" Jonathan asked.

"I was with Master Janus in the Jerusalem garrison for three years and have been here in Caesarea for seven years," Samir replied, his voice steady but distant, as though reciting facts about someone else.

Jonathan leaned forward slightly. "And before that?"

Samir's hands stilled in his lap. "I was sentenced to hard labor in the mines of Wadi Hammamat." His voice dropped lower. "I had been there for almost eight years when I met Master Janus. A snake had bitten his horse, and I saved it." For the first time, a hint of pride crossed his face. "Because of this, Master Janus bought me, and I became his slave. I traveled with him to Jerusalem and then here to Caesarea."

"Was it Black Lightning that you saved from the snake bite?" Jonathan asked.

"Yes," Samir said, his posture straightening despite his injuries. "Since then, I've earned Black Lightning's trust and the trust of his mate," he added, a rare note of pride entering his voice.

Jonathan watched as Samir's entire demeanor transformed when speaking about the horses. "Do you take care of all the horses in these stables?" Jonathan asked.

"Yes, I do, along with some stablehands." Samir gestured toward the door where the boy had disappeared. "Occasionally, I'm also sent to other garrisons as my master directs."

"You know a lot about horses, Samir," Jonathan said, genuinely impressed. "Where did you learn all of this?"

"I grew up in a family whose livelihood depended on caring for horses. My father, from Nabataea, met my mother in Tyre and started a family. He was the head of the stables in one of the Roman garrisons in Tyre. My father's ancestors all cared for animals, particularly horses and donkeys, for their livelihood, just as we did in Tyre. My father was the first in his family to rise to such an exalted position.

"All the men in our family had to learn everything about horses and donkeys at a young age. My older brother, Raqmu, is a farrier who trims and shoes horses in the garrison, and I was a stable hand.

"As the head of the stables, my father knew how to do everything a horse or donkey needed. He is one of the best stable masters in Tyre," Samir said.

"Janus is lucky to have you caring for his horses, Samir," Jonathan commended.

"I believe I am the lucky one, Master Jonathan. Master Janus saved my life and gave me the work I have always loved to do. Horses are not only beautiful, majestic creatures; they remind me of my family," said Samir. His voice softened with a melancholy that spoke of profound loss.

"I hope you heal well soon before the horses start missing your scent," Jonathan said, rising from his seat. Samir stood up immediately upon seeing Jonathan rise. "And I hope one day Black Lightning will let me come near him," Jonathan added with a smile.

Samir smiled back. "Then let's see how close you can get today," Samir said. He opened the door and beckoned Jonathan to follow.

Jonathan followed Samir into the stables, his eyes drawn again to the web of scars across the man's back. *Did the Roman soldiers do this to him in the mines of Wadi Hammamat?* he wondered. Some scars ran deeper than others, and some cuts were longer, suggesting that someone had taken pleasure in the man's pain. Jonathan's stomach tightened. He was finding it increasingly difficult to reconcile the Romans he had known in Crete with what he was witnessing here in Judea.

They passed several horses being groomed, the sweet-sour smell of hay and manure mingling with the earthy scents of horsehair and leather. The stable floor was made of packed earth, swept clean but still releasing dust that caught the slanting rays of sunlight streaming through the small, high windows. The steady rhythm of brushes against coats and the occasional soft nickering created a peaceful backdrop until they reached the end of the stables, where a large black horse stood silently, watching Samir approach.

The stallion's coat gleamed like wet obsidian, muscles rippling beneath the surface with each slight movement.

Jonathan stopped a few feet away when Samir gestured for him to halt.

Samir greeted the black stallion in a soft, calming tone. He used a language of clicks and whispers that seemed as natural as breathing as he stroked its neck lovingly. The stallion's nostrils flared, taking in Samir's scent, before it nuzzled against Samir's neck, making a gentle huffing noise that sent warm breath visibly curling in the cooler stable air.

Samir turned to Jonathan and asked him to take a few steps closer. Jonathan did. Black Lightning stopped nickering and looked at him, shaking his mane.

"Please take a few more steps," Samir said. Jonathan did so, and the horse stood alert, as if sensing danger. Samir stroked the stallion's head, whispering that everything would be all right.

"I suppose that's as close as you can get today, Master Jonathan," Samir said. "Visit more often. He'll learn to recognize your smell and presence and know you mean no harm."

Jonathan nodded. "Thank you, Samir, for the excellent information. I'll try to visit again soon. Take care of yourself," he said, turning to leave. As he walked away, he couldn't help but notice how Samir's posture remained rigidly formal until the very moment Jonathan passed through the stables' door.

Samir

"Horses are not only beautiful, majestic creatures; they remind me of my family."

THE ECHO OF JONATHAN'S DEPARTING FOOTSTEPS HAD BARELY FADED when Samir's carefully crafted facade collapsed.

He turned toward his room, no longer needing to pretend that he was well. Each step sent pain rippling through his body. His arm ached as he pressed it tightly against his side for support. It still hurt badly.

The last two days had been miserable—his back and shoulders stiff with pain, his breath shallow from the strain. Every movement reminded him of the bruises, the torn muscle. But staying in bed would only prolong the healing process. He had endured worse injuries, bruised, cut, and bleeding, yet he had always survived.

This is nothing, he told himself.

Raqmu would have scolded him for dwelling on the pain. "Forget it,

Samir. Move. Stop thinking," he remembered Raqmu telling him over and over.

If his brother had been here, maybe, just maybe, he would have found the courage to finally answer back. *It's not the wounds you can see that hurt. It's the ones buried deeply in your head that won't let you forget.*

Samir sighed, slow and heavy.

Lately, the nightmares had returned. They were vivid and suffocating, leaving him gasping in the dark, slick with sweat despite the cool air.

Start moving, Samir.

The thought pulsed through his mind in a rhythm that matched the throbbing pain.

Start moving.

Don't think about Raqmu.

Don't think about the past.

But even as he formed the words, the memories pressed harder, pushing against the walls he had built and threatening to flood through at any moment.

It's done. It's done.

The horses were his sanctuary, perhaps his only sanctuary, in a world where the past never truly released its grip.

8

JOSEPH

The pottery wheel stood silent as Amos stepped through the doorway, cloak dusty from his journey. Later, he would barely remember the ride to Ramah, his mind consumed with the space where his son should have been.

Three months had passed since Jonathan vanished, and still, there was no word.

Now, standing before Joseph's wall of vessels, Amos felt both pride and pain surge through him. The afternoon light streamed through the high windows, catching each curve and contour of the assembled masterpieces. Their smooth surfaces gleamed with subtle variations, deep amber glazes, midnight blues, and the distinctive gold-flecked finish that had become his signature.

The room carried the faint scent of beeswax and cedar oil from the carved shelving, mixed with Ramah's ever-present dust that settled on everything despite the servants' constant attention. His contribution among these treasures, which bore his now-famous fish sigil, commissioned years ago before his world had fractured, seemed to mock him with its perfection, its dancing light and shadow a cruel contrast to the darkness that had settled over his life.

How could I have shaped such beauty, coaxed such grace from formless clay, while failing to see my son's growing desperation?

His gaze lingered on his piece. Though proud of the work selected for this distinguished company, he knew his hands had shaped finer vessels. *But will they ever do so again?*

"Amos!" Joseph's warm voice interrupted his dark thoughts. "What a joy to see you, my friend! What brings you to visit? Please, sit!"

This visit marked the final stop in Amos's unscheduled patron visits. He had deliberately saved this client for last, the one whose early faith in his talent had opened doors to Judea's elite households and paved the way for him to become one of the region's most sought-after artisans.

Joseph was one of the few people Amos considered a friend. He owed so much to the man who had made his success possible and ultimately secured a better future for Jonathan.

Joseph was one of the most successful traders in all of Galilee and Judea. His trade routes and network of contacts extended across the sea to distant lands. Despite his wealth and connections to Roman officials and Jewish leaders alike, Joseph remained kind and fair in all his dealings. His reputation for wisdom and integrity earned him respect from people at every station.

For Amos, Joseph was more than a patron. He was the rare friend who had believed in him when others saw only a struggling young artisan with a mysterious infant.

"I apologize for the abruptness of this visit, my friend. Thank you for seeing me," Amos said.

"Oh, Amos, you and Dan can visit anytime, and I say this honestly and with joy. Tell me, what made you travel to Ramah to see me? What can I do for you?" Joseph looked intently at Amos.

Amos sighed. "My son ran away three months ago, and we can't find him," he said in a whisper.

A look of surprise initially crossed Joseph's face before immediately turning to concern. "Jonathan ran away? But why?"

"Because he thought that not following in my footsteps to become a pottery artisan would break my heart," Amos replied, trying to keep his voice from breaking.

"I'm sorry to hear this," Joseph answered, his concern evident.

"My son not doing pottery would never break my heart. My son running away did," Amos replied. "Jonathan's assumption that I would love him only if he did pottery was painful. And the worst part was that I made it seem like he was right. I never spoke or did anything to correct him and tell him he was wrong."

The two men remained silent.

Joseph broke the silence and asked, "Is there anything I can do to help?"

"You made a sizable down payment a few months ago, commissioning me to create a piece for an esteemed colleague." Amos looked at Joseph and cast his gaze downward as he pulled a small bag out of his pocket. "I am here to return your advance payment."

Joseph's face registered surprise, which quickly faded to concern. He looked at Amos, silently asking for an explanation. The closeness between the two old friends was evident. Like Dan, Amos didn't need to hear Joseph ask why. He knew his friend and greatest patron needed to hear why he couldn't finish the commission.

Amos's voice dropped to a whisper, the words scraping his throat. "Ever since my son ran away, I can no longer do any work." His calloused hands spread before him, trembling slightly, fingers curling as if searching for clay. "My mind is not at ease, and my hands..." He clenched them into fists, then released them helplessly, studying the lifelines etched across his palms like cracks in dried clay.

"The wheel spins, but the form won't come. I position the clay, center it perfectly, but when I begin to shape..." He shook his head, a master describing the inexplicable failure of skills honed over decades.

"I *can't* do pottery anymore."

Amos looked devastated. The lines around his eyes had deepened into crevices since Joseph had last seen him, like clay that had dried too quickly and started to crack. His skin had taken on the sallow hue of someone who had spent too many days indoors, away from the sun that had once bronzed his face as he worked in the open courtyard of his studio. A new hollowness had settled in his cheeks, and his work-thickened fingers, usually so steady and precise, now trembled slightly when he gestured.

Even his clothing hung differently on his frame, suggesting he had been eating little. The weight of his loss was etched across his face like a potter's tool scoring wet clay: deep, deliberate, and permanent.

"Amos, I'm sorry about your son. And I'm saddened to hear you've stopped making pottery." Joseph's voice lowered, reverent. "You have a rare gift: the ability to transform a lump of clay into something extraordinary."

He met Amos's eyes. "I wish I had that. All I can do is admire the work of those who possess it." He gestured toward the wall where his vessels were displayed.

Amos raised a hand, then looked at his own. "It's gone," he said. "My wheel spins, but nothing takes shape. The clay stays clay. I can't make it beautiful anymore."

Joseph studied him, this master potter he had always admired, now looking lost. Silence settled between them. Then Joseph spoke again, his voice steady.

"You see what others miss. You find meaning in what others overlook. Your vessels transform daily tasks into sacred moments."

He motioned toward the shelves with quiet conviction. "Where others cut stone or melt glass, you take humble clay, the dust under our feet, and shape it into something that endures. That's not just skill, Amos. That's transformation."

Amos's gaze dropped.

Joseph leaned forward. "The ability to turn the ordinary into something beautiful is a sacred gift. And sacred gifts don't vanish. They wait, not in silence, but in expectation." His voice softened. "When it returns, you'll create something greater than ever before."

Amos gripped Joseph's hand as if drawing strength from his friend. "I will not accept the money you are returning, my friend," Joseph said, placing his hand over Amos's hand, which held the small bag of coins. "I will wait for you to create beautiful things again," he added, feeling the pain of his friend's broken heart.

"But... I can't..." Amos tried to respond, but he stopped.

"Your son will return to you," Joseph said, his voice carrying a certainty that his eyes couldn't quite match. He leaned forward, resting a hand on Amos's shoulder. "Trust that you have raised him well, that the truth you have planted in him will guide him home."

A moment of silence stretched between them, filled with unspoken fears.

"Jonathan will find his way back when the right time comes," Joseph continued, more softly now. "Truth always surfaces, like beauty from clay. I will also send word to all my emissaries and traders throughout Judea and Galilee to watch for him and send any news of his whereabouts. This I promise you, my friend."

Amos clasped Joseph's arm in wordless gratitude before taking his leave, his shoulders slightly less burdened than when he arrived.

As Amos's footsteps faded down the corridor, Joseph remained seated, the weight of their conversation settling around him. Seeing his old friend, a man who had always stood tall despite life's burdens, now so broken, unsettled something fundamental in Joseph.

The afternoon shadows lengthened across the floor, marking time's passage as Joseph remained motionless, replaying every word, every gesture, and every unspoken undercurrent that had passed between them.

Only when the last ray of sunlight withdrew from the room did he finally move, lighting the oil lamps whose gentle glow transformed the chamber just as twilight transformed the world outside: neither day nor night, but a space between worlds where reflection came most naturally.

The Fish Sigil of Amos

Amos placed his fish sigil in every pottery piece he made, usually at the bottom.

Joseph sat in quiet contemplation long after Amos had gone. The household moved around him with hushed efficiency, the servants well aware that he was not to be disturbed when he withdrew in this manner.

Amos had always been guarded, his emotions carefully kept behind steady hands and measured words. But today, the walls had crumbled. Joseph had never seen him so unguarded.

Their conversations had always been honest, respectful, and marked by genuine concern. Joseph had walked beside Amos and Dan through hardship and triumph, witnessing how both men learned to shape beauty from struggle.

He remembered the day he first met them. They were young and determined, searching Caesarea for a wet nurse with little more than hope in their eyes. He had used his connections to assist them, shielding them from unwanted attention, and watched as they pursued a dream not just for themselves, but for the sake of the child.

Joseph had opened doors for them, recognizing their talent early and introducing them to patrons who would help them thrive. Over time, they had become masters of their craft.

Joseph's gaze drifted to the vases lining his wall. Visitors often stood in awe before the collection, but for him, the pieces were more than art. They were reminders. Vessels of potential realized.

He had spent hours in the workshops of Judea's finest craftsmen, not as a patron but as a student, marveling at the way gifted hands could draw beauty from what others dismissed. He believed this ability to see the extraordinary in the ordinary was divine.

Sometimes Joseph could not understand why sorrow touched the lives of people like Amos and Dan. But just as artisans are given sacred sight to perceive hidden beauty, perhaps suffering, too, held a purpose beyond understanding.

Amos was one of those rare souls who could bring forth that beauty. And so was Dan. Their pottery bore both their marks: Amos's steady form, Dan's intricate detailing. Together, they created more than either could alone.

Gifts like theirs do not vanish. They lie dormant, waiting for the right season. When Amos returns to the wheel, and Joseph had no doubt he would return, what he creates will not merely rival his past work. It will surpass it.

The flame beside him flickered once, then steadied. Shadows of the vessels danced across the walls as Joseph rose and closed the door behind him.

Joseph

"The ability to turn the ordinary into
something beautiful is a sacred gift.
And sacred gifts don't vanish.
They wait, not in silence,
but in expectation. When it returns,
you'll create something greater
than ever before."

9

CANA

JONATHAN WASN'T IN CANA. ONE YEAR AND FOUR MONTHS AFTER HIS son's disappearance, Amos found himself standing in yet another unfamiliar town, chasing yet another ghost.

The whispered sighting was enough for Amos and Dan to leave their workshop and rush to Cana. A trader claimed to have glimpsed a boy who looked like Jonathan working in a vineyard. Amos and Dan immediately sought two seats in Joseph's caravan bound for Bethsaida that same day. It would pass through Cana, the small town known for its wines and stone vessels.

The air in Cana carried the distinctive perfume of ripening grapes, different from the salt-tinged breezes of Caesarea. Stone buildings caught the heat of the day, and the packed-earth streets resonated with the quiet rhythm of a town whose life moved in harmony with its vineyards. Even the dust that rose beneath their sandals seemed different, richer somehow, mixed with the crushed fragments of grape seeds and the ancient soil that produced Cana's renowned wines.

The roads no longer felt foreign to Amos. For over a year, he and Dan had traveled throughout Judea, Galilee, Samaria, and as far as Tyre, pursuing every whisper of Jonathan's whereabouts. Each journey began with hope and ended with the same hollow ache, but neither spoke of giving up.

Joseph's trading network had become their lifeline, providing both transportation and information. With each failed search, Amos clung to the belief that they were one day closer to finding his son. These months on the road had transformed both men. Where Amos had grown stronger, the constant travel had taken its toll on Dan, who now paused for breath on even gentle slopes. One basked in newfound vigor, while the other denied his growing weakness.

The one thing both men had in common was that neither wanted to be left alone in the house, so they traveled together in Joseph's caravans, sharing every piece of news they heard about Jonathan and hoping for an outcome they both nurtured in their hearts.

Traveling with Dan brought back so many memories for Amos. Some he willingly embraced as he remembered them, and others he allowed to enter his mind to lessen the pain with each remembrance.

He finally realized that the more he refused to acknowledge the bad memories, the stronger they became. The more he allowed them to come and go as they pleased, the less pain he felt with each recollection.

Amos admitted that his most painful memories were turning points in his life that had shaped him into the man he was today. He believed that the challenges he had faced then were not meant to destroy him but to shape him.

It was like pottery, he told himself when looking back. The clay will retain its form for a while, but exposure to the kiln hardens it into its final shape. My most painful memories were like the kiln. Exposure to them has hardened me into form.

On the day they arrived, they visited two vineyards, each at least two miles apart. The paths were steep and manageable for younger men, but a true test of strength for older ones more accustomed to sitting before a potter's wheel. Amos rose to the challenge with quiet resolve. Dan followed willingly, his strength fading with each step, every incline carving a deeper toll. Rest became his rhythm, not by choice, but by necessity.

Amos noticed the extended rests. He worried about Dan, though he kept it to himself. Pressing the issue would only spark one of Dan's trademark monologues, that stubborn refusal to let anyone speak for his body but him.

Amos still remembered how the last monologue ended. He would not risk provoking another one.

So he watched, quietly and carefully, as Dan pushed uphill with effort that grew heavier with each step.

The vineyards stretched in orderly rows, their vines bowed with ripening fruit. The air carried the sweet tang of fermenting grapes, mingled with the warmth of sunbaked soil.

After two days of scouring the outskirts of Cana, they had found no sign of Jonathan. The silence between them during the descent spoke of their shared disappointment. The downhill path offered Dan some mercy, but Amos noticed the way he braced himself against trees now and then. Dan's expression hid his disappointment, but not his exhaustion.

They needed to hurry - one of Joseph's caravans would leave before dawn.

They had to reach the town center before nightfall to secure a place to sleep. Amos hoped the easier path would spare Dan's strength. His pauses were longer now, his breath slower. Dan would resist if confronted, but Amos made a quiet vow: once they returned to Caesarea, he would take him to a physician.

Twilight settled over Cana. Oil lamps flickered in windows, casting a warm light across the narrow streets. The stone walls, still holding the day's heat, radiated a gentle warmth as the air cooled. Evening prayers drifted from homes, mingling with the voices of weary travelers.

The town was crowded. Many had arrived over the past two days, and like the first lodge, the second had no space left. There were only six beds, and they were all taken.

Darkness was near. Sleeping outdoors was not an option, not for Dan.

The two men stepped back into the streets, the shadows lengthening as the sun sank low. The setting sun bathed the stone buildings in golden hues.

"Comfortable beds have made us soft, Dan," Amos said with a wry smile. "The ground would feel harder now than when we first left Capernaum."

They laughed, both thinking of that same long-ago journey, and the strength it once demanded.

As they walked, Amos noticed a shop displaying stone vessels beside ones made of clay. Dan saw it too and slowed his pace.

Cana was known for wine, but the vessels mattered just as much. In Caesarea, wine was stored in clay amphorae. In Cana, however, wine for ritual use was stored only in stone vessels. The Law held that stone could not take on impurity. It remained clean, fit for sacred use.

Neither man spoke, but they drifted toward the display.

Exquisite stone vessels stood before them, their smooth surfaces catching the light.

Amos marveled, as always, at the strength and skill they required. Shaped not by hand but by hammer and chisel, these vessels required perfect precision; one wrong strike could ruin the piece entirely.

He and Dan ran their fingers over several that caught their eye, both reverent in their silence. Both knew how much a craft could demand of its maker. While the clay vessels were equally fine, their eyes kept returning to the stone and its simplicity, its quiet strength.

A man cleared his throat, and both turned toward the sound.

"Good day, sirs. How may I help you?" said the shopkeeper from behind the counter.

"We admire your wares," Amos replied. "They're beautiful."

"You've got an eye," the man said with a grin. "You went straight to the most valuable ones. Are you traders? Winemakers?"

"Neither," Amos said with a polite smile. "We're on our way back to Caesarea. We were drawn in by your display. We've been looking for lodging, but every place so far is full."

The man stepped around the counter, moving with the ease of someone who knew every board beneath his feet. He looked to be in his early forties, stocky and broad-shouldered, with a shock of gray hair and a neatly trimmed beard. Warm brown eyes crinkled beneath a generous smile.

"Welcome to my shop. I'm Eli. And yes, lodges fill quickly this time of year. The wine traders have started arriving to collect their orders." He paused. "You look like you could use a hand."

Amos nodded faintly, cautious but hopeful.

"As it happens, the two men I hired to run this place didn't return as promised. So here I am, minding the store myself when I should be elsewhere. I can offer you the back room for the night. There are two beds: basic, but dry. This isn't an inn, after all."

Eli chuckled softly. "Will that do?"

Amos and Dan exchanged a look, too stunned by his kindness to speak at first. Dan shook his head, smiling.

"Your kindness is a gift we gladly accept, Eli. A simple bed is more than enough after our long search."

"Well then," Eli said, already heading to the door, "let me close up, and we'll get a meal at the local inn before I leave you to rest. You must be hungry. I know I am."

He locked the door behind them, whistling a cheerful tune as the three stepped into the twilight.

EVERYONE IN CANA SEEMED TO KNOW ELI. AS THEY WALKED THE narrow streets, faces lit up at the sight of him, and hands reached out in greeting.

The same friendly reception followed them to the inn. The inn owner, leaning heavily on his cane, emerged from the back room, his weathered face breaking into a smile that erased years from his features. He embraced Eli like a brother before leading them to the finest table in the house.

"You seem to know every soul in this town," Dan observed, settling onto the bench.

Eli's eyes crinkled with mischief. "There's no mystery there," he whispered, leaning in. "I'm invited to every celebration, every milestone, birth, marriage, harvest. When you bring the wine, you witness life's sweetest moments." His infectious laughter rolled through the room.

The innkeeper placed before them earthenware bowls of steaming lentil stew, fragrant with coriander and garlic, alongside flatbread still warm from the hearth. The local wine Eli insisted they try was nothing like the watered-down fare served to travelers. It was earthy and robust, carrying hints of dried fruit and spice that spread comfort through Amos's chest with each sip.

The wooden bench beneath them bore the polished smoothness that comes only from years of bodies sliding across its surface, and the low murmur of evening conversations created a gentle backdrop to their meal.

The warmth of the meal and Eli's genuine interest loosened their tongues. Between bites of bread and sips of wine, Amos and Dan found themselves sharing the story they'd guarded so carefully: Jonathan's disappearance.

When they finished, silence settled between them. Eli stared into his cup, swirling the dark liquid thoughtfully.

"You know," he finally said, his voice softer now, "I've come to believe people enter our lives as gifts, sometimes wrapped in joy, sometimes in sorrow. Each day, I try to unwrap the gifts life has brought me." He looked up, meeting Amos's gaze. "Even the difficult ones."

Dan glanced at Amos, noticing how his friend leaned forward, hanging on every word.

"It's in our darkest moments that we discover what we're made of," Eli continued. "Not when the path is clear, but when we can't see the next step... when there is no certainty, only the choice to move forward with trust that we have been prepared well for what lies ahead."

He set down his cup. "You are searching for your son. I lost mine." The words came with effort. "My only boy, my heir. Unlike your Jonathan, who may yet find his way home, my Eliab died in my arms." He looked down at his hands as if he were still feeling the weight.

"When the illness took him, I felt betrayed by the world itself. I watched him fade day by day, powerless. I abandoned everything, my vineyard, my wife, my daughter. I couldn't see past my grief."

Eli's fingers traced the rim of his cup. "One night, I heard Hannah praying in her room, sobbing. 'Take me instead,' she begged. 'If you take me, only Mother will grieve. But if you take Eliab, no one in our home will ever know joy again.'

"Her words cut through my selfishness. We all loved Eliab, but I'd been too blind to realize that my wife and daughter were drowning in the same sea. That night, I promised Hannah that if her brother died, we would grieve together and learn to live again as a family.

"I chose to remember my son every day. The pain is nothing compared to the gift of having been his father. Courage isn't about avoiding pain," he said, his eyes never leaving Amos's. "It's about continuing even when the hurt seems unbearable.

"Eliab gave new meaning to my winemaking. Every bottle I make celebrates his brief, beautiful life. When families open a bottle of my wine at their celebrations, a part of Eliab joins their joy. In this way, I became more than just a vineyard owner. I've realized my purpose."

That night, sleep eluded Amos. Eli's words echoed in his mind.

Purpose.

Deep in his heart, Amos knew he had also discovered his own.

It had been calling to him, but he had failed to respond.

Eli

"I've come to believe people enter our lives as gifts, sometimes wrapped in joy, sometimes in sorrow. Each day, I try to unwrap the gifts life has brought me... even the difficult ones."

TWO WEEKS AFTER THEIR RETURN FROM CANA, DAN HEARD THE pottery wheel spinning. He rushed to the studio, wondering who would dare touch Amos's wheel so early in the morning.

"Who told you to…" Dan stopped mid-sentence.

Amos was bent over a lump of clay, spinning the wheel in deep concentration. The man who had set pottery aside since Jonathan disappeared was working again.

His hands, coated in slip, moved with remembered rhythm. The clay pushed back against his palms, soft but substantial. Muscle memory awakened, and the scent of moistened earth filled the studio once more, displacing the dust of disuse.

"Amos!?"

Both were startled by the sudden interruption of the morning quiet. Dan's face was pale. Amos jumped. For a moment, neither spoke, and then they both erupted into laughter.

Amos laughed until tears ran down his cheeks. "My friend," he said, "you looked like you'd seen a ghost!"

"I did," Dan answered, recovering from the shock. "And the ghost was doing pottery!"

Their laughter echoed through the house, sweeping out the quiet heaviness that had lingered since Jonathan left.

"This will be a long morning," Dan said with playful exasperation as he stepped out to prepare breakfast.

Later, they sat in the courtyard, sipping their favorite mint and herb drink. Dan broke the silence.

"You're doing pottery again."

Amos wasn't sure if it was a question or a statement. It didn't matter, not with Dan.

"I've been thinking about it since Cana," he said.

"Eli," Dan murmured. "He's been on my mind too."

Amos nodded. It didn't surprise him anymore—their thoughts often moved in tandem. Bound by craft, by memory, by Jonathan.

"I finally realized something," Amos said. "Pottery was never my purpose. It was just the path."

Dan smiled.

"The day Jonathan entered our lives, purpose called to me—but I didn't recognize it. It often comes that way, I suppose. Dressed like a burden."

He paused. "I tried to shape a future for Jonathan where he'd never want for anything. But I was wrong to believe I could control it. He didn't need a legacy. He needed a father. And I wasn't the one he found that in."

"He would have been happiest with both," Dan said gently. "He's always looked up to you."

Amos fell silent. Regret lined his face. Dan said nothing. He knew whatever he might offer, Amos had already told himself, more harshly and with less mercy.

"I want to make something new, Dan," Amos said at last. "Pieces that carry the lessons I've learned about loss, about purpose, and I don't plan to sell them.

"We've saved enough," Amos added softly. "More than enough for us… and Jonathan. Whatever he decides to do."

"Whatever he decides," Dan echoed.

"This time, I'm making pottery for myself," Amos said. "For him. So that when he returns, he'll know he changed me. He shaped me. Not just as a craftsman, but as a father. As a man." Tears rimmed Amos's eyes. Dan gave him a quiet nod. Nothing more was needed.

"But I'm afraid I won't live to see him come home," Amos whispered.

"Don't say that," Dan replied. "You and I will be here, standing, waiting to welcome him."

Amos opened his mouth to protest, but Dan stopped him with a look.

He sighed and settled into his chair, tea warming his palms.

We'll both be here when Jonathan returns, Dan thought. *He needs us. We just have to wait a little longer.*

The old wheel will turn again. What beautiful things might it shape now?

What if I am no longer around by the time my son returns home?

The question haunted Amos, though he never voiced it to Dan. There were so many things left unsaid between him and Jonathan. While Dan would gladly speak on his behalf, Amos knew he needed to express everything as he would tell it to his son if he were present.

I need a journal where I can speak as if Jonathan were beside me. If I die before he returns, my words will remain. Truth will be preserved on the page when I can no longer speak it with my voice.

Morning light spilled across the courtyard as Amos reached for a small, leather-bound book. His fingers, accustomed to shaping clay, trembled slightly as they touched the unmarked pages. This would be his most important creation: a vessel of words rather than clay that must contain what was most precious to him.

He sat beneath the olive tree, dipped his quill into dark ink, and began to pour his heart onto the page.

"I finally did it, Dan," Amos said, closing the journal. "I wrote my first entry."

"And what did you write about?" Dan asked, not looking up from his work.

"I wrote about Capernaum and how we met," Amos answered.

"And when are you planning to write the rest of it?" Dan pressed, now looking intently at Amos.

"I can't," Amos sighed, his hand trembling. "That part... It's still too raw, too close to the bone."

"But you know you must, right, my old friend?" Dan asked, concern evident on his face.

Amos didn't answer. The thought of documenting those memories filled him with dread, a story that should have been told years ago.

His heart broke each time he remembered, so he pushed the thoughts away to maintain the balance needed for his craft. Now he felt compelled to willingly recall every painful detail he had fought for two decades to suppress.

"When will you stop blaming yourself, Amos?" Dan asked. "Why not start forgiving yourself instead? You have done what you could and more. No one could have done better. It's time to let go."

Amos's sad eyes met Dan's. *People become their own worst enemies,* he thought. *They don't forgive themselves as quickly as they forgive others. I don't believe there will ever come a time when I can forgive myself.*

Amos glanced at his old friend, deeply grateful for the one presence that had held him steady in the most difficult of times.

Amos wondered if people realized that Dan was the linchpin holding everything together. He shook his head. Everything he accomplished was made possible by this selfless man who, as a boy, had decided to throw his lot in with Amos when he wanted to leave Capernaum.

I couldn't have done it without Dan. Nothing would have been possible without him. Dan was the other side of the coin. I'm just on the front-facing side of it. One can't be without the other, Amos thought. He found it amusing that people thought he could have accomplished so much alone.

I will be the front-facing side of the coin. He and Dan agreed on a plan to secure Jonathan's future.

Jonathan. My son!

10

CARAVANSERAIS

BENJAMIN GREETED JONATHAN WITH A TIGHT HUG AND A WARM SMILE. Benjamin's father, Ezra, had organized the caravan, and the air at Caesarea's eastern gate hummed with pre-journey commotion.

The tang of oxen mingled with sweet hay and the metallic clink of harness rings. Merchants called to one another in a symphony of bartering and instructions. The sun, still climbing, cast long shadows onto the dust-covered road that would carry them to Joppa.

Traders from across Caesarea lined the street with wagons and carts, ready to roll through the city gates. The excitement among travelers made it feel like a festival.

The loud beat of drums signaled the start of the journey. As caravan head, Ezra led the way in the first wagon, pulled by a sturdy team of oxen. Benjamin and Jonathan walked alongside the carts, joining those who preferred to stretch their legs. They had a full day of travel ahead.

Benjamin explained that they would spend the first night in

Apollonia, the second in Antipatris, and arrive in Joppa by midday on the third day.

Benjamin chuckled, noticing the bow slung over Jonathan's shoulder and the quiver of arrows on his back. He remembered how, as a child, Jonathan would run up to Roman soldiers and ask permission in fluent Greek to touch their bows. Jonathan's gift for languages had always impressed Benjamin.

Jonathan caught the chuckle and grinned. "Have you traveled by caravan before?" Benjamin asked.

"This is my first time," Jonathan said, eyes wide with excitement. "It looks like fun."

"It is fun, but also about safety," Benjamin said. "There's security in numbers. The summer heat can deplete you quickly, and bandits target small caravans with high-value goods and few guards. Many names in the traders' ledgers belonged to merchants who never came back."

He gestured to the carts behind them. "See those guards? I always travel with armed men, trained to fight. Galilee can be dangerous. I plan for the worst, and pray it never happens."

Jonathan glanced at the beautifully crafted short sword on Benjamin's back. "Do you fight with that sword?" he asked, teasing.

"Can you shoot arrows with that bow?" Benjamin shot back, grinning.

They laughed, their voices echoing along the sun-warmed road.

The rhythmic creaking of wagon wheels and steady footfalls gave way to easy conversation. Eventually, they spoke of Caleb.

Benjamin shared that Caleb had left Caesarea unexpectedly. Everything he knew came from his father, who stayed in touch with Caleb's father, Samuel. In the quiet left by his friends' absence, Benjamin had focused on learning swordsmanship from retired soldiers, skills tested more than once by real bandits along trade routes.

Though his father believed hired guards were a better investment than trained merchants, Benjamin saw combat training as a necessary form of insurance. He had also studied trade, examining where goods came from, who bought them, and how they were transported. For six years, he'd walked routes and learned their rhythms.

Jonathan nodded. They had both changed. Each had honed new skills. He wondered about Caleb, how much he had changed, and where he was now.

The sun traced its arc overhead as the caravan pressed on. Dust rose from countless hooves and wheels, casting a golden haze. Jonathan's legs ached, but the steady rhythm of walking gave him time to absorb everything: the calls of the guards, the creak of wagons, the gentle tinkling of bells on the pack animals. The coastline of Caesarea had long since faded behind them, replaced by rolling hills and scattered olive groves.

As the afternoon waned, the journey began to shift. The caravan slowed slightly. Guards rested their hands closer to their weapons. Conversations quieted. Eyes flicked more often to the horizon, now deepening into dusk.

Jonathan noticed how Benjamin's posture changed. He was alert, scanning, and silent. The road climbed slightly, offering a view of the land ahead. Distant points of light appeared, flickering like early stars.

Soon, the drums announced the day's end. From the shadows emerged a large, well-lit structure behind high walls. Benjamin informed Jonathan that it was the caravanserai of Apollonia. They have arrived. Jonathan's eyes lit up. He had never seen one before.

Benjamin, seasoned by travel, explained that caravanserais were roadside inns built for security. With enclosed courtyards, they protected travelers, animals, and goods from danger and weather. Stables and storage occupied the lower level, while sleeping rooms were located on the upper level.

The structure unfolded before Jonathan like a compact city. His craftsman's eye traced the clean joints of the limestone, the symmetry of arches, and the clever placement of supports. Every detail is married to function with grace from aromatic kitchens to timber-beamed rooms, ventilated stables to locked storage.

"Do all trade routes have these?" he asked, eyes wide.

"Only the major ones," Benjamin said. "Smaller routes don't have enough traffic to justify them."

"Come on," Benjamin added, tugging at Jonathan's cloak. "Let's eat. I'm starving."

The aroma hit them before they stepped inside. The dining hall enveloped Jonathan in thick warmth, with the cooking smoke, stone walls, and layered scents of bay leaves, garlic, and slow-roasting meat. Travelers spoke in a dozen dialects, their voices humming beneath bursts of laughter.

Their earthenware bowls were filled with lamb stew, the meat so tender it fell apart in broth thickened by lentils and barley. Flatbread, warm from the oven, served as both spoon and companion to the dish. Jonathan took one bite and closed his eyes. Flavor exploded on his tongue, and he realized how deeply travel could awaken the senses.

~

JONATHAN SLEPT LIGHTLY. THE BED WAS PASSABLE, THE ROOM WARM, but Benjamin's snoring made sleep elusive. He rose quietly, gathered his things, and slipped outside to greet the morning.

From the balcony of their room, he looked down into the courtyard where men were feeding and securing the animals. Men checked harnesses, repaired wheels, and hitched donkeys. The sun was still low, but the caravan was already stirring.

Jonathan leaned on the railing, taking it all in: the quiet bustle below, the scent of bread baking, the clink of gear being packed.

He went off in search of something simple to eat, letting Benjamin sleep a little longer.

~

Benjamin and Jonathan walked a long way that morning. When the sun grew too hot, they hopped onto one of the wagons for a break. Then they exchanged stories about what they had learned and the places they had seen over the last six years.

Benjamin's eyes lit up as he described his journey into swordsmanship, his hands moving in practiced gestures while he explained the intricacies of blade work. Each movement spoke of years spent learning the dance of steel, transforming from a merchant's son into someone who could defend his father's caravans.

Jonathan listened, recognizing in his friend's passion the same fire that burned in his own heart for bowcraft.

The wagon swayed beneath them as they spoke, their voices carrying the weight of hard-won wisdom.

Jonathan's eyes drifted, and his voice grew softer. "It's *strange,* Benjamin. I finally understand what my father meant about seeing the form hiding in raw material, waiting to be freed. He saw it in clay, and I..." His voice faltered. "I see it in wood. One look at a piece, and I see what it could be."

His hands fell still in his lap, and in a tone that was barely a whisper, Jonathan shared, *"How I wish I could run to Father now, tell him I understand what he tried so hard to teach me. I have the vision he spoke of, but not in clay.* He swallowed hard, grief and regret mingling in his voice.

"But it's too late. My father is gone, and I can never tell him."

The wagon struck a rut, jolting them both. For a moment, Jonathan felt the weight of the journal in his pack, the vessel his father had left behind. Perhaps some conversations transcended death after all.

They rode on in silence, the creaking wheels and quiet chatter of travelers around them forming a shell of privacy. Their lighthearted talk had given way to something heavier, like the inland roads they now followed.

Benjamin's mood shifted. He sat straighter, more guarded. Jonathan sensed the change and knew something was about to happen.

Some truths, like distant hills, couldn't be avoided forever.

Seated side by side, Benjamin began.

"No one knew where you were, Jonathan. No one. My father ran into Amos somewhere near Caesarea Philippi. I saw your father and Dan in Tiberias... I think. They were traveling everywhere, looking for you."

Jonathan listened. There was no anger in Benjamin's voice, only frustration.

"For them to go to such lengths... what were you thinking?"

Jonathan explained. He spoke of the vase he had shattered, of his fear of telling the truth about having no skill or passion for pottery, and of his decision to run rather than explain his longing for something else.

By the time he finished, he felt small and foolish.

"If you didn't want to be a potter, all you had to do was say so," Benjamin said.

"Benjamin, you know my father." Jonathan mimicked his father's stern expression. "He doesn't talk. He just looks at you with those eyes... like he already knows what you've done. Remember how you and Caleb never came with me when I had to ask him for permission?"

"Then you should have asked a yes or no question, like 'Father, is it all right if I don't do pottery for a living?'"

"I could never do that."

"And look where it got you."

Jonathan said nothing.

Benjamin pressed on. "So... did Dan tell you what your father's plan was?"

Jonathan ran his fingers through his hair before answering.

"Dan said there was no plan. He explained that the pottery lessons weren't meant to shape me into a potter but to show me the craft that feeds our family. He said the choice was mine to make."

Benjamin shook his head. "I hate to say it, Jonathan, but running away was a terrible decision."

He saw that his friend looked lost, so he softened, placing an arm around Jonathan's shoulder.

"But look at the bright side. Now you have two trades. You can shape clay, or bend wood... or both. You can be anything you want."

Jonathan's voice dropped to a whisper.

"All I ever wanted was to be his son."

The last rays of sunlight painted the sky in deep purples and gold as the caravan approached Antipatris.

Unlike at their first stop, where wonder had made everything feel new, Jonathan now watched their arrival with heightened awareness. He noticed the way guards shifted into place, how traders secured their goods with swift efficiency. The drumbeat announcing their approach sounded different now, its rhythm touched by the weight of the day.

Torchlights flickered from the caravanserai's walls, calling them forward. Jonathan's legs ached, but the heaviness in his chest was greater. Rest was near, but sleep? Sleep might be harder to find.

The caravanserai loomed before them, larger and more refined than the one in Apollonia. Its courtyard sprawled wide, its architecture elegant with Roman influences, both practical and grand.

Jonathan admired the carefully cut stone archways with their precise fittings and no visible mortar. In the center, a well with a clever pulley system displayed the same precision he sought in his bowcraft.

Inside, the wooden bed frames showed the work of master joiners, no nails, just wood fitted perfectly to wood. Even the oil lamps showed thoughtful design, crafted from fine clay, their deep blue glaze dancing with the light.

Benjamin and Jonathan joined Ezra and several Caesarean traders for dinner.

Some, knowing that Benjamin now helped manage his father's business, asked his advice on transporting goods. Jonathan watched as his friend responded confidently, offering sound and strategic answers.

Across the table, Ezra's face glowed with pride. For Jonathan, witnessing this moment sent a sharp pain through his chest. He felt pain not just for the pride he'd never receive, but for the man whose heart he had broken.

He wondered if he had inherited any of his father's quiet strength, or only his capacity for silence and solitude.

He looked down, afraid the tears might come. The thought of what his father had endured—the long search, the unanswered questions, the ache of not knowing—was almost too much.

Benjamin continued, fielding questions and offering insight.

Quietly, Jonathan slipped away.

Their room welcomed him with its cool stone and flickering oil lamp. He sat for a while, listening to the hush settle around him. This day had begun with laughter, but somewhere between the hills and the road, something had shifted.

Their friendship remained intact, but something had deepened. It was no longer just about memories or inside jokes. Now it was about hard truths and the silence that followed them.

Jonathan remained near the window, still looking out at the rugged landscape. The rocky soil, the olive trees clinging to the hillsides, and the shepherd guiding his flock through challenging terrain all spoke of survival.

Would he find his place in this world?

The question stayed with him as he reached for the journal at the foot of his bed.

The leather was worn, and the scent of clay lingered.

Would the pages hold answers? Or only more of the past?

With quiet hands, he opened the journal to the first page. His father's voice waited inside.

11

JOURNAL ENTRY 1

CAPERNAUM

We had enough to live comfortably. Not wealthy like the tax collectors, not poor like the day laborers. We lived somewhere in between, comfortable, steady, and never lacking.

My father owned a fleet of fishing boats. Some were rented, while others were used for trading. The fishermen who hired the boats either paid outright or gave a share of their catch as payment. My father would salt the fish and barter for something more profitable. If the boats weren't rented, my father and my older brother would take to the water themselves. But a good rental offer could turn them from fishermen into traders for a season.

We were luckier than most children in Capernaum. My father hired a tutor to teach my brother and me to read and write in Aramaic. It was costly and rare for the sons of fishermen, but my father saw it as an investment in our family's future.

"A man who trades must read his agreements." He had big dreams, and our family shared them with him.

My brother eagerly followed in his footsteps. He was becoming a shrewd trader, which freed me to pursue something else: something my mother had nurtured in me since childhood —pottery.

My mother was a skilled potter who never sought recognition for her work. She created simple yet beautiful pieces that sold well enough to contribute to the family's earnings.

She taught me early how to spot good clay, soak and clean it, shape a base, and work the wheel. I remember the cool slip of wet clay between my fingers, the resistance as it centered, and the satisfaction of watching walls rise under steady pressure. My mother's hands guided mine, teaching me to feel thickness rather than see it. The earthy scent of fresh clay filled our courtyard, and when a pot was finally ready, the hollow tap of a fired vessel told me it was strong.

We worked well together, and the money we earned covered the cost of my additional training with local potters who taught for a fee.

My father's trade thrived, my mother's pottery flourished, and my brother grew skilled. It was a blessed life.

Our home stood near enough to the lake that morning mist slipped through the windows, carrying the murmurs of fishermen preparing their nets. From the roof, I could see the shimmer of the water, with boats scattered like seeds, and sometimes catch the scent of smoke from fish-drying racks along the shore.

That was the life I knew.

Then I met Dan.

He stood by a pottery wheel, his hands already knowing the clay as if it were a part of him, as if he were born from it. We were nearly the same age, though I was taller, but skill belonged to him. Dan was an orphan taken in by our teacher as a potter's assistant. What other pottery students struggled to learn in years, Dan mastered in months.

He was a great potter and a masterful finisher. His touch turned good pieces into ones that people wanted to buy. I learned more from watching him than from any formal lesson.

We rarely spoke at length. Sitting on the bench outside the studio after class, I'd talk about home, my brother's work, and my father's trade. Dan listened, curious and always learning. But he never spoke of his family or what had brought him to Capernaum. I never asked.

Dan and I kept to ourselves. Some mistook our silence for meekness, and we were often bullied. I fought when I had to, though I hated it. It always left me bruised.

The easiest way out of a fight was to call my older brother.

I admired him. He was my opposite: big, loud, strong, built for the sea. When he returned from fishing, the house filled with his presence, the slap of wet sandals on stone, the briny scent clinging to his clothes, his laughter rolling through the walls. My father clapped his shoulder with pride. My mother met my eyes across the room—the quiet ones understanding each other.

His crew adored him. He called them his family. And when injustice fell upon any of them, he felt it keenly.

Everything changed the year the new tax collector came.

The demands were impossible, but the Romans backed him. My brother began attending meetings after dark. My father worried but said nothing. My mother had to cook for more mouths than usual.

Then, a soldier died, and the Romans arrested my brother. They called him a rebel and sentenced him to execution.

My father sold everything in an attempt to free my brother.

The boats went, one by one, until there were no more. Pottery lessons stopped. My mother and I could not sustain three people on clay alone.

It wasn't enough. My brother was executed. My father did not survive the loss. My mother followed soon after.

I buried them all.

The ground of Capernaum holds everything I once had.

There was nothing left for me there.

The town had become a collection of fragments of what had once been whole. Like a vessel fired too quickly, everything had shattered. Pottery in Capernaum was used primarily for salting fish, not as an art form. And yet, years later, fish surfaced in my work, like a potter's thumbprint, impossible to erase.

I wanted to create the finest pottery. Caesarea was the ideal location, a city of traders, wealth, and art. I was leaving Galilee for Judea.

I told Dan my plan and asked him to come. Truthfully, I might not have found the strength to leave if he had refused. But Dan's eyes lit up. "It'll be an adventure," he said.

That was enough for me.

Dan had little to leave behind. He bid farewell to our teacher while I settled the remaining matters of my life.

Five days later, at dusk, we met at the place we had agreed upon, just outside the town's edge.

I didn't know then that this choice would lead me to you. I only knew I was leaving behind ghosts for something I might build with my hands.

The clay of Caesarea would be different, the water would mix differently, and the kilns would burn at unfamiliar temperatures. But potters understand this: when a vessel is flawed from the start, you don't patch it. You break it down, soak it, and begin again.

Dan and I walked away carrying nothing but the hope that we could remake ourselves as carefully as we shaped our vessels.

I remembered our final conversation:

"Five days," Dan had said, his voice steady.

I nodded. "At dusk."

It was settled.

We would meet there, beyond the gates, where the path turned, where the past ended, and something new began.

12

TRUST

JONATHAN SAT QUIETLY AT BREAKFAST, LOST IN THOUGHT. HE RE-READ his father's first journal entry, trying to imagine what he would have done in his father's shoes. His father had never discussed his sad and difficult childhood.

Jonathan's grandfather was a fisherman. While his uncle followed those footsteps, his father chose pottery as his path. This confirmed that Amos never expected him to follow in his footsteps, for Amos himself hadn't followed his father's trade. Jonathan shook his head, realizing how wrong he had been to assume otherwise.

And then there was Dan. Jonathan had always known they were close, but never guessed that their friendship had begun when they were boys. Two orphans setting out to find their place in the world. What a journey that must have been!

The pottery wheel belonged to his grandma; no wonder his father valued it so much! On it, his father had learned to work with clay. Through pottery, his father sustained the family after his uncle's death. Amos raised him and earned a living using the same wheel.

Jonathan carefully tucked the journal back into his travel pouch as the camp stirred to life around him.

The morning preparations for departure provided a welcome distraction for Jonathan. His mind kept returning to the image of his young father and Dan, two orphaned boys making their way into the world, leaving Capernaum together.

The caravan left Antipatris before dawn. As the sun climbed toward its zenith, Benjamin noticed his friend's unusual silence. Jonathan had barely spoken a word since they'd set out, lost in whatever thoughts the journal had stirred in him.

Benjamin asked if he was feeling well. Jonathan nodded and said he was okay, but didn't elaborate further. Benjamin knew something was bothering Jonathan, but he didn't dare ask.

They were just a few hours from Joppa, and everyone was excited to participate in the trade fair. People were laughing, some were singing, and others couldn't stop talking about what they planned to eat or buy at the fair. It's one of Judea's most significant trade events, and the most prominent traders will all be in one place, showcasing their best products.

"We'll be in Joppa in a few hours," Benjamin said to Jonathan, breaking their silence. "The markets open earliest near the harbor. The prime locations command double the usual rates during the fair." His merchant's calculation gave way to a grin. "But enough about profits! I'm trying to imagine the look on Caleb's face when he sees us together, that's a transaction worth more than any silver!" Benjamin started laughing, and Jonathan joined in.

As they approached Joppa, the landscape changed. The inland hills gave way to coastal plains, and the wind carried the unmistakable brine of the Great Sea. The road widened as more travelers converged toward the ancient port, and the distant cries of gulls announced their proximity to the coast. Merchant caravans that had traveled from Damascus, Egypt, and beyond slowed their pace, forming a colorful procession of humanity stretching toward the city gates.

Jonathan felt the energy shift, the weary determination of the journey yielding to the anticipatory excitement of arrival.

Joppa's skyline finally loomed before them, and the caravan erupted in cheers.

Joppa is an old, grand city with a rich history. Unlike Caesarea, which Rome built for Roman use, Joppa is an ancient and blessed city. Its natural harbor made it an ideal location for maritime trade, bringing traders from around the region and other parts of the world to showcase their wares and establish connections to expand their networks.

The *Maritime Fair* transformed Joppa's harbor district into a maze of colorful tents and stalls. Jonathan's trained eye immediately assessed the structures, noting the sturdy cedar frames supporting canopies dyed in deep hues, reminiscent of Tyrian purple in their faded elegance. The clever joinery of temporary stall counters, built to be swiftly assembled and disassembled, spoke of seasoned merchants accustomed to the rhythms of trade.

The air was thick with the mingled scents of exotic spices, fresh-caught fish, and salty breeze from the sea. Merchants' calls competed with the creaking of ship masts and the cries of seabirds, while the constant rhythm of waves against the harbor's dressed-stone walls provided a steady backdrop to the calculated chaos of commerce.

Everywhere, traders displayed their wares on vibrant carpets, gleaming metals from Damascus, delicate glass from Sidon, and rich textiles from lands far beyond the Great Sea.

The rhythmic jingling of harness ornaments marked the arrival of Bedouin merchants, their caravan-weary camels resting in designated areas. Nearby, metalworkers demonstrated their craft, the sharp ting-ting-ting of hammers on copper punctuating the air as they shaped intricate jewelry and practical implements. The smell of hot metal mixed with the scent of roasting lamb from food vendors who moved through the crowds with practiced agility.

At makeshift tables, merchants bent over papyrus sheets, reed pens scratching as they calculated values and recorded transactions in multiple languages. Everything here had its price: goods, services, even information, with everything negotiable in the ancient dance of commerce.

Ezra, Benjamin's father, has expanded his trading network through his visible presence in Joppa, especially during the Maritime Fair.

This year, Ezra plans to expand his network further.

Like all Hebrew men, his son will be getting married soon, and the family will grow quickly. Ezra is determined to secure Benjamin's future and that of his grandchildren.

Ezra scanned the caravan and saw his son, Benjamin, and his friend, Jonathan, rush into the crowd that had become too thick for the caravan to move further. *They'll have to set up tents elsewhere and showcase what Caesarea traders can offer to the world.*

"Jonathan, over here!" Benjamin shouted, waving his arms in the air so that he could see him through the crowd, which had become too thick to move.

"I'm coming!" Jonathan shouted, pushing his way through the sea of people, each trying to reach their destination.

Within sight of each other, the two friends started moving again, with Benjamin leading the way. Benjamin was searching for the tents of the Cana traders, knowing Caleb would be waiting in his father's tent. *I'll have Jonathan wait a moment before entering,* Benjamin thought. *I want to see Caleb's face when Jonathan reveals himself!*

The Cana traders' section filled the air with rich wine aromas. Rows of stone jars caught the midday sun, their polished surfaces reflecting light like water. Workers rolled aged barrels between tents while merchants and buyers haggled over samples of Cana's renowned wine. There stood Caleb at his father's tent entrance, all grown up and talking confidently with another trader!

Caleb had dark brown hair and a neatly trimmed beard. He was almost as tall as Jonathan. Caleb, who appeared tan with a medium build, looked like he had been working frequently under the sun. As in childhood, his eyes crinkled with the same permanent, almost infectious smile.

"Caleb!" Benjamin's voice carried over the crowd. Caleb spun around, his face lighting up at the sight of his old friend. He quickly excused himself from the trader he'd been talking to and rushed forward, embracing Benjamin with the enthusiasm of years of separation.

"Benjamin! It's so good to see you! Finally!" Caleb's voice cracked with emotion. "It's been so long! How are..." He broke off mid-sentence, his eyes widening as he caught sight of another familiar face. "Jonathan? Jonathan!"

Jonathan covered the last few steps between them, throwing one arm around Caleb and the other around Benjamin. His eyes bright with joy, he pulled them both close. "Now we're complete! My friends!"

The three young men playfully jostled and patted each other on the back, laughing as they sized each other up. They discussed how much each had changed, as Caleb led them inside his father's tent.

~

Inside Samuel's tent, the outside world faded away. Fresh grape clusters hung from the tent poles in small woven baskets, the grapes' deep purple skins glistening in the filtered light. The air was cooler here, rich with the scent of fermenting wine that emanated from the polished stone jars arranged in carefully displayed rows.

Intricately woven carpets, featuring patterns specific to Galilean craftsmanship, cushioned their feet from the packed earth floor. Oil lamps cast a warm, amber glow that brought the stone jars' surfaces to life, the jars' polished exteriors reflecting the light like still water. From somewhere nearby came the soft melody of a reed flute, providing a gentle backdrop to their reunion.

"Please sit!" Caleb told his friends. "You must be hungry!"

Caleb returned with a tray of warm bread, honey-glazed and spiced with fennel.

The smell made both Benjamin's and Jonathan's stomachs growl. Caleb also brought in a jar of his father's best wine and a platter of sweet grapes. The three friends shared a simple meal and discussed their adventures over the past six years.

As the sun began to set, laughter filled Samuel's tent.

The friends sat in a corner, talking and drinking wine. Caleb admired Jonathan's bow, impressed by its craftsmanship. Feeling content after drinking some of Samuel's best wine, Benjamin remembered something he had always wanted to ask Caleb.

"Caleb, why did you leave Caesarea so suddenly that we didn't even get to say goodbye?" Benjamin asked.

Caleb explained that his father's trading business was failing. Nothing sold well except wines from Cana. When his father heard that a vineyard owner in Cana wanted to sell his property, Caleb's father quickly sold everything in Caesarea to buy it. The family moved to Cana to learn about running a vineyard and making wine. "It was a challenging start for us. Cana was also where I went through the most difficult period of my life," Caleb added.

Benjamin and Jonathan exchanged a glance, silently wondering if the other knew what Caleb was discussing. They realized that neither of them knew what Caleb meant, so they turned their attention to Caleb. Jonathan was the first to ask.

"What happened in Cana?" Jonathan leaned forward, his voice gentle but insistent.

"Why didn't you reach out to me?" Benjamin asked, his words tumbling out, his face a mixture of hurt and concern. "I could have been there for you!"

Caleb's fingers tightened around his wine cup as he looked between his two closest childhood friends. He drew a deep breath, his shoulders sagging slightly. "I went blind."

The silence that followed was heavy with shock. Jonathan and Benjamin exchanged glances, neither knowing how to respond. Finally, Benjamin leaned forward. "Tell us what happened," Benjamin said.

Caleb nodded, pausing to gather his thoughts before continuing.

"My father built his reputation on reliability," Caleb said, leaning forward. "When traders from Jerusalem to Damascus ordered wine from him, they knew it would arrive exactly when promised, exactly as described."

He swirled the wine in his cup, watching the light catch its ruby depths. "Our regular clients were ecstatic when we acquired our vineyard and began producing wine. Orders doubled, then tripled."

Caleb set down his cup, his fingers tracing patterns on the wooden table. "Two truths govern our trade. First, wine trading for small vineyards like ours lives or dies on trust, just as vines depend on the trellis that supports them. Second, winemaking is subject to forces beyond human control. The same sun that nurtures can scorch; the same rain that nourishes can drown; and the same soil that gives life harbors disease. The vintner proposes, but nature disposes."

His voice dropped slightly. "Harvests can be fickle. Some years, the vines bend with abundance. Other years offer barely enough to fill a cup." A shadow crossed his face. "The year I became engaged was one of those lean years.

"But my father pressed forward with plans for my marriage. He had arranged a match with another vineyard owner's daughter in Cana. This union would join our lands and elevate our family among the winemakers of Cana. 'It's providence, Caleb,' my father told me. 'We'll never want for grapes again.'"

Caleb smiled softly. "My bride and I agreed to wait until our wedding day to meet, but we exchanged letters that were shy at first, then increasingly honest. Through ink and parchment, I fell in love with her mind and heart."

His fingers stilled on the table. "Then came the accident that changed everything. I was pruning vines when I fell from the ladder. The injury to my head seemed minor at first, but by the third day, darkness swallowed my world."

Benjamin and Jonathan sat motionless. The air between them was suddenly heavy.

"The finest healers came and went," Caleb continued, his voice steady despite the weight of his words. "None could lift the veil that had fallen over my eyes."

"Nothing?" Jonathan's whisper was barely audible over the distant sounds of the fair. His hand instinctively reached toward Caleb before dropping back to his side. "You couldn't see anything at all?"

"Light and shadow, nothing more." Caleb's voice took on a distant quality, as if he were revisiting that darkness. "It was like trying to see through a sandstorm - your eyes are open, but the world remains hidden." His fingers traced an unconscious path across his face where the blindfold had once rested. "I began wearing a blindfold so people wouldn't be confused by my open, unseeing eyes.

"I begged my bride to release me from the engagement. What bride deserves a blind husband who cannot work the vines or even find his way across a room?" His voice caught. "But she refused. She would not break her promise."

Benjamin reached for the wine, pouring another measure into his cup with hands that weren't entirely steady.

Caleb leaned forward, his voice dropping to continue:

As the wedding drew near, relatives arrived from all corners of Judea to help with preparations.

One evening, as I sat alone in the courtyard, a woman joined me, a relative of my father. Her voice was gentle, like water over stones.

She asked if there was anything she could do to help me.

I laughed, a bitter sound that surprised even me.

"All I want is to see my bride's face," I told her.

She touched my shoulder, a quiet gesture.

"I've known your bride since she was small," she said. "You don't need eyes to see her beauty; your heart will know it. She will make a good wife. Your father has chosen well."

I turned toward her.

"I am not the man for her," I said. "She has no future with me."

The silence stretched between us. Then she spoke, her voice steady.

"Worrying about tomorrow changes nothing. It only steals today's joy."

Her calm certainty unsettled me.

"I am blind," I reminded her. "I can barely care for myself. How can I not fear what lies ahead?"

I expected her to walk away, to leave me to my thoughts. But she didn't.

Instead, she sat quietly before speaking, a whisper meant to settle rather than to argue.

"Everyone is stronger than they believe. We forget that strength comes from those we love, and even more from those who love us."

Her hand covered mine, warm and steady.

"There is a greater power that brings certain people into our lives for a reason."

"And what dark reasoning could that be?" I asked bitterly.

She didn't recoil.

Her words felt as if they came from somewhere beyond herself.

"Trust that every day you've lived has prepared you for what comes next. You have everything you need. And if the challenge exceeds your preparation, help will come through the people placed in your path."

A pause. Then, soft... certain.

"Perhaps this is why she has entered your life, to be your strength when yours fails. It is not for us to know until it unfolds. Face tomorrow with gratitude, not fear. Gratitude comes from a full heart; fear comes from an empty one."

She leaned closer, speaking words I would never forget.

"Believe you have everything you need inside you, Caleb."

We sat in silence after that.

After a time, I tried to lighten the moment.

"Will you be at the wedding?"

"My son and I will be there. We will celebrate with you. Have faith."

She placed a finger on my chest, pressing the word into me as if willing me to hold it.

"Trust."

Then she left.

Caleb's voice fell silent, his expression distant, as if he were still absorbing the memory of that moment. Benjamin and Jonathan exchanged glances, neither knowing quite how to respond to the extraordinary story they had just heard.

"This is why I didn't invite you, Benjamin. I couldn't bear for you to see me blind."

Benjamin nodded, words failing him. Jonathan stared at his hands, equally silent.

"The wedding proceeded with only family who knew my condition. After the ceremony, my bride asked me to remove my blindfold to see my face fully." Caleb's voice quickened. "When I lifted the cloth and opened my eyes, expecting nothing but badly blurred visions, I saw her. I saw my bride. Not shadows, not light, her face, her eyes, every detail. My heart nearly burst from my chest. I held her face between my hands and whispered, 'I see you, Hannah... I see you.'

"She didn't understand at first. She wept when she realized what I meant, embracing me before running to tell my father."

"What happened?" Benjamin lurched forward eagerly, his wine cup teetering dangerously in his grip. His eyes were wide with wonder. "What caused your sight to return?"

"I don't know." Caleb's voice softened with the memory, his fingers absently tracing the rim of his cup. "I wasn't expecting anything when I removed the blindfold. Then suddenly, there she was, so beautiful I forgot to be astonished that I could see at all."

"But how is that possible?" Jonathan shifted closer, his craftsman's mind struggling to make sense of it. His brow furrowed as he asked, "How does blindness vanish in an instant?"

"I have no answer." Caleb spread his hands in a gesture of surrender, resignation reflected on his face in the lamplight as he tried to make sense of everything. "I've been asked a thousand times, and I always say the same thing: I honestly don't know.

"My father's celebration became legendary. The feast lasted days, with guests marveling at wine finer than any they had tasted. The wedding filled Cana with music from drums and lyres, and dancers moving in circles. The scent of roasting meats, fresh bread, and honey cakes hung in the air while children darted between tables. As night fell, olive oil lamps created pools of golden light, and guests' faces seemed to glow, not just from wine, but from something indescribable. The memory of that wine still lingers, rich and dark, with flavors that seemed to spread from the tongue to the heart.

"Your father and Dan were there, Jonathan!"

Jonathan's eyebrows shot up in surprise.

"Hannah's father considers them family, though not by blood. They met years ago and formed a bond that transcends kinship."

Jonathan shook his head in wonder. *His father, forming deep friendships? The man he knew kept the world at arm's length.* Jonathan kept silent, allowing Caleb to continue telling his story.

"As word spread about my restored sight, more guests arrived daily. My father congratulated Hannah's father on the exceptional wine served at the feast. My father-in-law returned the compliment, thinking my father had provided it. Only then did we realize neither knew its source."

"Your wedding was full of mysteries!" Benjamin threw his hands up in mock outrage, wine sloshing in his cup. His eyes sparkled with genuine regret. "I'm furious to have missed it!"

"A servant later told us something strange. Wine was running out as the entire community continued arriving to celebrate. One of my father's female relatives instructed the servants to await instructions from one of my cousins. He told them to fill all available jars with water. The servants did, securing every jar they could find, filling them with water, and leaving my cousin alone. That's all we know."

Caleb's expression brightened as he turned to Jonathan, leaning forward over the low table between them. "Hannah has a beautiful amphora that your father, Amos, crafted for her family years ago.

"The design shows a father and a young son in a lush vineyard, brightly lit by a warm sun," Caleb continued. "The amphora is adorned with grapes, grapevines, and leaves. It's so beautiful, Jonathan! It's their family heirloom, and Hannah's father gave it to us as a wedding gift! And the most remarkable thing? It bears the word 'Trust' engraved on its base."

Jonathan stood abruptly, his fingers instinctively moving as if practicing the engraving technique his father had perfected. "It had 'trust' engraved on it? In what language? Was it cut deep or shallow? Did the letters show a slight rightward slant?"

"In Aramaic. It's your father's handwriting, Jonathan," Caleb confirmed. "Isn't it remarkable that the word my relative left me with was already engraved on the amphora your father created and gave to Hannah's father years in advance? What an extraordinary connection.

"During the wedding chaos, a servant took Hannah's precious amphora and filled it with water alongside the other jars. When the servants returned later, every jar, including Hannah's amphora, held wine of unparalleled quality instead of water."

Caleb's voice dropped to a whisper. "When Hannah reclaimed her amphora after the celebration, it still carried the fragrance of that delicious wine, as if bearing witness to something beyond understanding."

Caleb

"Light and shadow, nothing more. It was like trying to see through a sandstorm - your eyes are open, but the world remains hidden."

"My head hurts from trying to understand all the strange and wonderful things that happened at your wedding!" Benjamin pressed his palm against his forehead, making an exaggerated show of distress.

"Your head hurts from too much wine!" Jonathan reached over to clap Benjamin's shoulder, his eyes dancing with amusement.

"It could be that, too!" Benjamin dropped his theatrical pose, joining in the laughter that filled the warm air of the tent.

Their laughter mingled with the clinking of wine cups. A servant's voice cut through the warm atmosphere, calling Benjamin's name from outside the tent.

"Master Benjamin?" The servant's head appeared through the tent flap. "Your father requests your presence. He is meeting with a potential trading partner."

Benjamin rose, steadying himself against the table. "Duty calls," he said with a rueful smile. "Father never misses a business opportunity."

"I should head back, too." Jonathan gathered his things, feeling the weight of exhaustion from their long journey. "The inn's waiting, and I need to rest."

The two friends bid Caleb goodnight and promised to return the following day to spend more time together, sharing more wine and stories to make up for the years they had been apart.

Joppa's skyline was ablaze with lights from hundreds of tents. Music spilled from taverns near the harbor, mingling with the laughter and haggling that continued well into the night. The city seemed determined to extract every moment of commerce and celebration from the fair before dawn brought another day.

But as Jonathan walked back to the inn, the revelry around him seemed to fade. The weight of Caleb's story, and its strange connections to his father, pulled him inward. His fingers traced the leather binding of the journal in his pocket, feeling its edges like a map to a territory he both feared and longed to explore.

He had "truth." Caleb and Hannah had "trust." Was there a meaning behind all of this?

Jonathan sat by the single oil lamp in the quiet solitude of his room. Its gentle flame cast dancing shadows across the walls as he carefully opened the journal. The parchment felt alive beneath his fingertips, carrying not just his father's words but his very essence. He noticed that three days had passed between the first entry and the next. The gap in the narrative spoke volumes.

Something about those missing days made his heart beat faster. The space between entries seemed to hold its own unwritten story, as if his father had struggled to write what came next...

What had happened after his father and Dan left Capernaum? How had they made their way to Caesarea? And most importantly, where did he fit into the story?

With these questions burning in his mind, he drew a deep breath and began to read. His father's voice seemed to rise from the page.

Trust

The design shows a father and a young son in a lush vineyard, brightly lit by a warm sun. It is adorned with grapes, grape vines, and leaves.

13

JOURNAL ENTRY 2

THE GIFT

I sold our house and all remaining property. Although the amount was less than expected, Dan believed it would be enough to start a small shop. However, after the sale, people came to collect payment for debts they claimed my father had incurred. I knew some were telling the truth, while others were lying. For several days, I met with debt collectors, leading to challenging conversations that made me wish I had my brother's negotiating skills, even just a fraction of them.

I finished negotiating with the last debt collector very late in the evening, the day before Dan and I were set to leave. I took a short nap, as we would be leaving in just a few hours.

I woke up in a panic. I had overslept! Dan must have been waiting for over an hour! I grabbed my belongings: a small bag of clothes and pottery tools, and the bigger one containing my legacy—my mother's pottery wheel—bound with rope to sling over my shoulder. I could have packed the wheelbase if I were as strong as ten men, but my frame could only manage to carry the top wheel for a few miles before collapsing from exhaustion. I would have to build a new base in Caesarea.

I ran as fast as possible, hoping Dan would still be waiting. Sweat trickled down my back, my lungs burning with each breath. The wheel bounced painfully against my spine with every step. The fleeting thought that Dan might have already left scared me, pushing me to run faster despite the strain. The streets leading out of Capernaum were deserted; fishermen had already gone to sea, leaving only the pungent scent of fish and the distant splash of oars. My sandals scraping against rough stones was the only sound breaking the morning silence.

About two miles outside town, I passed a couple beside their small cart, which had a broken wheel. Their donkey was tied to a nearby tree. The woman smiled, but worry was evident in her pale blue eyes as she asked if I could assist them. The man needed help repairing and remounting the wheel, less than an hour's work, I reckoned. I almost laughed at the irony—here I was, straining under my mother's wheel that felt as heavy as a stone anchor, while they needed help with their broken one. I waved as I passed, explaining I couldn't stop because I was late to meet someone. I continued my dash to meet Dan.

After walking more than two miles, I considered leaving my mother's pottery wheel by the roadside to run faster. The weight hurt my back and arms, but I changed my mind. I estimated I had less than a mile to go. I could carry the load by mustering my last remaining strength until I reached Dan, who could help me with the load.

When I reached our meeting place, my arms felt like lead. Red streaks, like whiplashes, appeared where I tightly held onto my things. Dan was not there, and I began to panic.

I looked around, hoping to see him sitting underneath a tree, sleeping, but there was no sign of him. Tears started to form. I bit my lip to avoid crying. I couldn't do this without Dan.

Had Dan turned back to Capernaum to look for me, or had he just left to go somewhere else without me? I was so tired that I slumped down on the dirt by the roadside to rest and gather my thoughts. I felt hope drain from me like water from poorly wedged clay.

Dan might have returned to Capernaum to look for me when he didn't find me here. Dan knew I wouldn't go to Caesarea alone.

A small voice inside my head asked, "What if Dan isn't back in Capernaum?"

Then I would sit and plan what to do next in Capernaum. Was I being defiant? I was trying to keep despair out of my head!

I was tired and had not gotten enough sleep. I was carrying a stone wheel that felt like it weighed a hundred pounds, and Dan was nowhere to be found. My day wasn't going as planned. I sighed and closed my eyes.

With all the resolve I could muster, I slowly got up, slung the rope that bound the wheel over my shoulder, and started to walk back to Capernaum.

I found myself whispering a prayer with each painful step, hoping to find Dan waiting for me somewhere in town. I felt the rope cutting through the skin of my shoulders. I was in pain.

Each step back toward Capernaum felt heavier than the last. The rising sun cast long shadows on the dusty road, marking the passage of time I couldn't afford to lose. My thoughts tumbled between worry for Dan and regret for oversleeping, both weighing as heavily as the wheel itself.

Then I saw the wagon. It was still there. Although I couldn't see the couple, the donkey remained tied to the tree.

As I got nearer, I saw two bodies lying still on the ground.

For a moment, I froze, then ran as fast as I could toward the couple I had seen earlier. What I saw stopped me from coming any nearer.

All strength left my body, and I let go of the bags I was carrying. The wheel thudded heavily into the dust, forgotten.

The metallic smell of blood hit me first, sharp and sickening in the warm air. The man had several stab wounds on his chest, blood clotted on his robe from bright crimson to deep red-brown. The woman had a cut at the base of her neck, her face frozen in pain, her eyes now glassy and vacant. Flies had begun to gather, their buzzing an obscene prayer over the dead.

Their belongings were strewn around. A robbery?

They weren't moving.

They weren't breathing.

They were dead.

I should have helped them. This wouldn't have happened if I had stopped. I could have prevented this! I sobbed uncontrollably as I dragged their bodies and laid them side by side. I whispered prayers and apologies that they would never hear.

"I'm sorry," I kept repeating.

The reality of what I had done, or failed to do, settled over me like a shroud. These people had asked for help, and my refusal had left them vulnerable. Perhaps if I had stayed... maybe if I had been the man my father raised me to be...

The weight of this truth was heavier than any pottery wheel. I began shaking uncontrollably as I grabbed a blanket off the cart to cover the bodies.

Then I saw something move under the pile of blankets inside the cart, a slight movement, then another. I stopped sobbing and froze.

The perpetrator could still be lurking. Had I arrived just as the killer was about to slip away?

The thought jolted me, heightening every sense. I was alone, a skinny boy with shekels in his pocket, an easy mark. I braced myself to run for my life...

Then I heard it, a soft, unmistakable sound that changed everything.

A baby cried out.

A baby?

It took a few seconds for me to start moving, to climb, and to look inside the cart where the sound was coming from. I started pulling away one layer of blanket after another and throwing baskets off the cart onto the ground.

Finally, I saw it—a baby!

It must have been fast asleep when everything happened.

A baby! And it cried again!

I carefully freed the baby from the tangled blankets and slowly climbed out of the cart. I stood staring at it. It was so small and crying, its skin warm against my calloused potter's hands. The blanket I wrapped around the tiny body smelled of cedar and something sweet, perhaps its mother's scent.

I wrapped my arms around the baby, trying to comfort it, silence it, and keep it warm, feeling its heart flutter against my chest like a trapped bird, but then I began to cry as well.

"I'm sorry I got them killed," I whispered to the baby.

"Now you're an orphan like me."

From the corner of my eye, I saw Dan running toward me from the direction of Capernaum. His face was white as he looked at the covered bodies. Between my sobs, I told him what had happened. He said he'd woken late and started running to meet me, passing a small group of Roman soldiers on the way.

"They'll be here soon," he said in panic, his face showing fear I had never seen before. "Romans! They're coming! The soldiers will think we did this, two orphans with coins! We have to go now!" Dan pulled, pushed, and grabbed my belongings as if they weighed nothing. I held the baby tightly, grabbing a cloth from the wagon to keep it warm.

"We have to move, Amos!" Dan said, urging me to start walking quickly.

This wasn't the fresh start I had planned.

I glanced at the dead couple. I looked at Dan in a panic as he grabbed his bags and mine, attempting to carry everything he could.

I looked at the baby.

It stopped crying. It was looking at me intently.

The baby's eyes were blue.

14

JOURNAL ENTRY 3

LEGACY

I have dreamt of the woman's blue eyes more times than I can count.

Each dream is different.

Sometimes, those eyes haunt me, reminding me that I did not stop when asked. I wake up gasping, my face wet, and my hands shaking long afterward. That will always be one of my greatest regrets.

Other nights, those same blue eyes plead with me, beg me to care for you. Those nights, I wake with a different fear, wondering if I have prepared enough for your future. Have I given you all you need? Will your education be enough? Your skills? Do you have everything to live the life I once dreamed of in Capernaum?

It isn't easy to see those eyes in you every day. Every time I look at you, I am reminded of what I failed to do. Your eyes bear witness to my greatest mistake.

I have long prepared myself for the possibility that you may never forgive me. Nor receive the grace of seeing you again before I die.

I admit my faults. I did not save the people in the wagon with you, and I did not tell you the truth that I wasn't brave enough to share while you were still here.

I have searched for you ever since you left. I have read and reread your letter, the one you placed on the pottery wheel. Trust me when I say that legacy was never part of my expectations for you. You were always free to choose your path.

I was fortunate that my older brother followed in my father's footsteps; it freed me from pursuing something I never loved as deeply as pottery. Pottery is a language I understand. It has taught me patience when guiding clay into form, forgiveness when a piece breaks, and joy when clay passes through the kiln successfully. Dan and I unconsciously used pottery as a language; we spoke through clay, form, and the steady shaping of earth between our hands.

When we taught you pottery, we hoped to share the lessons that had shaped us and that you would take them with you. But we failed. It was wrong of me to assume you would understand these lessons without explanation.

I come from a family of simple means.

Growing up, I learned that a legacy is not something left behind.

True legacy isn't seen with the naked eye.

It's not an inheritance. Not a burden. Not a duty.

It's a choice.

Legacy is how you live, how you honor the people who love you, the ones who believe in you.

It's in the daily choices that pay tribute to those who shaped you, a conscious effort to make your life a living testament to their care and devotion.

It's how you carry forward the hopes and beliefs of those who saw something in you before you ever did.

I hope mine shows you how much you have always meant to me.

Forgive me if I have caused you pain and failed to make you feel how precious you are.

You were never meant to carry my past.

Only your future.

Your father.

15

FAMILY

THE STARS HAD STARTED TO FADE, BUT THE SILENCE LINGERED. AND IT was comforting.

Jonathan sat alone in the dim gray light of dawn, watching as the last stars faded above Joppa's harbor. The wooden bench beneath him bore silent witness to a truth too heavy to speak.

Beside him lay his father's journal, a small thing to contain the ruins of a life.

The rhythm of waves against the pier was the only sound in these hushed hours. Occasionally, the distant call of gulls and the groan of ship timbers broke the silence. The familiar scent of salt, fish, and tarred rope hung in the air. Soon, the docks would stir, the shouts of merchants, the creak of cargo being loaded, but for now, this space belonged to him and his undoing.

How strange that he had once escaped to harbors like this one in Crete when homesickness for Caesarea weighed on him. And yet, home again, he longed for the foreign shore he had left behind.

He was constantly yearning for the place he wasn't.

Last night, he had begun reading his father's journal at the inn, grateful that Benjamin wasn't there to witness the storm that broke within him.

Rage. Grief. Betrayal.

Emotions had come in waves too powerful to name, colliding inside his chest, tightening his throat, leaving him gasping. He had fled into the night, seeking anonymity among strangers, needing the world to blur while he unraveled.

Three times, he had read those pages.

The first sent fury racing through his blood, a fire so pure and consuming that he finally understood the prophets' words.

The second left him weightless, untethered, adrift in the wreckage of everything he had believed.

By the third, numbness had settled in, slow and inevitable, as if his heart had surrendered to exhaustion.

Now, in the gathering light, understanding finally came, sharp and unforgiving.

This was why Amos had never truly looked at him, not entirely, not directly.

Jonathan's face was not that of a son, but a wound Amos could never close.

And in Jonathan's eyes, blue eyes unlike any in their family, Amos saw the woman he had refused to save.

Could he blame Amos for keeping the truth buried?

Had Jonathan been in his place, would he have had the courage to take in an orphaned infant and call him his son? Would he have found the words to explain that everything the child believed about himself was a lie?

Jonathan exhaled slowly, watching his breath fade into the morning cold, just as certainty had disappeared from his life.

If Dan and Amos had not been delayed on their way to Caesarea, they would never have encountered the robbery. The Romans would have placed him with a Jewish family or institution. Either way, he would still be someone other than who he'd believed himself to be.

The soft ocean breeze lifted the hair from his forehead as he closed his eyes. *His mother's eyes were blue, his birth mother, whoever she had been.* In all his travels, he'd never met another soul with eyes the same shade as his own. He was grateful for the lingering darkness, for the anonymity it provided, as his world realigned itself around one simple truth: *he was no one.*

The pain in his chest was sharp and sudden, like when he'd split wood against its grain and felt the resistance give way. Jonathan regretted coming home for the first time since leaving Crete, not because there was nothing to return to, but because what awaited him was more complex than any bow he'd ever crafted.

It was almost noon when Jonathan started walking back to the inn. The harbor merchants had long since opened their stalls. The midday heat pressed against him, but he barely felt it. Time had passed, but he was still standing in the wreckage of last night. The streets blurred, voices, movement, and the press of bodies. He moved through it all, yet none of it seemed to affect him.

By the time Jonathan returned, Benjamin had been frantically searching for him with a few men from Ezra's crew. Caleb was also at the inn, looking worried. He was with a man whose wild gray hair and carefully trimmed beard gave him the appearance of both a sage and a warrior, someone who had seen enough of life to understand its most profound truths.

Benjamin saw Jonathan and ran toward him. "Where were you?" he asked, his voice laced with anger and worry. "I've been looking for you all night!"

Jonathan murmured, "I was at the docks. I'm so sorry. I needed to clear my head."

"Clear your what?" Benjamin asked, perplexed. Jonathan averted his gaze, his fingers tightening around the journal in his hands.

Caleb rushed to Jonathan and hugged him. "We were worried about you," he said, relief evident in his voice. "I came to the inn to see you this morning." He gestured toward the older man. "My father-in-law arrived last night. When I mentioned you were Amos's son, he insisted on meeting you right away."

Caleb looked at the man who hurriedly stood beside him and continued, "Jonathan, meet Eli, the father of Hannah."

Eli drew close and hugged Jonathan tightly, surprising him. "I have heard so much about you from your father, Jonathan. It is a true pleasure to meet you and welcome you home. Your father would have been so happy to see you back!" Eli said.

Jonathan's smile was strained. "Father," he said, the word hollow as he looked at Eli. *Amos is not my father,* Jonathan wanted to say to the man, but he chose to keep silent. Jonathan looked lost. "I should have come home sooner to see him while he was still alive. Did you know him well, Eli? Do you come from Capernaum, too?" Jonathan asked, looking dazed.

"I was born and raised in Cana. I met your father and Dan during one of their trips to Galilee, looking for you," Eli replied. "Is Dan here in Joppa? I haven't seen him since your father passed away," Eli said.

"Dan is in Caesarea," Jonathan said, his voice flat.

Benjamin said, "And speaking of Caesarea, Jonathan, I can't return tomorrow as planned. I need to help my father finish some trade negotiations. Can we go back the day after tomorrow instead?"

"Sure, Benjamin," Jonathan replied. "I'm in no hurry to return to Caesarea," Jonathan said numbly, thinking of Dan and the painful confrontation that awaited both of them.

"Then, may I invite you to have a meal with me in Samuel's tent?" Eli asked. "I have heard so much about you from the stories your father proudly shared. Would you oblige me? I'd like to hear about the places you've been during all those years when Amos and Dan searched for you. Caleb hasn't shared any information about you since I arrived." Eli looked at Caleb, who grinned.

"Yes, of course," Jonathan replied. *He suddenly realized he hadn't slept a wink and was tired, but needed to keep up appearances. Besides, this man was Caleb's father-in-law and had known Amos. Jonathan had to make time.* "Please give me an hour to freshen up, and then I'll join you."

Caleb asked, "Is that agreed, then? We will wait for you in my father's tent!" Jonathan smiled at Caleb and nodded. Caleb and Eli began walking away.

Benjamin said, "I will be with my father, Jonathan. And don't ever go missing again, especially not without telling me!" Benjamin laughed loudly as he walked with his father's men. "I'll catch you later, okay?" Benjamin shouted.

Jonathan turned toward the inn. A difficult day lay ahead, and he wondered *how long he could keep pretending that everything was all right.*

~

THE WINE FLOWED LIKE LIQUID AMBER, CATCHING THE LAMPLIGHT AS Eli poured another measure into Jonathan's cup. Jonathan had never tasted anything like it, rich and complex, carrying echoes of sunlight and earth that lingered long after each sip.

"Your wine is extraordinary," Jonathan said, the words inadequate for what his senses experienced. The earthy clay cup felt warm in his hands, its rough texture a contrast to the smooth liquid within.

Oil lamps cast dancing shadows across the woven tapestries lining Samuel's tent, their flickering light catching the amber depths of the wine. Eli's weathered face creased with quiet pride. "The vines for this vintage were planted after Caleb and Hannah's wedding. It was a blessed year." Beside him, Caleb smiled at the memory. The scent of freshly baked bread and roasted lamb mingled with the wine's bouquet.

"Caleb tells me you trained in Bowery in Crete for nearly six years under a master," Eli said, studying Jonathan with eyes that seemed to see beneath surfaces. "Will you be establishing your workshop soon?"

Jonathan's fingers traced the rim of his cup. "I had planned to open a shop in Caesarea, take on apprentices, accept commissions." He hesitated. "But now, I honestly do not know."

Eli waited. His silence was an invitation.

"I ran away believing my father intended me to follow his path as a potter," Jonathan continued, his voice dropping. "Days ago, I learned from Dan that he never had such plans. The choice was always mine." Caleb's expression shifted, concern shadowing his features as he watched his friend.

"And just before leaving for this journey, I discovered something unexpected: I have a gift with clay." Jonathan's laugh held no humor. "I created a piece I had never managed under my father's watchful eye. This time, I shaped it for the joy alone, with no one to please." His voice caught. "There's no one to please now that Amos is gone."

The silence that followed felt tangible, heavy with unspoken weight.

"So," Eli finally said, "you possess two talents, one for wood, another for clay. Which brings you joy?"

Jonathan looked up, startled. "That's exactly what Dan asked me days ago, if being a bowmaker would make me happy."

"And your answer?"

"I said I don't know." Jonathan's gaze fell to the table.

"Something troubles you," Caleb said softly. "You haven't been yourself since this morning."

Jonathan attempted a smile, but his eyes remained troubled. "It's nothing. It will pass."

Eli watched him with the patient attention of one who had witnessed many storms. "I met your father in Cana five years ago," he began, his voice taking on a storyteller's cadence. "He was examining my stone jars. In Cana, we store our wines in stone rather than clay. The vessels come in countless forms, each with its character."

Jonathan looked up, wanting to hear more despite himself.

"Your father was drawn unerringly to the most valuable pieces without knowing their prices. Do you know how he knew?"

Jonathan shook his head.

"He recognized the vessels that required the most time and devotion to create," Eli said. "Not the most elaborate or ornate, but those into which the craftsman had poured the greatest measure of himself." His eyes held Jonathan's. "They were all carved from the same stone, yet your father could tell the difference."

Eli leaned forward. "It's the same with all of us. We value most those with whom we've shared our lives, those who have witnessed our struggles and triumphs. The people who have seen us at our worst and remained. These are life's true treasures."

The lamplight caught the silver in Eli's beard as he continued. "I met Amos when he was searching for you across Galilee and Judea. He traveled with merchant caravans to every place rumors placed you, hoping to find you and ask for your forgiveness."

"Forgiveness?" Jonathan echoed, surprised. The word was hollow in his throat.

"For the truths he never dared to speak," Eli said quietly.

Jonathan's eyes widened. "Did he tell you everything?"

Eli nodded once; the gesture was heavy with understanding.

"I only learned about it last night," Jonathan whispered, his voice barely audible over the soft crackle of the oil lamps.

Confusion crossed Caleb's face. "What did you learn, Jonathan?"

"That I am not truly his son." The words fell like stones between them. "He found me as an infant beside a road, the sole survivor of what appeared to be a robbery that left two people dead." Jonathan's head bowed under the weight of the truth. Caleb's arm came around his shoulders, a wordless offering of support.

"I hope you understand," Eli said gently, "how difficult it was for your father to carry this knowledge, just as I recognize how painful it must be for you to receive it. The one certainty I gained when I first spoke with Amos was this: he chose you. He loved you, not out of obligation, but wholeheartedly." Jonathan's throat tightened at these words, each one striking him like a physical blow—truth he wasn't prepared to face.

"Amos is *not* my father." The words burned, yet felt hollow in his throat. *"I am no one."* The silence pressed in, vast and unrelenting. But Eli held his gaze steadily.

Eli responded thoughtfully, "You are cherished deeply by Amos and Dan. Both have always given you their unconditional love. This kind of love from those who choose to be part of our lives shapes who we are."

Eli leaned forward, his eyes holding Jonathan's with the intensity of someone about to share a profound truth.

Eli's voice deepened with each carefully placed word. "Family goes *beyond* mere blood relations. It's not just about blood ties but about the people who fill the gaps in our lives with their presence. For some, family includes friends who share your joy or mentors who guide you through the darkness. For others, it consists of those who steadfastly stand by you, choosing you just as you choose them.

"For the truly fortunate, family consists of those who enter your life, enrich it immeasurably, and decide to *stay*, even when there's no reason to do so."

The truth of Eli's words pressed against Jonathan's chest like a physical weight. "By these standards, consider yourself blessed beyond measure, Jonathan. Those two men who found you as an infant could have continued their journey unencumbered. They were young, having just begun their lives after enduring hardships. They stood at the threshold of their dreams, and in that moment, they decided you would be a part of those dreams."

Jonathan's breath caught in his throat. Each word Eli spoke was balm and blade, healing and cutting simultaneously.

"Can you imagine the sacrifice? Caring for an infant while establishing a trade, building a life? They were scarcely older than you are now." Eli's voice grew softer.

"The essence of family lies not in shared *blood* but in shared *moments*, in the sacred bonds formed when someone decides, without obligation, that you are precious to them and will forever hold a place in their heart."

Eli rose and moved to sit beside Jonathan, his arm coming around the young man's shoulders. "So please, don't say you are no one. You know *exactly* who you are. You are the beloved son of Amos, Caesarea's Master of Clay. I witnessed your father and Dan search for you without rest when you left, and I rejoice that you have returned. Your father would have been overjoyed to see you home. I am grateful that Dan continues to experience this blessing."

Jonathan's head remained bowed, his vision blurred with unshed tears, his shoulders hunched as if bearing the weight of revelations too heavy to carry alone.

All night, Jonathan had combed through the past, seeking traces of betrayal, blind to the quiet grace that had been shaping his life all along.

Two men had chosen him and had woven him into their lives, their dreams, and their home. Without obligation. Without condition. He had never been lost. He had always been theirs.

The anger that had burned in his chest since reading his father's journal began to dissolve, replaced by a single, overwhelming truth: he had been chosen. He had been loved, not out of duty or obligation, but wholly and freely.

Now, all that remained was the bitter knowledge that he could never ask forgiveness from the man who had given him everything. Jonathan could only hope that with Dan, he might somehow atone for the pain he had caused.

"Are you all right, my son?" Eli asked softly.

Jonathan could only nod, words beyond him as he turned and embraced the older man, holding on as if to anchor himself in a world suddenly transformed by understanding.

~

THE NIGHT PASSED IN FITFUL SLEEP, JONATHAN'S DREAMS A JUMBLE OF faces: Amos, Dan, the blue-eyed woman he would never know. Morning came with a clarity he hadn't expected, as if Eli's words had washed something clean inside him.

The journey back to Caesarea felt different now. Each step carried both the weight of revelation and the lightness of understanding.

Jonathan found himself studying the faces of travelers he passed, wondering how many carried their own unspoken stories of chosen families and unexpected grace.

The world seemed both larger and smaller at once. It was larger in its possibilities, smaller in its intimate connections that bound people together in ways blood could never explain.

As the road stretched before them, Jonathan's thoughts gradually shifted from the storm of recent days to the broader world around him. The familiar sights and sounds of the trading route began to filter back into his consciousness. Life continued its relentless forward motion, regardless of personal revelations.

Jonathan was on his way home.

Home, he said to himself. He looked forward to hearing everything from Dan; there should be no more secrets.

Truth. He would finally hear the truth from one of his fathers.

Jonathan resolved to make amends for all the pain he had caused by leaving.

All this time, he had misunderstood. They had never wanted an heir. They had only wanted a son.

And Jonathan only wanted a father.

How simple the last six years could have been if there had been no secrets, only truth.

As they traveled, Jonathan found himself settling into a strange peace. It wasn't contentment, but acceptance. Only then did his thoughts turn to the slain couple. *Were they his parents? They must have been. At the very least, he was related to the blue-eyed woman. Who were they? Where were they headed when they met their fate near*

Capernaum? Had they left any clues about their origins? Would Dan know?

Would Dan also know about the amphora Amos had given to Eli? Why would his father inscribe that particular word on a piece of clay for that specific person? Jonathan felt sure it was no coincidence that both the amphora and Caleb's relative had emphasized the same word, "trust."

Jonathan's clay box bore the word "truth." He knew why he had the word "truth." He knew that Dan had made a clay piece with the word "teach" for his friend Levi. *So, how many pieces had been made by Amos and Dan? And who had them?*

Jonathan shook his head as he walked. *Truth. Trust. Teach. He couldn't make sense of it.*

Ezra's small caravan made good progress along the coastal route.

The spring air carried the scent of wildflowers and salt spray, while the packed earth of the Roman road stretched before them, worn smooth by countless travelers. They stayed in the same caravanserais they had occupied in Antipatris and Apollonia, their stone walls offering welcome shelter from the night winds.

They would travel for about one more day before reaching Caesarea, their pack animals' hooves creating a rhythmic accompaniment to their journey. If all went well, they would arrive in Caesarea close to midnight.

Jonathan was looking forward to having breakfast with Dan. He had so many questions to ask!

Benjamin walked briskly up to Jonathan.

"Hey, did you hear what the newly arrived guests at the caravanserai were talking about this morning?" Benjamin asked Jonathan.

Jonathan shook his head. "No, I didn't. Anything interesting?" Jonathan asked.

"They said the Romans were trying to crush the rebellion in Jerusalem. They added that the rebels' numbers were growing, and the Romans weren't happy."

"I hope no one was hurt," Jonathan said.

"Jonathan! Your six-year stay in Crete has sheltered you from the reality of living under Roman rule in Galilee and Judea! You have no idea, do you? The Romans thrive on violence, just as merchants thrive on profit. They calculate it, invest in it, and expect returns on it! They have the largest army in the world and all the weapons that *shekels* can buy. What trader would practice restraint when controlling all the goods?" Benjamin looked both serious and troubled.

"I told you, I've seen the worst side of Roman cruelty. It's called crucifixion! I pray you never witness one. I still have nightmares about the one I witnessed." Benjamin's eyes held a wild look as he spoke.

Jonathan remained silent. He could not relate to Benjamin's description of Roman aggression and cruelty. All the Romans he had met were good people, except for the one at Caesarea's docks, who was a drunk and a thief.

"I'm sorry, my friend. I have no idea what you are saying. My perspective stems from my experience in Crete, where the Greeks and Romans lived peacefully. Just give me time, and I'll be able to understand what you're saying," Jonathan assured his friend.

Benjamin looked at Jonathan, unable to believe that his friend didn't understand Roman violence.

"Here, I bought you something," Benjamin said, handing Jonathan a hard object wrapped in beautiful red cloth.

"What is it?" Jonathan smiled at Benjamin and opened the wrap. It was a small knife with an intricately detailed handle and Jonathan's name engraved on it. "It's beautiful," Jonathan exclaimed, putting an arm around Benjamin's shoulder. "Thank you!"

"I saw the smith who made this in Joppa," Benjamin said, pointing to his sword. "He had put up a tent to display his best work. I saw this beautiful little knife and asked him to engrave your name on the handle. I'm glad you liked it. I figured that your bow would only be good for targets at a distance. This knife will be good when the enemy is much closer." Benjamin gave a hearty laugh.

"He'll only get closer if I miss," Jonathan replied, laughing.

Once again, Benjamin shared what he had learned from his extensive sword lessons over the past six years. He showed Jonathan how to handle the small knife and the various ways it can be used for basic defense. Jonathan was impressed by Benjamin's knowledge of swords and enthusiastically went through the motions Benjamin had demonstrated. He was pleased that his friend had not only mastered trading but also swordsmanship. Jonathan felt happy for his friend and proud of him.

"Will you come to my wedding?" Benjamin asked Jonathan.

"Of course, I wouldn't miss it for the world. When will it be?" Jonathan asked.

"I'll be married in about a month. The house is ready, and all preparations are complete," Benjamin laughed. "I'm going to be a husband," he said.

Jonathan put an arm around Benjamin as they walked. "I'm so happy for you. I'm looking forward to meeting Priscilla. Her name is Priscilla, right?" Jonathan asked Benjamin, smiling.

"You remembered! I bet you'll like her!" Benjamin smiled.

As Jonathan had anticipated, they arrived in Caesarea after midnight.

16

JERUSALEM

DAN LEFT FOR JERUSALEM THE NIGHT BEFORE JONATHAN LEFT FOR Joppa. Though he estimated his return to Caesarea would be too close to Jonathan's arrival, Dan was counting on traveling fast enough to be home before Jonathan returned from Joppa.

Jacob pleaded to come with him, but Dan insisted that he could manage alone, as he felt much better. Joseph's caravan, already headed to Jerusalem, could provide only one more seat on such short notice, and Dan wouldn't allow Jacob to make the journey on foot.

As in all his previous trips to Jerusalem, Dan dressed plainly, wearing nothing that would distinguish him from the average traveler or identify him as one of Caesarea's upper class. The only new addition was a cane; he had finally admitted he needed one, and Jacob had managed to find one for him before his departure.

The trip was long overdue. It had been two months since Dan had visited Jerusalem to check on Levi and his brothers, as he hadn't been feeling well for the past six weeks. Jonathan's arrival had further delayed his journey.

Telling Jonathan everything about Jerusalem, beyond what Amos wanted him to know, would require time and ask a great deal from the young man, who already had more than he could handle. *This can wait*, Dan said to himself.

Dan couldn't shake the feeling that something was happening in Jerusalem. He hadn't heard from anyone in weeks, and it had been too long since he'd received news about Levi.

Amos and Dan both knew Levi from their childhood in Capernaum. Though younger, he shared Amos's Aramaic writing instructor and was the fastest learner in the group. When they met on the street, Levi would warn them where bullies were hiding, waiting for Amos and Dan to pass by. He was one of the few people Amos and Dan genuinely liked.

They met again, years later, when Levi was given a different name.

During a visit to Joseph's home, Dan and Amos witnessed something unexpected. A government official from Capernaum arrived with desperation etched on his face. The man's child was dying, and he sought guidance in finding a Galilean healer whose name had begun to ripple through the region, carried by hushed conversations and urgent pleas.

Joseph knew of the healer the official was looking for and offered to guide him to Cana, where the healer was staying at the time. He invited Amos and Dan to join him on the journey to help the official find the healer.

When they reached Cana, Joseph led them directly to the healer. After hearing the official's plea, the healer said, "Go back to your son. Your son will live."

The certainty in the healer's voice left no room for doubt. The peace that settled over the official's face struck Amos deeply. The man had received not a promise but a fact already accomplished.

Amos also noticed a familiar face among the healer's companions as they stood there. "Levi, is that you?" he called out.

The man, with dark curly hair and a neatly trimmed beard, turned toward them. Recognition dawned in his eyes as memories of Capernaum surfaced. "Amos! Dan!" he exclaimed, embracing them both with genuine joy.

The unexpected encounter reunited Amos and Dan with Levi, whom the healer's followers referred to as Matthew. Levi referred to his companions as his "brothers," and they all addressed the healer respectfully as "Rabbi."

Joseph, Amos, and Dan accompanied the official back to Capernaum, where servants rushed out with astonishing news: the child had recovered at the exact hour the Rabbi had spoken those words in Cana.

Amos felt something stir within his carefully constructed world.

From then on, Amos and Dan answered Levi's invitations and joined the Brothers when they could, sitting and listening to the Rabbi and his teachings. The Rabbi based himself in Capernaum, the very town Amos and Dan had fled from in their youth. Now, both men found themselves drawn to the place they had left, drawn by something more valuable than the fame and fortune they had sought and found in Caesarea.

Although many names circulated about the healer, Amos and Dan referred to him as "Rabbi," just as the Brothers did. His teachings offered them a fresh perspective on the Scriptures they had known all their lives, but not as profoundly as they now understood them.

They soon discovered that Joseph also quietly followed the Rabbi. The three men began discreetly traveling together whenever possible, listening to the Rabbi's words, asking questions, and gradually transforming their understanding of faith.

During one such journey, the three men decided to provide discreet, regular financial support to the Rabbi and his followers.

Together, the three men formalized their commitment, ensuring that the Brothers would never lack resources for their mission.

Joseph, however, went a step further by lending the upper room of one of his houses on the southwestern hill of the city to the Rabbi and his group whenever they were in Jerusalem. It was one of two houses not known publicly to be his.

For Amos and Dan, what had begun as curiosity transformed gradually into conviction, then devotion. The three men's commitment deepened with each passing month. They arranged their business affairs to generate steady support for the growing movement. When they couldn't travel, they ensured that supplies reached the disciples through Joseph's caravans.

It did not surprise any of them that those critical of the Rabbi finally convinced Rome to put an end to the Rabbi's teachings. What shocked them was the extremity of the silencing: they had asked the Romans to crucify him, and Rome complied.

Amos and Dan learned about it too late, but Joseph heard about it just in time to secure the Rabbi's body and offer his own tomb for use.

What happened next continues to baffle everyone.

The body has vanished.

Joseph saw the empty tomb, and Levi swore to the three men that he had seen the Rabbi alive.

Amos and Dan, who had not witnessed anything but had listened to the Rabbi so many times and had seen so many things that could not be explained, knew that everything was possible.

All three men believed Levi.

So, the Brothers continued to spread the Rabbi's teachings. Joseph, Amos, and Dan continued to support them. To the three men, the Rabbi was no longer just their teacher but the Messiah.

The quiet realization that they were doing the Lord's work renewed their spirits. The Brothers spreading the Lord's teachings were now called the Apostles.

The community is growing, and support has begun to flow in. However, the Romans had grown suspicious of all followers of the Messiah, sometimes even hostile. They believed the community was aligned with the rebels plotting a revolution against Rome.

They had all become suspects.

Their community was under surveillance.

Dan heaved a sigh. He had been anxious for weeks, waiting for news of Levi or the Apostles. He had to visit the upper room to gather news from the others who had been on the road for an extended period, spreading the teachings at the risk of their lives and limbs, traveling great distances to fulfill their mission.

Amos would want Dan to continue with the support; Dan was sure of this.

The caravan pushed relentlessly, kicking up dust that clung to skin and clothing like an unwelcome shroud. The rhythmic creak of wagon wheels and the jingle of harnesses marked their progress while the pungent scent of animals and unwashed travelers grew stronger under the relentless sun. By the third day, Jerusalem's walls rose before them, golden in the late afternoon light, the limestone blocks catching fire in the sun's dying rays. Dan's body ached from the journey, his joints protesting each jolt of the wagon, but urgency drove him forward.

The streets grew more crowded as they approached the city gates. Pilgrims in their festival garments, merchants hawking Passover wares, and locals hurrying to complete preparations jostled together in a human current that swept Dan along once he parted from the caravan. The scent of baking unleavened bread mingled with the sharp tang of vinegar used for cleaning, while lambs bleated from the Temple markets, their cries echoing off stone walls. The familiar weight of tension hung in the air, the unmistakable pressure that always preceded Passover in an occupied city, marked by the metallic glint of Roman helmets visible above the crowd.

Joseph's house stood in the upper quarter, a quiet sanctuary amid the chaos. The caretaker's eyes widened in recognition as Dan approached.

"Master Dan! We weren't expecting you."

"The upper room," Dan said, his voice rough from travel and thirst. "Are any of them there?"

The caretaker hesitated. "Three apostles arrived at dawn, but they left before midday. Some errand in the Lower City."

"Was Levi… err… Matthew among them?" Dan leaned forward, unable to mask his urgency.

"I cannot say for certain." The caretaker lowered his eyes, aware that he was of no help.

Dan handed over his travel bag, suddenly feeling its burden. "Please take this upstairs. I will find them. Thank you."

The shadows were lengthening as Dan made his way down the narrow streets. Jerusalem before Passover was a powder keg; Roman patrols were more frequent, and zealot whispers were more fervent. The air itself seemed to hold its breath.

Dan thought they'd be in the eastern quarter by the Pool of Siloam, where the community of believers often gathered in an elder's home. Despite his exhaustion, his pace quickened.

As he turned onto a broader street leading to the *Shuk*, the crowd ahead thickened suddenly. Young men with hard eyes and clenched fists had gathered, their voices rising in a dangerous chorus.

"How long will we bow to Rome's boot on our neck?"

"No more yoke!"

"Death to traitors!"

Dan tried to skirt the edges of the gathering, but the crowd had swelled, blocking all passage. Sweat beaded on his forehead as he pushed forward, his cane going before him, muttering apologies. He needed to pass through, now.

The first shout of alarm came from behind him. Roman soldiers appeared at both ends of the street, their armor catching the dying sunlight as they advanced in formation. The crowd compressed like a fist, trapping the protesters, including Dan, in its center.

"Stand your ground!" someone shouted.

The first rock arced through the air, striking a soldier's shield with a hollow thud. More followed, a hail of stones against metal. The soldiers raised their shields and advanced with mechanical precision.

Dan's heart hammered against his ribs. "Let me through," he pleaded, but his voice was lost in the growing roar.

The mood shifted in an instant. Dan saw the flash of steel, hidden daggers drawn in desperate hands from the corner of his eye. A young man lunged at the nearest soldier, his blade seeking the gap between armor plates.

"No!" Dan reached out, but it was too late.

The street erupted into chaos. The air was filled with the guttural roar of angry voices and the sharp metallic clash of drawn weapons. A rock struck Dan from behind, the impact sending white-hot pain through his skull. The taste of copper filled his mouth as he bit his tongue. He staggered, the cobblestones suddenly tilting beneath his feet. His vision blurred, the crowd becoming a smear of colors and movement. Someone crashed into him, a body thrown backward by a Roman shield. The impact forced the breath from Dan's lungs, and he lost his footing.

His knees hit the street hard. Around him, sandaled feet scrambled toward the fight. Voices became a meaningless roar. Dan tried to stand, but another surge of bodies knocked him to the ground.

He curled inward, arms protecting his head as the crowd became a stampede above him. A foot came down on his outstretched hand, another across his back. The pressure on his legs built until something gave way with a sickening crack.

Pain exploded through his body, then strangely receded, replaced by a terrifying numbness below his waist. The world began to darken at the edges.

At that moment between consciousness and oblivion, Dan heard a voice cutting through the chaos, as familiar as his heartbeat.

"Dan! DAN!"

The voice seemed to come from everywhere and nowhere at once. *Was it real?* Dan tried to turn his head toward the sound, but his body refused to respond. The voice called again, closer now, yet somehow farther away. It couldn't be Amos; Amos was... Yet, who else would call his name with such desperate familiarity?

As darkness claimed him, Dan faintly heard Amos calling out his name.

Amos? The thought formed and dissolved. Dan wondered if death wore the voices of those he loved most.

Miles away in Antipatris, Benjamin and Ezra's trade discussions continued, and wine flowed. Jonathan had just excused himself to return to his room to read his father's first journal entry.

~

When Jonathan arrived in Caesarea past midnight, Jacob was still awake. He had not been sleeping well since Dan left. When Dan failed to arrive three days ago, Jacob frantically scanned the road outside the courtyard from morning until night. He kept blaming himself for not insisting on coming with Dan to Jerusalem.

Now Jonathan was here, and he had to tell him everything.

Jacob opened the door even before Jonathan could knock.

"Thank you for opening the door, Jacob. You can go back to sleep now. I can manage from here," Jonathan said. Jacob didn't move. He didn't know where to begin.

"Is there anything wrong, Jacob?" Jonathan asked.

"Dan *isn't* here," Jacob said.

"Where is he?" Jonathan asked, looking confused.

"Dan left for Jerusalem nine days ago. He was supposed to be back yesterday at the latest," Jacob explained as calmly as he could, trying not to show how worried he was about the whole situation.

"Dan was gone even before I left for Joppa?" Jonathan asked, his brow furrowed in confusion.

"Yes," Jacob answered. "He promised he would be back by the time you arrived from Joppa," Jacob added, his eyes downcast.

"What is he doing in Jerusalem, and why didn't he tell me about it?" Jonathan's voice betrayed his feelings, a mix of anger and worry over his surrogate father missing for several days.

"Your father and Dan travel to Jerusalem monthly to meet with some people there. They usually join Joseph the Trader's caravan when traveling to and from Jerusalem. When your father died, Dan continued visiting Jerusalem via the caravan. Sometimes, he travels with Joseph, and sometimes, he travels alone." Jacob explained that Dan had not traveled to Jerusalem for two months because he was not feeling well.

"To be clear, Jacob, you are referring to the caravan's owner as Joseph of the Sanhedrin, correct?" Jonathan asked.

"Yes, he is the one," Jacob confirmed.

Jonathan paused. He knew Joseph the Trader, a prominent member of the Sanhedrin. He was one of his father's closest friends, if not his closest friend, next to Dan. Jonathan grew up familiar with the man, a successful trader in Galilee and Judea. Jonathan knew this prominent figure from Arimathea was instrumental in making his father's pottery pieces highly valued in Judea. Joseph was his father's most valued patron.

"Where does he go in Jerusalem?" Jonathan asked.

"He goes to the house of Joseph the Trader in Jerusalem," Jacob answered.

"Has Joseph transferred to Jerusalem?" Jonathan asked, still as confused as ever. "What I know is that Joseph lives in Ramah. My father and I go there when we have to deliver some commissioned pottery pieces," said Jonathan.

Jacob confirmed that Jonathan was correct, that Joseph lived in Ramah, but he added that the trader had another house in Jerusalem. "This is what I know," he said.

Jonathan took a deep breath, trying not to panic over the fact that his surrogate father had been away for more than a week and had not returned as anticipated.

"Is there anything else I need to know, Jacob?" Jonathan asked.

Jacob was momentarily silent, wrestling with himself over something Jonathan should know but didn't.

"Dan is sick," Jacob said. "He is seriously ill."

Jonathan looked at Jacob, visibly shaken by what he had heard. "How *sick?*" Jonathan asked in a whisper.

"All the physicians we have seen said we should make his life as comfortable as possible because there is nothing more they can do," Jacob said as he bowed his head.

"What do you mean?" Jonathan asked Jacob as his heart started beating wildly.

"They said he could have an episode anytime when he could no longer breathe well, and..." Jacob stopped talking.

"And he *didn't* want me to know?" Jonathan asked Jacob, trying to keep his voice from breaking.

"Yes," Jacob answered with his head bowed.

The memory hit Jonathan like a physical blow - that day in the courtyard when Dan asked him to work on a pottery piece for his friend Levi, Dan paused mid-sentence, his hand briefly pressing against his chest as he caught his breath. Jonathan had dismissed it then, attributing it to the heat of the day. That moment replayed in his mind with devastating clarity, along with other signs he should have seen: the shortened walks and the more extended rest periods between tasks. How long had Dan been hiding this?

There was a long silence between the two young men. Jacob felt torn about informing Jonathan of Dan's condition despite Dan's instructions for secrecy. Jacob, whom Dan had taken in as a pottery apprentice after witnessing his plight as an orphan hauling clay for potters in the streets of Caesarea, knew he had broken his promise to Dan. Jacob considered Dan not just his mentor but also his father. Jacob felt Dan might never forgive him for this.

"Thank you, Jacob. I will leave for Jerusalem before dawn. I will gather my things tonight. You may go now," Jonathan said, his fingers already mentally measuring what supplies he would need for the journey, his craftsman's mind automatically calculating distances and materials even as worry clouded his thoughts.

Jacob nodded and left.

Jonathan took a deep breath to steady himself. The last few days had taken much from him, starting with his father's revelation and ending with the stories Eli shared. He was coming to understand the man his father was and how much he had loved him.

Now, he would journey toward his other father, Dan, in Jerusalem. He fervently hopes that Dan is safe somewhere, as he cannot bear the thought of losing his only remaining family member.

Where are you, Dan? Jonathan wondered.

Jonathan's footsteps echoed in the empty corridor as he approached Dan's room. Each step felt heavier than the last, driven by a desperation he couldn't name. Was it the comfort of Dan's steady presence he sought? Or was it the primal fear of losing the last anchor to his world, just as he had lost his father? The thought sent a shiver of cold through his body.

The three had always maintained invisible boundaries, sacred spaces never crossed without invitation. A knock before entering, a pause before speaking, these small courtesies had formed the architecture of their shared life. But tonight, the rules no longer applied.

Tonight, Jonathan needed to search Dan's room for any information, any clue, anything that would explain why he and Amos had regularly traveled to Jerusalem without informing him.

Jonathan's hand trembled as it closed around the door handle. The hinges whispered as he pushed the door open, making him feel like an intruder in a sanctuary.

Moonlight spilled through the small window, casting a quiet glow over a space that echoed Dan's essence. The familiar scent of balsam and dried herbs lingered, mingling with the faint earthiness of clay that seemed woven into the very bones of their home. No ornate furnishings, no indulgent displays, only the bare necessities arranged with quiet dignity: a bed with its woven blanket carefully smoothed, a small table where a bronze oil lamp stood sentinel, and a wooden chest worn smooth by the passage of years.

The simplicity struck Jonathan anew, a silent testament to the man who had shaped his life with steady, unspoken devotion.

His gaze was drawn immediately to the shelf against the far wall, where Dan kept what he treasured most. Jonathan's breath caught in his throat as he approached it.

In the corner lay his father's favorite tunic, folded with such care that it might have been a royal garment. Jonathan's fingers hovered over it, not quite daring to touch. Beneath it rested what appeared to be an old *sudra,* something he had not seen before. He unfolded the fabric with reverent hands to reveal faint embroidery, a woman's profile wearing what looked like a crown shaped like a tower's battlements.

Something about it felt deeply personal, a story Jonathan wasn't meant to know. He carefully refolded it, returning it precisely as he had found it.

A small clay bowl held dried mustard seeds, whose purpose was a mystery, begging for questions Jonathan might never get to ask. Beside it stood a simple wine cup, unremarkable except for its place among Dan's treasures.

And then, Jonathan's heart constricted painfully. Half the shelf displayed misshapen, awkward pieces of pottery. His pottery. Every failed attempt, every frustrated creation, he had assumed his father had discarded in shame. They were all here, fired and glazed with the same care given to masterpieces.

With unsteady hands, Jonathan lifted one particularly malformed piece.

He remembered the day he had made it, how he had torn it from the wheel in a rage. He hurled it against the wall, breaking his father's commissioned piece, which led him to run away to Crete. Here it was, carefully preserved, the cracks sealed with a gold-flecked glaze that transformed its brokenness into something precious.

The words Dan always said after Jonathan's failures echoed in his mind: *"Sometimes our greatest masterpieces come from our broken pieces."*

The weight of it in his palm became unbearable. Jonathan sank onto Dan's bed, the rough wool blanket scratching against his skin. His vision blurred as he stared at the evidence of a love he had never fully comprehended, a love that treasured even his failures, that saw beauty in his broken attempts.

"Please," he whispered into the empty room, his voice breaking on the word. *"Please don't take him too. Not before I can..."* The prayer died in his throat, too raw to complete.

The silence of the room pressed against him like a physical weight. Outside, the wind stirred, rattling the shutters. Dan might be injured, suffering, or worse, somewhere. The thought sent a wave of nausea through Jonathan so intense that he had to bend forward, clutching the misshapen clay piece to his chest.

Fear, pure and primal, coursed through him. Not the fleeting fear of a child in darkness about to face his father, but the bone-deep terror of a man facing the possibility of irreparable loss.

In the quiet of Dan's room, surrounded by humble treasures that spoke of a life devoted to others, Jonathan finally understood what it meant to be truly afraid.

Somewhere between the moon's slow crawl across the sky and the distant promise of dawn, Jonathan realized that waiting could be its own kind of death. Each creak of the house carried a message he dared not receive. The dark messengers kept knocking inside his head and his heart, leaving him at their mercy in the dark.

His fingers closed around the mended pottery piece, its rough surface familiar against his callused skin. By first light, he would be on the road to Jerusalem.

To Dan.

To whatever truth awaited him there.

17

TRAVELERS

JONATHAN LEFT AT THE CRACK OF DAWN. HE TRIED HIS BEST TO prepare for his first journey through Judea alone, without the security of a caravan. Benjamin had shared with him stories about the dangers of traveling alone during their trip to Joppa. He made sure that he had enough arrows for his bow, that the small knife Benjamin had given him yesterday was in his pocket, that he had an extra tunic, water, and all the dried food he could find in the cupboard at home.

He hoped to cross paths with fellow travelers, maybe even join a passing caravan. An extra layer of protection. A moment's ease. But ease was a luxury he couldn't afford.

He tucked Marcus's pin inside his tunic, concealing it beneath a top cloth. Visible only when needed.

Jonathan tried to shake off all the negative thoughts that had kept him awake since he arrived from Joppa. He needed to be in Jerusalem as soon as possible.

It was a three- to five-day walk to Jerusalem. He intended to make it in three days.

The road stretched ahead of him, dusty and endless. His sandals, well-worn from work around the workshop, weren't made for such long-distance travel. Each step reminded him of this fact, but he pushed the discomfort aside. There would be time for blisters to heal after he found Dan.

Distant bells from shepherds' flocks echoed across the valleys, and the metallic jingle of merchants' coin purses marked the rhythm of commerce already beginning. The familiar coastline gave way to rolling hills dotted with olive groves, their silvery leaves shimmering in the gentle breeze. Each step took him further from the predictable rhythms of his life by the sea into terrain that grew increasingly foreign.

He patted his pocket to check for the hand knife that Benjamin had given him. He adjusted the straps that held the bow against his back. The weight of his provisions seemed to grow heavier with each step, but he couldn't risk being underprepared. Dan needed him to make this journey quickly.

A sudden commotion ahead made Jonathan's heart leap. Two men burst from behind a rock outcropping, chasing what appeared to be a stolen goat. The animal darted across the road, its pursuers following recklessly. Jonathan instinctively stepped back, his hand finding the knife Benjamin had given him. The men paid him no attention, but the encounter left him shaken. Benjamin's warnings about traveling alone echoed in his mind.

~

THE LANDSCAPE HAD SHIFTED AS THE MORNING WORE ON. THE gentle coastal plains had given way to more challenging terrain. Loose stones shifted treacherously under his feet, and thorny bushes encroached on the path's edges. The sun, now high overhead, beat down mercilessly, drawing strength from the rocky ground that reflected its heat like a potter's kiln.

Jonathan sought refuge beneath the sprawling branches of an ancient fig tree. Two men were already resting there, their travel-worn faces brightening as he approached.

"Please join us," the older man called, gesturing to the space beside him. "No one should bear this heat alone."

They introduced themselves as Uri and Ethan. Without hesitation, they shared their simple provisions: dried fish that tasted of the sea and flatbread still carrying the memory of morning fire. Jonathan accepted their offering, grateful for both the food and the company.

"Where does your path lead?" Uri asked, passing a waterskin.

"Jerusalem," Jonathan replied, trying to keep his voice steady. "My father traveled ahead of me. I'm going to bring him home." He didn't mention the knot in his stomach that tightened every time he thought about what condition he might find Dan in.

"We know Jerusalem well," Uri said softly. His eyes held something, concern, perhaps, that he didn't voice.

As they ate, Jonathan noticed how naturally the two men cared for each other. When Ethan winced while adjusting his pack, Uri quietly moved to check the strap without being asked. When a group of rough-looking travelers passed, eyeing their provisions with evident hunger, Ethan offered his water without hesitation. The men refused with suspicious glares, but Ethan's gesture remained genuine.

"Why?" Jonathan asked quietly after they had gone.

Ethan shrugged, tearing his bread to share more widely. "Thirsty people don't always know they're thirsty."

It was such a simple response, yet something about it reminded Jonathan of Dan's quiet kindnesses… the way he'd always appear with food when Amos worked late, or how he'd tend to Jonathan's pottery disasters without scolding.

"You speak of your father," Uri observed. "Is he unwell?"

The question opened something in Jonathan's chest. Before he could stop himself, words spilled out: his fear for his father, who had not returned on time, and the urgency that drove him forward despite his weeklong journey to Joppa.

Neither man offered empty reassurances. Instead, they listened with the kind of attention that made confessing feel safe.

"We had a teacher," Uri said eventually, his voice carrying a weight of loss. "He used to say that love isn't something you feel; it's something you do, especially when it seems impossible."

Ethan nodded, touching a small pouch at his belt. "I've seen men cross great distances for those they love. The distance isn't the miracle; it's the willingness to walk it."

Something in their words struck Jonathan like flint against steel, igniting a sudden spark within him. His mind raced to his father's journal, pages brimming with love, struggling across time and distance to finally speak the words left unsaid.

"What is your teacher's name?" Jonathan asked. Ethan gave him the name. "I'm sure you've heard of him," he added, looking at Jonathan intently.

Jonathan shook his head. "I apologize. I've been away for years, traveling from a distant land," he said. "I have not received any news from home. Where is your teacher now?"

Uri's gaze drifted toward the horizon. "Gone to his father," he murmured. Then, after a pause, he exchanged a glance with Ethan. "Though... strange things have been reported. Friends say they've seen him in familiar places, doing familiar things."

"Do you believe them?"

"I believe they saw what they needed to see," Uri replied.

As the afternoon heat lessened, they gathered their belongings and continued together. The conversation flowed naturally between footfalls and breaths, stories of their teacher that emerged not as lessons but as memories shared among friends.

Jonathan learned that their teacher had been a carpenter, like many in their region. He had worked with his hands, understood the patience required to shape stubborn materials, and the satisfaction of creating something useful from rough beginnings.

"He had potter's hands," Ethan mentioned, noticing Jonathan's calluses. "Could feel when the clay was ready, when it needed more water, and when to stop pushing."

The comparison made Jonathan's chest tighten. "Was he also a potter, besides being a carpenter?"

"No, but he understood the principle. He said people were like clay; some needed gentle pressure, others needed to be broken down and started over. But he never gave up on a piece."

Uri's teacher sounded so much like Dan, and it made Jonathan worry all the more. Jonathan remembered his conversation with Dan the day after he arrived. *If a form doesn't hold in pottery, we unmold the clay and begin again. Pottery gives us the space to learn from our mistakes. In pottery, we only fail when we stop trying.*

Uri and Ethan spoke of how their teacher had gathered followers, not through grand speeches, but through small acts that revealed his character. A woman caught in adultery was shown mercy instead of stones. A Roman centurion's servant was healed without question, despite the man's uncertain allegiance.

"He confused everyone," Uri admitted with a chuckle. "Rabbis, Romans, rebels—none of us could fit him into our understanding of how the world works."

"Will he be back?" Jonathan asked, looking forward to hearing the Rabbi speak for himself.

Uri smiled at Jonathan and answered, "So many have seen him back. I wasn't there for that part. But those who were... they're different now. Changed... And I believe them."

As they approached Antipatris, its limestone walls glowing amber in the setting sun, Jonathan quietly reflected on everything he had heard. The stories revealed a man who saw worth in the worthless, who chose love when it seemed foolish, and who forgave even those who had wronged him.

Forgiveness.

"You could stay with me tonight," Jonathan offered as they reached the caravanserai. The two men were grateful for the invitation.

Over a simple meal in the courtyard, surrounded by the drone of multiple languages and the smell of cooking fires, Jonathan felt something settling in his chest. Not answers—he had more questions than ever—but a sense that he was walking a path others had walked before him. That he was meant to be on the path.

When Uri and Ethan spoke of their teacher, they didn't sound like men trying to convince him of anything. They sounded like men who had been loved well and were trying to learn how to love in the same way, sharing that love with others.

After his companions had retired, Jonathan sat alone in the torchlight, his father's journal heavy in his hands. The day's conversations had stirred something in him, not revelation, but recognition. The love that had shaped him, the distance he was willing to travel for those who mattered, perhaps he had been walking in this teacher's footsteps without knowing it.

I was chosen. I am loved, he reminded himself, the words feeling different now, colored by what he had witnessed in two quiet men who carried their teacher's love like a flame.

Tomorrow would bring him closer to finding Dan. But tonight, he felt less alone than he had since leaving Caesarea.

Uri and Ethan were without their teacher's presence right now, but their way of loving, choosing, sacrificing, and forgiving lived on in ordinary people making extraordinary choices.

Extraordinary choices.

If given the opportunity, would he do the same? Would he freely choose the right thing to do over the easy path?

Jonathan fingered the edge of his father's journal, thinking about how truth could be passed down through written words, spoken stories, and the silent testimony of lives well-lived. He nurtured hope that Dan was safe as he prepared to read what his father had left him.

The flickering torchlight reminded him of the workshop's evening glow, where Dan should be right now. Instead, his second father's whereabouts remained a mystery. But Jonathan had learned something today about love that travels distances, about the willingness to walk impossible roads for those who matter.

Whatever awaited in Jerusalem, he would face it with the same love that had shaped him, the same love that had shaped the teacher whose followers now carried light to strangers beneath fig trees.

Impossible roads.

18

JOURNAL ENTRY 4

BLESSED

In Capernaum, I thought coins meant happiness: more boats, more coins, a better life. My father said it was simple math.

When our pottery shop started doing well in Caesarea, I counted our earnings each night, just as my father counted fish. At first, watching the numbers grow felt right. But then something changed. My hands still shaped the clay, but the feeling I once had was gone.

The pottery wheel became like my father's fishing nets. A way to live. That's all.

I remember counting coins at night after you had fallen asleep. Each one meant better clay, tools, and food for you. Dan and I were just boys from Galilee. What did we know about raising a child?

Nothing.

Sometimes worry made me burn whole batches of pottery. I worried about how to feed you, teach you, and keep you safe. Then you'd come into the workshop, little hands and face covered in clay from "helping," and the ruined pots wouldn't matter anymore.

You changed everything. Changed Caesarea. Changed our work. Changed us. Every pot we made was for your future.

People asked why Dan and I never married. The answer was simple: we had no fathers to arrange it, no family to offer dowries. We were just two orphans who arrived in Caesarea with empty pockets and heads full of dreams. You became our family. You became enough.

Life taught me that we are never alone. When I was lost, help always came: not things, but people, the right people at the right time.

I learned this during my most challenging years.

Weeks before my family died in Capernaum, Dan appeared. He pulled me through one of the worst times in my life. When we couldn't feed you, a stranger came to our aid. When pottery wouldn't sell, someone taught us how to make it better. When I didn't know how to be a father, you showed me I already was.

It took me years to see it.

Help always came. Not always in ways I understood. Not always in ways I expected. But always when we needed it most.

Some call it luck. I know better.

These were not accidents. And when no help came, when we had to wait, to struggle, that taught me something, too.

Sometimes the clay is already in your hands. You have to trust that you know how to shape it. Trust that your fingers remember. Trust that you are enough. That everything you need, you already have.

I'm not sure if I'll still be here when you read this. There's so much I wish I had said in person. Words never came easily to me, you know that better than anyone.

But my hands know clay, so I made these instead: pieces for the people who helped me when I wanted to give up. Each one has a word carved into it, a lesson I needed, a truth that changed me.

My hands shook while making them. It's hard to thank people who gave you hope when you had none. This is the best way I know how.

The first piece is yours, the one with 'truth' etched into it. I used the same red clay from the coastal beds as I did for the first bowl I gave you. Remember that day? Your small hands gripped too hard, clay squeezing between your fingers, and your face was so serious. You couldn't make it hold its shape, but you kept trying.

That's what you did with my life: you worked at it until it became better. After you came, every pot had a purpose. The glaze looked brighter. The forms felt stronger. They weren't just pottery anymore. They were what would feed you. Clothe you. Give you a future.

I made two more, hoping you'll find the people I gave them to. When you do, I hope you learn from them, as I did.

If I have the strength, I'll make one last piece. If I finish it, you'll find it beneath the stone slab that holds the pottery wheel.

I've watched you grow and watched you learn. Watched you become strong.

Now, I pray for the people you'll meet on your journey, the ones who will see in you what I've always seen, those who will help you when I can no longer be there. They will come, just as others came for me.

Some will teach you new ways to shape and create, helping you bring your visions to life. Others will show you how to stand, even when your strength feels gone.

And a few, just a few, will change your life the way you changed mine.

Know this, my son: every piece I ever made, I made thinking of you. Every truth I learned, I learned because of you.

When my fingers shaped the clay, they shaped it for you.

You were chosen. You are loved.

You always were.

19

THE UNEXPECTED

THE THREE MEN ATE A QUICK, HOT MEAL IN THE CARAVANSERAI, prepared for early travelers. The flatbread was still warm from stone ovens, fragrant and smoky from the fire with herbs and olive oil, accompanied by goat's cheese. The three men left before first light, when the eastern sky had just begun to soften from black to deep indigo. The air held the sharp chill of night, their breath forming small clouds that dissipated quickly in the darkness. The crunch of sandals on gravel and the occasional snort of pack animals were the only sounds breaking the pre-dawn silence.

Jonathan mentally traced their route like a bowyer making a precision cut: Lydda first, where Uri and Ethan would stay, then onward alone to Emmaus for the night, with Jerusalem still a day's journey beyond.

As they walked, Uri shared more stories of their teacher. Not grand proclamations, but small moments, a meal shared with tax collectors, a child lifted onto shoulders, and fishermen mending nets while listening to parables that made them laugh before they understood.

"He was a carpenter," Ethan mentioned. "He worked on wood." He gestured at Jonathan's callused fingers. "He understood what it meant to shape something out of it."

Wood? Jonathan found himself drawn to these details.

"What about you?" Uri asked. "What do you do, and where are you from?"

"I am from Caesarea. I just returned from Crete, where I learned to make bows."

"A bowyer from Crete?" Uri's eyes widened. "That's impressive. Where will you set up your trade?"

Jonathan shook his head. "Nothing is certain anymore. Everything I planned has changed since I returned."

They walked in comfortable silence for a while. The road stretched ahead of them, dusty and familiar to his companions, foreign to Jonathan. A group of travelers passed, going in the opposite direction, their donkeys loaded with pottery, simple, functional pieces, unlike his father's.

"We left everything to follow him," Ethan said suddenly, his voice matter-of-fact. "Fishing boats, healing practice, family expectations. People thought we'd lost our minds."

"Had you?" Jonathan asked.

Uri laughed. "Some days I wonder. But then I'd watch him with people, the way he saw worth in a tax collector everyone else despised, how he touched lepers when healers kept their distance." He shrugged. "It's hard to call that madness when it works."

"Worked how?"

"Changed them. Changed us." Ethan touched a small pouch at his belt, his healer's tools, Jonathan realized. "I learned to treat ailments of the body. But I watched him heal wounds that went deeper, shame, hatred, the kind of brokenness that keeps people from sleeping."

Jonathan remembered his sleepless nights in Crete. Some wounds were invisible, but no less real.

They crested a small hill, and Lydda came into view, white limestone buildings catching the morning sun, smoke rising from cooking fires, and the bustle of a market town coming to life.

"That's where we part ways," Uri said, pointing toward the settlement. "You'll continue alone from here?"

"I have to." Jonathan adjusted his pack straps, feeling the weight of the journey ahead. "The man I'm seeking, he's all the family I have left."

Ethan studied him with a healer's assessing gaze. "Family isn't always blood."

"No," Jonathan agreed, thinking of Dan. "Sometimes it's a choice. An extraordinary one."

They arrived in Lydda as the market square filled with morning traders. The town bustled with activity, merchants haggling over goods, the rhythmic clang of a blacksmith's hammer, and the tangy scent of curing hides from the tannery. Children darted between stalls displaying grains, olives, and the famous purple dyes that made Lydda a prosperous city.

Uri led them to a small cookshop where the aroma of roasting meat and fresh bread made Jonathan's stomach tighten with hunger. Over the shared meal, he watched as his companions interacted with the world around them. Uri slipped extra coins to the serving girl without fanfare, while Ethan quietly treated a child's scraped knee, the child's mother counting out payment for the food.

Small acts. Unremarkable to most. But Jonathan had spent enough time crafting to recognize passion when he saw it.

"If you need help in Jerusalem," Uri said as they prepared to part, "find Barnabas. He's our brother, you'll know him by how he treats strangers."

Jonathan thanked them, watching as they disappeared into Lydda's narrow streets. He shouldered his pack and set out immediately, knowing the most dangerous part of his journey lay ahead.

Alone again.

The afternoon stretched longer than expected. Despite pushing his pace, the sun was dropping fast, and Jerusalem remained stubbornly distant. Each traveler he passed confirmed what he already knew: he wouldn't reach Emmaus before dark.

As he walked, Ethan's words echoed in his mind. *It wasn't about forgiveness, which would have felt like preaching. But about healing wounds that went deeper than the surface, about the kind of brokenness that kept people awake at night.*

Jonathan knew that brokenness intimately. He had carried it from Caesarea to Crete and back again. But somewhere along the way, in his father's journal, in Dan's patient love, healing had begun.

He'd come seeking forgiveness, only to learn he needed to forgive his father for hiding the truth. The pain of that truth had shown him something unexpected: how deeply he had been loved all along.

Now, Dan needed him. The urgency to reach Jerusalem burned in his chest, driving him forward even as darkness crept across the land.

The road stretched empty before and behind him. The night was coming, and he would face it alone.

But he no longer felt abandoned. Uri and Ethan had shown him something without trying to teach it, that love travels in small acts, that healing happens in ordinary moments, that the most profound truths often come disguised as simple kindness... and that the hardest choices are usually the right ones.

Whatever awaited in Jerusalem, he would meet it with the same love that had shaped him, the love that had moved his father to choose him, Dan to raise him, and two strangers to share their bread beneath a fig tree.

Jonathan's legs burned with each step, but he pushed forward relentlessly. The urgency in his chest had crystallized into a single driving thought: *find Dan.* Every mile covered brought him closer to Jerusalem, to the answers he sought and to the man who had been more of a father to him than blood could make.

The sun hung lower now, painting the dusty road in shades of amber and rust. Soon, darkness would claim the hills, and with it would come the dangers Benjamin had warned him about. He needed shelter, a caravan to join, fellow travelers to share the night's watch, or at the very least a defensible place where he could rest without exposing himself to whatever prowled these roads after dark.

His eyes scanned the horizon for cooking fires, for the telltale dust clouds of approaching travelers, for any sign that he wouldn't face the coming night alone. The weight of his bow across his shoulders felt both comforting and insufficient. Benjamin's knife pressed against his leg with each step, a small reassurance in an increasingly hostile landscape.

The sun will set soon, he told himself, *and then the real test begins.*

It wasn't long before Jonathan heard a wolf's cry split the silence, a long, mournful howl. Jonathan waited, bow ready, but no answer came. The pack had not gathered yet.

His hand found Benjamin's knife in his pocket, and he checked the straps on his bow. *Ready?* The growing darkness sharpened his senses, and every shadow suddenly took on significance.

A flicker of firelight caught his eye, a campfire under an oak tree just off the road, its orange glow a beacon against the deepening twilight. The dancing flames cast shifting shadows on the surrounding rocks, illuminating the silhouette of a solitary figure. Relief flooded through Jonathan, cooling the fear that had tightened his throat, as the stranger's profile became familiar with each step. The curve of the shoulders, the way the head tilted slightly forward, he recognized that posture before he could make out the features.

Samir.

"Samir!" The name burst from him before he could think.

The man turned, his face breaking into a smile of recognition. "Master!"

Jonathan reached the warmth of the fire, the surprise of finding Samir momentarily overshadowing his weariness. He studied the man's familiar movements around the fire, efficient, practiced, much like his own approach to crafting bows.

"What brings you to this road?" he asked, careful to keep his voice even despite his relief at finding company. The flames cast dancing shadows across Samir's familiar features, their orange glow a stark contrast to the blue-black darkness beyond their circle. The sweet resin scent of burning cypress mingled with the earthier aroma of the oak tree above them, its branches forming a sheltering canopy that trapped the smoke and welcomed the warmth.

"A horse in Jerusalem needs tending," Samir said. "The garrison's centurion requested that I come specifically." He prodded the fire. "Usually, I'd travel with the soldiers, but they left days ago. And you, Master Jonathan? Why do you journey alone?"

"Looking for a relative in Jerusalem," Jonathan said, keeping his voice steady. "Someone there will know where to find him."

"You're fortunate then," Samir said, gesturing to the fire. "I know Jerusalem well. The garrison stable boys can help search."

Jonathan settled on a log, the night's earlier fears ebbing in the warmth of the firelight. He pulled out his food bag and offered it to Samir. "Hungry?"

The slave took it with grateful hands; above them, the moon rose, casting a pale light over the countryside. A wolf's cry pierced the night. An answer came. The pack had gathered. The wind turned cold, pushing them nearer to the flames.

Samir added more wood to the fire, checking whether his gathered wood would last the night.

"We need to keep the fire going and make sure we have enough wood until first light," Samir said.

Jonathan nodded. Together, they ventured just beyond the fire's light, gathering fallen branches that snapped crisply in their hands. The dry wood was rough against Jonathan's palms as they collected an armful each, the night air cooling his face while his back remained warm from the fire. They piled the branches carefully near the flames, arranging them so they would dry completely before being needed.

"Try to get a few hours of sleep, Samir. I will wake you when it's your turn to take over the watch. We will take turns," Jonathan said. Samir agreed.

The night sky was ablaze with stars.

Jonathan loosened the straps that held his bow securely behind his back, preparing it for use, just in case.

Samir began to sing an old Hebrew melody, and something in it stilled Jonathan. Dan had sung that same tune when Jonathan was a boy… softly, to lull him to sleep. Now, the sound pulled Dan's memory from the depths with startling clarity. And with it came the ache. The need to find him rose like fire in his chest.

"Where did you learn that?" Jonathan asked.

"My mother used to sing it when we were children," Samir said. "Her voice... I can still hear it. It always brings me peace."

"Your shoulder," Jonathan said, watching Samir feed the fire. "Has it healed?"

"Three days ago," Samir said, flexing his shoulder slightly. "I even trimmed Black Lightning's hooves before leaving."

"This was your family's trade, wasn't it? Horses?"

"My father's legacy." His voice dropped. "Or it was."

"Was?"

"He's in jail. He might be dead now; I don't know," he admitted, his hands stilled on the firewood.

"A Roman officer's stallion died under my father's watch, the finest one in the garrison, spirited like spring winds. Other stable hands poisoned the horse's feed, jealous, like a pack of animals fighting for the lead position.

"My father was the head groom. The blame fell to him," Samir's mouth twisted.

"And I became a slave."

The silence stretched between them, broken only by the fire's crackle and pop. Jonathan studied the man across the flames, surprised that the same skillful hands that tended horses with joy had a past bereft of it. The weight of unspoken questions hung heavy in the night air. The slave broke the silence.

"Ask." His voice was barely audible above the fire's whisper. "*About how I became a slave*. Sometimes, remembering is necessary."

Jonathan's throat felt dry, his pulse quickening. The craftsman in him recognized this moment as one where any hesitation would leave the work forever flawed. "Tell me."

Samir fed another branch to the flames as if drawing strength from the fire. "My father rose from stable hand to head groom in Tyre. He earned every step. Made our clan proud." His voice hardened. "Too proud. The others couldn't stand it. They sabotaged Lucius's stallion, the *Primus Pilus* himself."

His voice rose in anger, and he began shaking his head. "Lucius was forced to put down his beloved stallion to end its misery! And my father was charged with negligence and sent to jail!

"My brother and I had protested as much as we could, but since my father was the head of the stable, everything technically fell on his shoulders. He was found to be negligent, causing the death of a valuable horse.

"We were told to raise an impossible amount to pay for the cost of the horse, which would also free my father from jail.

"How much was the amount that they asked you to raise?" Jonathan asked.

"It was several hundred Tyrian *shekels,* which my brother and I could never raise, not in this lifetime, nor the next, not even if we were chained to the stables until we breathed our last."

"I'm sorry to hear this, Samir," Jonathan replied.

Samir's fingers traced patterns in the dirt beside the fire, like mapping the path his life had taken.

"My brother Raqmu came up with a plan," his voice dropped lower, forcing Jonathan to lean slightly forward to hear.

"We would go outside Tyre, find the trade routes where merchants traveled with valuable goods and animals." The firelight cast deep shadows across his face as he continued. "We'd offer to help with their horses or donkeys, charging a fee for our services."

He hesitated, his words catching in his throat. "If nothing were wrong with their animals, we'd... invent ailments. Diagnose problems that didn't exist." His eyes remained fixed on the flames, unable to meet Jonathan's gaze.

"It was wrong, but Raqmu insisted it was necessary.

"I was young. I didn't like what we were doing, but Raqmu said it was the only way to save our father. He kept telling me to grow up and be a man, and he would hit me every time I protested. He was only focused on freeing our father."

Samir fell silent for a moment, poking the embers of the fire with a stick. The wood hissed, and a fresh plume of smoke curled into the night air.

"The shekels poured in," he continued, his voice barely a whisper. "It was more than what we would earn in a year working in the garrison in Tyre, but we needed more. Raqmu suggested we slightly harm some animals so we could charge more. He said we would not hurt them seriously, but just enough for travelers to stop and check what ails their beasts. And then we would arrive and help them.

"This escalated to tampering with wagon wheels," Samir continued, his hands moving in demonstration. "Like when you loosen a horse's shoe just enough so it won't fall immediately, only later on the road. We'd target the smaller caravans, ones with just one or two men. They'd halt along the road we walked, wheels wobbling like a new foal's legs, and we'd appear to help. They always paid well for our services."

Jonathan suddenly felt his heart skip a beat, then pound against his ribs like a smith's hammer.

Smaller or single caravans.

The words echoed in his mind as a cold sweat broke across his forehead and back. His mouth went dry, and the fire's warmth couldn't touch the chill that had settled in his bones. He shifted his position, trying to appear merely uncomfortable rather than shaken to his core.

"That escalated to robbery in a matter of weeks, so that we could return quickly to Tyre. Half of the required amount was swiftly raised, but then something went wrong.

"The two caravans we were following split near Magdala," Samir continued, his fingers tracing fork-like paths in the dust beside the fire. "Two men in one wagon, arguing loudly, alert, weapons visible on their belts. The other had just a single driver." Samir's voice grew distant, his eyes reflecting the dancing flames as if seeing that dusty crossroads again.

"The lone wagon creaked under its heavy load. We could hear the driver singing to himself, unaware." His hand stilled in the dust.

"We chose the lone driver."

Jonathan's hands began to shake. He slipped them beneath his cloak.

"The wheel came loose exactly where we planned. While the driver struggled with it, Raqmu grabbed him in a headlock." Samir stared into the flames. "Usually, they just faint. Usually."

Jonathan surged to his feet, lungs refusing to work. Every instinct screamed at him to run, to stop listening, but his feet wouldn't move. His hands found refuge inside his cloak, fingers wrapping around Benjamin's knife like an anchor to sanity.

Lost in his memories, the slave didn't notice as he fed another stick to the flames. "But this man fought back," he continued, his voice hollow. "Raqmu drew his knife, drew blood. Then..." He swallowed hard. "A log crashed into Raqmu's head. Someone else was there. Hidden in the wagon."

Jonathan could see the pain etched in Samir's face, the way his shoulders hunched as though carrying a physical burden. The man seemed lost in his memories, barely aware of Jonathan's presence as his grip tightened on the knife until his knuckles burned.

"I ran to help. I grabbed the attacker from behind." Samir's voice dropped to a whisper. "A woman! I shouted to Raqmu, but he was already up, blood streaming down his face. The knife..." His words faltered. "She crumpled. Just... crumpled."

Jonathan abruptly stumbled back and braced himself against the tree, half of his face hidden in the shadows.

The rough bark pressed against his palm, its solid presence the only thing anchoring him to the moment. He bit his lip hard to stop himself from screaming, teeth breaking skin until he tasted blood, warm, metallic, strangely grounding. His throat constricted around the cry that fought to escape, turning his breath ragged.

"Raqmu started going through their things," Samir continued, his voice dropping even lower. "He was shouting at me, blood still running down his face, demanding that I find something of value."

Samir paused, staring into the fire as if he were seeing the scene unfold in the flames.

"I climbed inside the wagon. My hands were shaking so badly that I could barely move the bundles. That's when I saw it..." His voice caught. "A child. Sleeping peacefully in a nest of blankets, as if the world hadn't just collapsed.

"I froze. For a moment, I couldn't breathe. My brother was in a rage I'd never seen before. If he found the child..." He shook his head. "I pulled a blanket over, covering the child completely. I couldn't save the parents, but this... this is one thing I could do.

"I grabbed everything of value, a bag of coins, and some jewelry, hoping the child wouldn't wake up and cry. I honestly don't know what I would do if that were to happen. I tugged at Raqmu, saying, 'It's done! It's done! I had found all I could.' I was so afraid the baby would make a sound. And we started to run.

"Raqmu leaned on me as we ran away from the wagon. His head was bleeding profusely, so we had to stop often to bandage it.

"That was when a squad of Roman soldiers found us. They tracked us by following Raqmu's trail of blood," Samir whispered.

"Do you remember where this happened?" Jonathan asked, trying to keep his voice from shaking.

There was a pause, filled only by the crackle of flames and the distant, raspy call of a raven.

"It was near Capernaum," Samir answered, looking straight into the flames, unaware that his words had just confirmed everything.

Near Capernaum...

The words splintered something inside him.

His lungs seized. The firelight blurred.

His mother is gone.

And then, the sound of his blood pounding in his ears.

The pain was unbearable, a physical sensation that seized his lungs and sent ice through his veins. He stifled a cry, biting his lip so hard that warm blood flooded his mouth with its metallic tang. It trickled from the corner of his lips, a crimson confession on his chin. Both hands shook uncontrollably, the tremors running up his arms and into his shoulders.

"I saw my brother die slowly," Samir whispered. "Raqmu was crucified for killing the two people in the wagon." His voice faltered, almost disappearing into the crackle of the fire. "I was sent to the mines of Wadi Hamamat as a labor slave for the rest of my life."

He fell silent, the weight of memory seeming to press down on his shoulders physically. When he finally continued, his voice had changed, and there was an edge of wonder in it.

"Then one day, a snake bit the prized stallion of the *tribunus*. I'd learned about herbs that could draw out poison from my father." His fingers traced patterns in the dirt. "Janus, who was still a

Tribunus Militum then, bought me after that. He saved my life." He looked up briefly. "I would have died in those mines. I would be dead by now."

Tears ran down Samir's cheeks as he stared into the flames. The story had been told. There was nothing more to say.

Remembering made Samir's chest hurt. Remembering Raqmu... and his father, who must have thought they had abandoned him... If he is still alive...

He barely noticed Jonathan, whose back was slightly turned and who was holding onto the tree. Samir kept staring at the flames and didn't notice Jonathan shaking with rage, taking deep breaths as if gasping for air.

Neither man saw the other suffering silently as the story was retold.

Each was immersed in his private pain.

The two men remained silent for a long time.

The fire popped and hissed, and an owl called somewhere in the darkness. The silence stretched between them... Jonathan with his terrible knowledge, Samir with his unburdened conscience.

Neither man spoke, as if words themselves had become dangerous things.

Later in the night, the wolves called again, their voices weaving through the darkness like a lament that matched the weight on Jonathan's chest. This second cry was sharper, more urgent, its nearness making the hair on his arms stand on end. In the stillness that followed, even the fire seemed to hold its breath.

"Sleep," Jonathan said numbly to Samir, who was quietly tending the fire. "I will keep watch. I'll wake you when it's your turn."

Samir nodded, placed his tattered cloak on the ground a few feet from the fire, and lay on it. His back was turned to the flames and Jonathan. *He didn't want Jonathan to see him cry.*

Jonathan fed the fire mechanically, each movement a battle for control, like trying to shape an uncooperative piece of wood that threatened to split with each cut. Across the flames, Samir's sleeping form presented a target his hatred couldn't ignore, as marked as the center point on a bow stave that had to be precisely shaped.

The knife felt heavy in his grip, smooth, deceptive in its ease. The fire cast just enough light to see Samir, curled in sleep, unaware. *One quick motion. That's all it would take.* The night would swallow any sound. No witnesses. No questions. Justice delivered in silence.

The weight of the blade. The breath of the sleeping man.

A single step forward. Just one.

The wolves howled again. Sharp. Piercing. The fates are watching.

Jonathan's hands shook violently. He closed his eyes.

Blue eyes. His mother's eyes. Like rare sapphires among common stones, unmistakable. Amos's words returned. *"You're special. There's no one like you anywhere."*

Jonathan had traveled enough to know the truth: how many women in Judea or Galilee had blue eyes? As rare as the straight-grained yew he had chosen for Amos's bow.

It would be so simple. Silent. Quick. Like Raqmu's blade at his mother's throat. The wolves would clean away the evidence by morning, or an arrow, clean through the heart, a bowyer's justice.

His hand trembled. *One life for another. An eye for an eye. The old law demanded it: clear, precise justice like a perfectly balanced scale.*

Yet across the fire, the scarred back before him testified to its own story: years of punishment served in a brutal mine, the lash marks counting out a price already paid. Those same hands that had participated in death had also covered a sleeping child, preserving life when destruction would have been easier.

Jonathan stared at the man who had both destroyed and saved his world, a boy who had hidden a baby from his murderous brother, a slave who had survived his darkness.

The simple justice of the knife grew more complicated with each passing heartbeat.

His grip tightened around the knife, sweat slicking the handle. The firelight wavered, as if undecided itself. His pulse hammered against his ribs, urging action and urging restraint.

Jonathan wrestled with the weight of the blade, each breath a silent battle. His pain whispered of vengeance, of release, while the faces of Amos and Dan held his hands still, their presence heavier than the blade itself. The night passed in this cruel balance, desire for justice in one hand, the weight of mercy in the other, each heartbeat a painful choice renewed.

Dawn's first gray light found Jonathan already moving; his decision had been made not in a single moment, but through a thousand small surrenders throughout the night. Behind him, the dying fire still smoldered. Samir still slept, breathing deeply and evenly, unaware that his confession had rewritten Jonathan's understanding of his beginning. Some distances couldn't be measured in steps.

Through the endless night, he'd relived it all through new eyes: young Amos discovering the carnage, the broken wagon, the bodies, the desperate silence of a scene where violence had so recently visited. Then, the discovery of a sleeping baby wrapped in blankets, deliberately tucked away from danger. Hidden. Protected. Jonathan could almost see Samir's younger self, terrified yet still human enough to shield an innocent child from his brother's rage. Saved by the same hands that had helped destroy everything else. The story of his beginning was more complex than he'd imagined, neither pure tragedy nor miracle, but something messier that defied simple judgment.

Samir's choice had preserved more than a child's life - it had given Jonathan two fathers instead of none. One who'd found him, one who'd raised him. Both who'd loved him beyond blood.

The knife felt heavy in his pocket now. Useless. A weapon against yesterday's ghosts.

What Ethan and Uri taught him pulled his hand away from the easy choice of hate and vengeance.

Forgiveness wasn't about deserving. Samir's hands had helped orchestrate his parents' deaths, but they had also saved him from Raqmu's blade. One choice didn't erase the other, but perhaps that was the point.

Vengeance wouldn't bring his mother's blue eyes back to life, change the past, honor either of his fathers who had shaped him, or fill the void that burned for Dan's safety.

Sometimes, what we think are the easiest pain-free solutions extract the most heart-wrenching consequences. Amos had learned that with his silence, and Jonathan by running away. Six lost years with his father had taught him the price of taking the simple path. Vengeance might satisfy for a moment, but its poison would last a lifetime.

His mother's death, if she were his mother, had stolen his past... but perhaps it wasn't his past to begin with?

But Amos and Dan had given him a future.

One father was gone now, but the other... the other still needed him.

Truth had its timing. Each revelation these past days had come when he was ready to bear it. He was who he was because of both tragedy and grace: Samir's mercy, Amos's love, and Dan's guidance.

Jerusalem waited. Dan waited. The rest could stay here with the dying fire, the questions, the grief, the rage. They would be waiting for him when he returned if he chose to reclaim them.

Two fathers. One was already beyond reach, a regret he would carry forever. The other, Dan, was still within saving if he hurried. This choice, at least, was clear.

Jonathan pushed himself harder along the road to Jerusalem, every sense alert in the growing light.

The morning air was cool against his face, carrying the scent of damp earth and distant wood smoke. His sandals crunched rhythmically on the packed dirt road, each step taking him farther from last night's revelations and closer to his remaining father.

Behind him, Samir would wake to an empty camp, finding only cold ashes where resolution might have been.

That wound would need time to heal on its own.

But his other father? He could be in danger.

Nothing else mattered now.

20

MERCY

JONATHAN REACHED JERUSALEM SOMETIME AFTER NOON. HE DIDN'T stop to rest despite his parched throat and hollow stomach. Each step was measured and deliberate as he moved through the streets, fueled by the desire to see Dan safe.

Jerusalem's sights and sounds differed from those of any city he had visited.

Crowds jostled for space as chanted prayers echoed off stone walls, while the bleating of sacrificial lambs punctuated the din. The sharp tang of animals mingled with sweet incense that clung to his sweat-dampened tunic, creating a heady mixture that seemed to embody the city's sacred chaos.

Money changers were everywhere. Their tables could be seen in front of the biggest shops on every street corner. Jonathan suspected they might even be inside the temple itself. Everything revolved around the giant temple that dominated the skyline.

He had one goal: Joseph's house. Jacob's instructions had been clear. *Dan would be at Joseph's house.* The thought was a lodestone, pulling him through the chaos.

He adjusted his cloak to display the Roman pin Marcus had given him.

Then he walked to the nearest Roman soldier and asked for directions in Greek.

The Roman soldier looked at the pin and courteously told Jonathan that Joseph, the trader, was known to have a house on the Western Hill of Jerusalem. The soldier gave him directions. Jonathan thanked him and started walking.

Jonathan found the streets of Jerusalem even narrower than those of Crete and far more crowded. He kept bumping into and jostling with so many people that he couldn't see more than a few meters ahead. Everyone he met was pulling an animal or carrying one toward the temple while he was going in the opposite direction.

The first hint of trouble came as a subtle shift in the crowd's rhythm. Bodies that had flowed around him now pressed closer, movement becoming restricted. Then came the voices, isolated shouts at first, quickly swelling into a chorus of anger. The words were Hebrew, unmistakable even to ears more accustomed to Greek: denunciations of Rome, calls for freedom, the dangerous language of rebellion.

Jonathan felt the crowd's mood shift from a bustling marketplace to a brewing storm in the blink of an eye.

He looked ahead and saw a group of young men with their fists raised above their heads, shouting for the Romans to get out of Judea.

The crowd surged forward again, and Jonathan found himself locked, body to body, with the rest of the people trying to move away from the marching young men demanding freedom from Rome.

"Romans!" A shout erupted behind him, and a fresh wave of panic rippled through the crowd. Jonathan glanced back and saw the same

Roman soldiers he had approached earlier marching toward the protesters behind him. Jonathan realized he was now trapped between the two opposing groups. *Violence was imminent, and he had to get to safety.*

He tried to force his way through the sea of bodies. But the surging crowd pressed forward, more violently this time, and he soon found himself facing the young man who was shouting and challenging the Roman soldiers to come and fight.

The young man looked at the Roman pin tucked in Jonathan's cloak and shouted to his friends, "Here's one of them! A *traitor!*" Two more men closed in on him and started hitting him with their fists. Someone struck the back of his head. A fist landed on his jaw. Then he felt more fists hitting him in other parts of his body. He raised his arms to cover his face.

Jonathan was hammered on all sides. A blow caught his face with a dull thud that reverberated through his skull. Another strike sent a splintering pain across his cheekbone. His left eye swelled instantly, warm blood trickling down his face like rain on parched earth. His face cracked under another hit. His head spun, the crowd's roar dulling to a distant rumble. Copper flooded his mouth as he tasted blood. His chest seized under a barrage of fists, each impact stealing another breath. His knees scraped against rough stone as he fell.

He was in excruciating pain and gasping for air until a body somehow covered him from receiving more blows... shouting... He couldn't make out the words. His ears were ringing from the blows he received on the side of his face...

He held on tight to the body that covered him, feeling the frantic rise and fall of the man's chest against his own. Sweat and blood mingled between them as his protector's muscles tensed and shifted, absorbing blows meant for Jonathan. Through the ringing in his ears, he could barely make out the hoarse shouts directed at his assailants, desperate words flung like shields into the chaos.

Then blackness. The world collapsed. The crowd roared on.

And Jonathan was gone.

WHEN CONSCIOUSNESS RETURNED, JONATHAN FELT A SPLASH OF water on his face. A hand wiped the blood he tasted in his mouth. He opened his eyes to find Samir looking worriedly at him, both of them still in the narrow street where the violence continued to rage at a short distance.

"Master, are you okay? I feared something had happened to you when I awoke and couldn't find you. It is good that I found you just in time. You are hurt badly."

Jonathan was hurt from the assault. His head was bleeding. He couldn't fully open one of his eyes, his chest hurt from the pummeling, and one of his ribs seemed to be broken. He couldn't breathe properly.

Samir was visibly distraught and bleeding badly, too. His face was red, one eye was closed shut, his lips were bleeding, and a few cuts on his head and shoulders badly needed stitching.

"You covered me?" Jonathan mumbled.

Hours ago, he had held Samir's life in his hands; now, Samir had chosen to shield him with his own body.

"I had to, Master! That crowd hated everything connected with Rome. To them, you were worse, a traitor. I tried to explain, but they wouldn't listen." Samir's voice held no trace of the previous night's anguish, only concern.

He looked at Samir, saw the blood pooling at his jawline, the pain etched deep into his skin, and felt the weight of it.

This was the man who had helped destroy his world.

A man whose life he had almost taken.

A man who had saved him again and again.

Jonathan's lips parted, but words never came.

Darkness claimed him once more.

HOURS LATER, JONATHAN AWOKE TO THE SMELL OF FRESHLY MADE bread and a sweetly scented herbal concoction. He slowly opened his eyes and found a young girl staring at him, shouting, "*Imma,* he's *awake!* Come!"

Jonathan looked at a beautiful little girl who was staring at him, her curious eyes wide beneath a crown of dark, curly hair. He was in a small room, lying on a cot stuffed with straw that crinkled beneath his weight. Across from him, a woman worked at a low table, the rhythmic sound of her pestle grinding herbs against stone punctuating the stillness. The walls bore the smooth finish of many years of careful maintenance, and a small window high above let in a shaft of golden afternoon light that caught the dust motes dancing in the air.

A woman almost the same age as Jonathan approached him and smiled. "Truly! We were worried that you were more seriously hurt than the cuts and a broken rib we were able to ascertain. Would you like to sit?" she asked.

Jonathan accepted their help, and both the woman and her child assisted him. He had a tight bandage around his waist. When he moved slightly to sit up, he felt a sharp pain in his midsection. He winced.

"Where am I?" Jonathan asked.

"You are in the City of David. We're in the Lower City of Jerusalem. Samir brought you here yesterday. He is a friend of my husband. My husband works in the garrison stable here in Jerusalem. Both you and Samir needed help yesterday. We're the nearest people he could reach. You were unconscious, and he was bleeding," she said.

"Where is Samir?" Jonathan asked quietly.

"He had to report to the stable with my husband. They left early," she answered.

Jonathan absorbed this quietly.

"I am Rebecca," the woman said. "And this is Leah, my daughter." The woman nodded toward her young daughter, who sat near Jonathan, looking intently at him. "Samir told us you're called Jonathan?"

Jonathan's eyes confirmed what she already knew.

"You must be hungry. Please eat," Rebecca beckoned toward the table, where bread and a fresh drink were waiting.

Jonathan slowly stood, testing his balance. Rebecca and Leah both moved to help him, the child placing his hand on her small shoulder as they guided him to the table.

He whispered his thanks as he sat. He began to eat, not realizing how hungry he was until he took a bite of the freshly baked bread. The crust crackled between his teeth, giving way to a warm, yeasty center that reminded him of mornings in his father's courtyard. He started taking larger bites, one after the other, the familiar comfort of simple bread momentarily overshadowing his pain. He was famished.

Rebecca smiled.

"Samir told us you are looking for your relative here in Jerusalem. Do you have any idea where he might be?"

"I seek the house of Joseph the Trader," Jonathan answered, his merchant's Greek giving way to the more careful cadence of local

Aramaic. "I understand he serves on the Sanhedrin as well." He noted the flicker of recognition in her eyes. "Might you know where I can find him?"

Rebecca's eyes widened in recognition of the name. She nodded but remained silent.

"Can you tell me where to find Joseph's house?" Jonathan asked.

Rebecca answered, "There is someone I can ask to bring you to that place. He usually comes around this area to distribute food to the less fortunate. I will wait for him to pass by and inform him of your request," Rebecca assured Jonathan.

"Thank you," Jonathan murmured, savoring the most refreshing herbal drink he had ever tasted, cool and sharp with mint, mellowed by the gentle sweetness of honey and an elusive warmth, unfamiliar but soothing. The liquid seemed to clear not only his throat but also his thoughts, though his bruised body continued to protest with each movement.

~

JONATHAN AWOKE TO A CALM CONVERSATION BETWEEN A MAN AND A woman. He had slept again after consuming the bread and drink that Rebecca had prepared for him.

He slowly opened his eyes to see two people staring at him from the far side of the room. Rebecca was talking with a man who was bigger than Jonathan and muscular, just like Samir. He had short, dark, curly hair and a well-trimmed beard, with eyes that seemed to hold both scrutiny and compassion in equal measure.

Although his presence commanded attention and respect, he wore simple garments of undyed wool, free from the gold emblems or rich purple borders that would seem to suit him more. His voice, when he spoke, carried the resonant timbre of someone accustomed to being heard. Some people might find this confusing, but not Jonathan.

Amos had the same effect on people.

The man stepped forward, moving with the deliberate calm of someone who carefully measured his actions. "Hello, Jonathan," he said, his voice carrying a warmth that seemed to fill the small room. "I am Barnabas. Rebecca has shared that you seek Joseph's house." He paused, studying Jonathan with eyes that seemed to see beyond his injuries. "May I ask why you are searching for him?"

Jonathan tried to sit up. Rebecca rushed to his side, followed by Barnabas. They propped Jonathan into a sitting position.

"Thank you," Jonathan said to both of them.

"I met Uri and Ethan on my way to Jerusalem, and they told me to find you," Jonathan said to Barnabas. "I'm fortunate that Rebecca knows you as well."

"I am Jonathan, son of Amos, whom some called Caesarea's Master of Clay," he replied, the pride in his heritage evident in his voice. "I search for my father's lifelong assistant and my second father in all ways that matter." His fingers unconsciously traced the edge of his bandage, as though shaping clay. "He departed for Jerusalem days ago and should have returned. I've traced his path to Joseph's house."

Jonathan met Barnabas's gaze directly. "Can you help me find him?"

Barnabas's eyes widened upon hearing Jonathan's answer, recognition dawning across his features. He closed his eyes and bowed his head slightly, his lips moving in what appeared to be a silent prayer of thanksgiving. His gaze held a new intensity when he looked up again, part compassion, part purpose.

Barnabas answered with the certainty of one delivering long-awaited news, *"I'll bring you to Dan."*

21

TRANSFORMATION

JONATHAN, BADLY BRUISED AND BANDAGED, WAS USHERED INTO A room on the second floor, where he found himself standing before his father's patron and lifelong friend, Joseph the Trader.

Joseph's hair and beard were neatly trimmed and groomed. Although he was dressed without the powerful symbols of his office, his appearance did not diminish the stature of this powerful and wealthy man. This was a man whose presence people could not ignore.

Joseph rushed to hug him. "Welcome home, Jonathan," Joseph said, his voice carrying the warmth and gravity of a man who recognized the workings of providence. "Your father would have been pleased to see you here; he always believed your path would lead you back when the time was right."

Jonathan nodded and smiled. He knew how much his father valued this man's friendship and patronage. Joseph was the one person who made it possible for Jonathan and his family to live well in Caesarea Maritima. Jonathan and his entire family would always be grateful to him.

"Please sit," Joseph beckoned to Jonathan.

They sat opposite each other near a window overlooking the courtyard, where they could see the dying light of the setting sun casting long shadows across the stone pavers below. The scent of cedar and beeswax filled the vast room, a space that could accommodate seventy to a hundred people, its whitewashed walls retaining the warmth of the day. The air felt charged somehow, as if the space itself remembered the momentous gatherings it had witnessed.

Prominently placed in the center stood a long table, surrounded by beautifully carved benches that were worn smooth by use. Their surfaces caught the amber glow of oil lamps that had just been lit against the approaching evening. It looked like a perfect setting for a simple banquet, an intimate gathering of friends and family.

Jonathan couldn't help but notice how Joseph's eyes kept studying his face as if searching for traces of his father there. The room itself seemed to hold its breath, its vastness making their intimate conversation feel both private and somehow momentous.

"Where were you, and when did you arrive?" Joseph asked.

Jonathan was initially surprised that Joseph knew he had been away, but he then remembered how close the two men had been; Amos would have told him about what happened. Jonathan narrated everything that had happened to him since he had been gone, up until two weeks ago, when he arrived from Crete to find his father dead... to yesterday, when he was caught in a melee. He omitted the part about Samir and the story that binds them together.

Joseph listened intently and asked questions. He was surprised that Jonathan went to Crete and was impressed by his bowyer training under Andreas. He said he had heard about the bowyer and his mastery of the craft.

Joseph asked if he could look at the bow Jonathan had with him. Jonathan handed Joseph the bow, explaining that it had been slightly damaged in the melee he had been caught in. He added that whatever damage the bow sustained could be repaired quickly when he returned to Caesarea.

Joseph looked at the bow quietly, tracing his fingers over every painstakingly carved part. Jonathan observed how the trader's hands moved with practiced discernment, evaluating the bow's balance and tension points just as he would assess a fine piece of pottery. *This man reads craftsmanship like Father read clay.*

"It's a beautiful piece of work," Joseph said.

"I made it for my father," Jonathan replied.

"And this would have made him so proud," Joseph responded, handing the bow back to Jonathan, who lowered it to his side.

The weight of the bow felt different now, lighter somehow, as if the burden of uncertainty had lifted with it. Jonathan ran his fingers along the familiar grain of the wood, remembering all the times he'd done this before, but never with such clarity of purpose. Each groove and imperfection told a story, much like the pottery pieces that had led him here. Now it also bore scratches from the melee that he did not intend to smooth out, erase, or hide.

When he finally secured the bow and looked back at Joseph, he noticed a subtle shift in the man's demeanor. The older man's shoulders tensed slightly, and his eyes took on a guarded look that made Jonathan's heart beat faster.

"Do you know where Dan is?" Jonathan asked, his voice barely above a whisper. Joseph nodded, looking directly at Jonathan.

The silence stretched between them, long, heavy, and full of unspoken words.

Joseph shifted his weight, and Jonathan recognized the familiar gesture that always preceded difficult news. His heart quickened. The peace he'd felt moments ago wavered like sunlight breaking through storm clouds.

"There's something you need to know about Dan," Joseph paused. The silence made Jonathan very nervous, but he tried to remain calm. He looked directly at Joseph.

"Dan was seriously injured in a melee," Joseph informed Jonathan. "The same kind you were caught in. One of our people found him unconscious and bleeding. He was brought here, but he has not woken up since. He is in serious but stable condition," Joseph said.

Jonathan's heart seemed to stop. He gripped his chair tightly, struggling to regain his composure.

"Since we found Dan, I have sent for the best doctors to check on him. They have done everything they can. Now that some of the Apostles have gathered in Jerusalem together, they have started prayer vigils for him," Joseph added. "Everyone is doing their best. Dan is one of our own."

"Can I see him?" Jonathan asked, his voice steady despite the trembling of his hands.

"Later," Joseph answered. "Two Apostles just arrived from a trip this morning, including Levi. We call him Matthew now. Both Apostles have been with Dan since. We can see Dan when they are finished," Joseph assured Jonathan.

"I can't lose Dan. He's the only family I have left," Jonathan said, his voice trembling. Tears threatened to fall from Jonathan's eyes, and his heart was breaking again. Joseph quickly rose from his seat and hugged the young man to comfort him.

Time seemed to slow as Jonathan absorbed the news. He sat in silence, barely noticing as visitors came and went, as prayers were whispered in corners of the room, and as the day's light shifted across the tiled floor. When he finally looked up, the room had emptied, and the shadows had lengthened considerably.

~

JONATHAN WAS STILL UNRAVELING HIS THOUGHTS WHEN JOSEPH approached, silent and deliberate, holding a small, beautiful water jar. Jonathan's heart lurched. Even in the fading light, he recognized his father's work immediately. The distinctive style, the perfect proportions, his fingers ached with muscle memory of how his father had taught him to shape such vessels.

"Your father gave me two matching pieces," Joseph said softly, watching Jonathan's face. "A large and a small water jar." He paused, letting the weight of the moment settle between them. "This is the smaller one." Joseph carefully extended the piece toward Jonathan.

Jonathan's hands trembled slightly as he reached for the jar.

The familiar texture of his father's work was both comfort and a fresh wound. The jar was heavier than it appeared, solid and perfectly balanced in his palms. The clay felt cool against his skin, yet somehow radiated warmth that seemed to come from within.

The clay piece was so beautiful.

As his fingers traced the raised leaves of the mustard tree, the slight roughness of the design contrasted with the smooth glaze. The moment felt sacred, as if he were receiving more than just a pottery piece; he was receiving a message from his father across time and distance.

Jonathan was speechless.

At the jar's center stood a towering mustard tree, its embossed leaves climbing the neck as though emerging naturally from the clay. On one side, the sun dipped below the horizon; on the other, it rose in quiet brilliance. The piece was bathed in the shifting hues of dawn and dusk, its glaze flawless, its craftsmanship exquisite. It stirred both joy and sorrow. Jonathan could see his father's touch in every careful stroke, and he knew precisely where Dan's hands had shaped it. It was a creation of skill and devotion, beautifully and lovingly made.

"And what words were engraved on this piece?" he quietly asked Joseph.

Joseph was taken aback. He had told no one about the inscription in the jar. No one! After a few moments, he found his voice.

"It bore the word 'transformation,'" Joseph answered, almost like a whisper.

There was a moment of silence between the two men. Joseph broke the silence. "How do you know?"

"Mine bore 'truth,' engraved on a clay box. I learned about an amphora that my father gave to a family in Cana, which bore the word 'trust.' Now, I know who holds the third piece my father made." Jonathan's voice grew quiet as understanding dawned.

"The truth piece made me question everything I thought I knew about my father, about myself." He touched the jar gently.

"The trust piece taught me that sometimes you must believe even when you can't see the whole path." He looked up at Joseph. "And now this, transformation. Father wasn't just making pottery, was he?" Jonathan touched the water jar reverently.

"These weren't just vessels. He was mapping a journey."

Joseph nodded slowly. "The truth frees us, trust opens our hearts, and transformation..." He paused, looking meaningfully around the room where so many miracles had occurred. "Transformation makes us new."

"Each word led to the next," Jonathan said softly. "Like stepping stones across a river."

"Or like clay being shaped on a potter's wheel," Joseph added gently. "I witnessed your father travel this path well."

"Where is it?" Jonathan asked Joseph. "Where are the Aramaic letters in this piece?"

"The inscription is not in this piece. It's in the larger one," Joseph said.

"Where is the larger piece, then?" Jonathan asked.

"It's in a tomb," Joseph answered.

Jonathan looked at Joseph, confused. *Did he hear right? A tomb?*

"Come, let us sit," Joseph beckoned.

They sat on two vacant chairs facing each other, with a small table between them. Joseph carefully and lovingly placed his water vessel on the table.

"The people in this house..." Joseph paused, as if choosing his next words carefully. "We followed a Rabbi." Joseph's eyes moved around the room as if seeing memories in the shadows. "We saw things, Jonathan. Things that changed us," his voice dropped. "Now we do what we can to share what he taught us.

"Your father and Dan believe the same thing. They support the Rabbi's teachings and his disciples, whom he calls his Apostles. Like me, your father and Dan quietly and regularly contribute to financing what needs to be done, despite the risks involved.

"People think we're rebels," Joseph's mouth tightened. "Romans watch us, Jews suspect us, but our Rabbi never spoke of overthrowing Rome. He spoke of changing hearts."

Joseph looked at Jonathan intently, trying to determine if he understood what he was saying. *Many people struggle to comprehend because they listen with their ears rather than their hearts.*

Jonathan nodded and said, "I believe I met some of your followers on my way here. Uri and Ethan told me unbelievable stories. They told me to seek out Barnabas if I needed help. I met Barnabas at Rebecca's house. Were all of them followers of the one you call the Rabbi?" Jonathan asked.

Joseph nodded. "As were your father and Dan."

Jonathan hesitated. "Uri told me the one you follow is with his father. Is he here?"

Joseph studied him carefully before answering.

"He was buried, Jonathan."

Jonathan's brow furrowed. "Buried?"

Joseph exhaled slowly. "He was crucified."

Jonathan stiffened. His lips parted slightly, but he said nothing.

"He was placed in a tomb," Joseph continued. "A tomb I gave him."

Jonathan's breath caught. "Your tomb?"

Joseph nodded once, but his expression softened.

"My servants prepared everything, oils, spices, burial cloths, and water for cleansing the body." He hesitated. "A new servant, in her hurry, grabbed the first water jar she saw, filled it with water, and rushed to the tomb." He gestured toward the space on the table between them.

"Your father's jar, the piece that carried the word 'transformation,' is still inside the tomb where he rose from the dead." Joseph's voice was barely audible, but the word 'transformation' seemed to settle heavily in the space between them.

Jonathan exhaled slowly. "Transformation," he repeated, as if testing its weight.

Joseph held his gaze. "It remains there, Jonathan."

Jonathan's heart pounded. He swallowed hard. "Then..."

Joseph leaned forward, his voice barely above a whisper. "He is not there. He lives."

Jonathan's body tensed. The walls of the room seemed smaller somehow; the air heavier.

"Two people who saw him alive after he had been buried for three days are with Dan now. More of them will be here soon. You can ask all of them yourself."

The silence stretched between them, thick with meaning.

"How do I learn more?" Jonathan asked.

Joseph gave a knowing nod. "Dan heard him speak. He sat and broke bread with him, just as your father did. He can tell you everything."

Both men fell silent. Joseph vividly remembered everything that had transpired, while Jonathan quietly pondered all he had heard.

"Did your father make more pieces with inscriptions?" Joseph asked after a moment. "Are there more out there?" Joseph leaned forward, interested.

"He wrote that there were three. He hoped to finish a fourth and told me where to find it if he succeeded. I intend to look," Jonathan said.

"Please let me know when you do," Joseph said.

"I will," Jonathan promised.

"Can you share the stories behind the pottery pieces that bear truth and trust?" Joseph asked. Jonathan nodded. It would be a long night, but Jonathan knew his father's friend needed to hear everything he had discovered.

As Jonathan recounted his journey, from the clay box in his father's workshop to the amphora in Cana, he watched Joseph's face. The older man's eyes brightened with unshed tears as the pieces of Amos's legacy fell into place.

The night had grown late when Jonathan finished, and profound silence filled the room.

"Your father understood something profound about faith. It's something I'm only beginning to see. Each piece he made was a step. Truth, then trust, and finally transformation. He was showing you the way."

Jonathan felt the weight of those words settle into his heart. The day's exhaustion, the emotional toll of all he'd learned, and the lingering worry about Dan began to press heavily upon him. As Joseph rose to leave, Jonathan remained in his chair, too overwhelmed to move.

"Rest," Joseph said softly, gently touching Jonathan's shoulder. "Tomorrow will bring its revelations."

As Joseph's footsteps faded down the corridor, Jonathan remained seated, pondering all he had learned and experienced. Three words echoed in his mind like the stages of his journey: truth, trust, and transformation. His eyes grew heavy as he contemplated the mystery, the room's gentle stillness enveloping him like his father's embrace.

Transformation

The clay piece was breathtaking. It had a large mustard tree at the center of the piece. The detailing was exquisite. The tree leaves were embossed on the neck of the vessel as if they were growing out of clay. The sun was setting on one side of the tree and rising on the other. An ending and a beginning.

"Wake up, Jonathan," a voice called to him. Jonathan stirred, disoriented. He had slept in the chair with his head on the table. His conversation with Joseph had ended just as the sun began to rise. Now, he realized it must be noon.

Looking at the person who had roused him, he saw a man, perhaps a few years younger than his father, regarding him with interest. The man had short black hair, a well-groomed beard, and eyes that smiled with warmth and joy.

"Forgive me," Jonathan said, straightening. "I fell asleep."

"Good afternoon, Jonathan. I am Matthew, but your father and Dan insist on calling me Levi," the man said, laughing. "I've known them since we were children in Capernaum."

"Good afternoon, Levi," Jonathan greeted, rubbing his eyes to wake himself up.

"Dan is asking for you," Levi said.

Jonathan jumped to his feet, surprised by the news. *Dan had awakened!* "Where is he?" Jonathan asked.

"Follow me," Levi said, smiling as he led Jonathan down a corridor into one of the rooms. He found Dan lying in bed, attended by a young man.

"Your son is here, Dan," Levi announced as they entered the room.

Dan lay in bed, thin and pale, his once-sturdy frame diminished. The blankets rose high above the mattress where his body should have filled the space. The room carried the sharp herbal scent of medicinal poultices and the sweeter undertone of healing balms.

Dan's breath caught as Jonathan stepped into the room. The sight struck him like a fist to the gut. Dried blood traced ragged lines across Jonathan's forehead. Two deep slashes carved his cheek. His swollen eye, raw and angry, remained half-closed. Dan gasped at the battered face of the young man he had always silently claimed as his son.

Jonathan rushed to Dan and wrapped his arms around him, feeling the bones beneath the thin tunic, hearing the papery sound of his breathing. A sob escaped Jonathan's lips as Dan's familiar scent (clay, olive oil, and something uniquely his own) broke through the medicinal smells.

Dan's weathered hands found Jonathan's face, tracing the features he'd feared he'd never see again.

"My boy," Dan whispered, his voice fragile yet fierce. "My stubborn, precious boy. I thought I had lost you forever."

"Never again," Jonathan whispered back. "Never leave without me."

"Never," Dan promised, pulling him close despite his weakness. His voice cracked.

Levi and the young man who had tended Dan quietly left the room, closing the door with gentle reverence for the reunion taking place.

For hours, they talked. The afternoon light shifted to evening's amber glow, and still they talked until Dan's eyes grew heavy with exhaustion.

"Rest now," Jonathan whispered, adjusting the blanket around Dan's shoulders. "I'll be here when you wake."

THE SUN HAD SET WHEN JONATHAN STEPPED OUT OF DAN'S ROOM.

He felt at peace.

No fear, no regret, and no hate. It was the first time he had ever felt that way.

The corridor was quiet except for the soft murmur of evening prayers from nearby rooms. Oil lamps cast dancing shadows on the walls, reminding him of nights in his father's workshop. But now, instead of restlessness, he felt a profound stillness in his soul.

The pieces of his life, his father's legacy, Dan's faith, and his journey, had finally fallen into place.

He was so absorbed in this newfound serenity that he almost missed the approaching footsteps. He encountered Barnabas in the corridor, and Barnabas greeted him in Greek.

Jonathan unconsciously returned the greeting in the same language, making Barnabas laugh heartily. "I suspected you spoke Greek fluently!"

"I have been in Crete for six years," Jonathan said with a smile.

"I hail from Cyprus! Why were you in Crete for six years?" Barnabas asked.

22

TREASURE

While Dan regained his strength for the journey to Caesarea, Jonathan spent his days in the upper room, absorbing wisdom from every disciple and Apostle who passed through.

Jonathan met Uri and Ethan again, and they were both ecstatic to see him in the upper room. The two couldn't believe that it was Dan whom Jonathan was looking for! Both Uri and Ethan knew Dan well.

Jonathan learned that Uri and Ethan were among the 72 men who traveled to spread the word of the Lord. He felt lucky to have met a handful of them, including Levi, whose friendship meant so much to his father and Dan.

Jonathan stood on the balcony, gazing out at hundreds of houses, each lit by a pinprick of light as darkness slowly enveloped the city.

The evening air carried the mingled scents of cooking fires, roasting meat, and the sweet fragrance of evening flowers just beginning to open. From somewhere below came the soft, melancholy notes of a shepherd's flute, rising and falling like a wordless prayer. He breathed in the cold night air deeply, feeling it sharp in his lungs, a counterpoint to the warm stone of the balcony rail, which still held the day's heat beneath his palms. Though he had witnessed the city's hidden brutality beneath its surface, he still found Jerusalem mesmerizing, a living contradiction of beauty and harshness, devotion and deceit.

And I think Father felt this way about Jerusalem, too.

He had learned that his father visited the upper room monthly with Dan and more often if his health permitted. His father had been on this same balcony, waiting for the Lord or the Apostles to arrive, so he could eavesdrop on their discussions and reflect on them privately. Dan said his father's transformation started from this.

The upper room had taken on a lived-in quality that contrasted with its solemn purpose; reed mats were rolled against walls where people slept, the scent of fresh bread and olive oil lingered from shared meals, and the limestone floor had been worn smooth by constant movement. Morning light streamed through eastern windows, filling the room with golden warmth, while evening brought the flickering glow of oil lamps and the mingled voices of prayers. The wooden beams overhead had darkened from years of cookfires and incense, bearing silent witness to extraordinary gatherings.

Each disciple seemed to take a particular interest in him.

Some shared stories of the sick being healed in distant villages. Others spoke of teachings delivered on wind-swept hillsides, where the Lord's words carried to thousands who had gathered to listen. With every conversation, another piece of the larger story fell into place, not just of the Lord but of Amos's quiet transformation while witnessing in Jerusalem.

Levi, especially, made time for Jonathan before setting off on another journey. He invited him on long walks through Jerusalem's winding streets, leading him beyond the city walls to quieter paths.

As they walked, Levi would pause, pointing to places where the Lord had taught, healed, or rested. "Here," he'd say, gesturing to an unremarkable corner, "he stopped to speak with a blind beggar everyone else ignored." Or, "In this courtyard, he silenced the learned men with questions they couldn't answer."

Each place took on new meaning through Levi's words, turning ordinary spaces into sacred ones. And slowly, Jonathan began to see the city differently, not just as it was, but as his father had seen it.

When the Apostle Peter arrived, Jonathan was baptized, just as his father and Dan had been before him. With Peter's presence in the upper room, the ordinary became luminous. What once felt routine now shimmered with purpose, every simple task a quiet rhythm of service, each movement an offering. The change in Jonathan was unmistakable, so palpable that he found himself smiling for no apparent reason. Words failed him, but joy did not. Now, he understood why his father had longed to be in Jerusalem as often as he could. Now he knew why his father had died happy.

Joseph also spent time with Jonathan, advising him to reach out if he needed anything, especially when starting his trade, regardless of what his chosen trade would be. "Your father has enriched my life in so many ways. I hope to continue to show my deep appreciation for his wisdom and friendship through his son." This time, Jonathan did not nod to acknowledge what Joseph had said; instead, he rushed to hug the man.

It was Barnabas, however, with whom Jonathan formed the strongest bond.

Barnabas made all of Christ's stories and teachings easier for Jonathan to understand. He answered every question Jonathan asked, even the ones he was hesitant to voice to others for fear of misunderstanding.

Barnabas seemed to know when Jonathan needed clarification and when he needed space to ponder what he had heard.

Jonathan continued to be amazed at how Barnabas, like everyone else, could leave everything he had to follow the Lord and spread his teachings.

As they spent more time together, Jonathan began to understand why. The teachings were simple in words but required much deeper thought to understand them fully. Each story had many layers to explore. One could listen with ears, head, or heart. Each approach revealed different truths, and Barnabas helped him ponder them all.

A few days before Jonathan and Dan were set to leave for Caesarea, Barnabas joined Jonathan on the balcony, looking out at the city bathed in the sun's last glow.

"I've been told that your father was often seen in this very same spot, staring at the same view you are looking at now," Barnabas told Jonathan. Jonathan smiled. His father always loved the simple pleasures in life despite being constantly surrounded by the ostentatious display of wealth in Caesarea.

"Amos was often seen in this very spot, as he quietly contemplated what he heard from the Apostles or the Lord himself. A disciple said that Amos once shared that he felt like he was slowly being transformed, that he was changing much like the clay he formed on the wheel."

"I wish I could have come home sooner to see my father change," Jonathan whispered. *"I wish we could have shared this moment,"* he continued, looking at the city below.

"You still have your other father with you, Jonathan," Barnabas reminded. "You can still share everything with him," Barnabas added.

Jonathan looked at Barnabas and nodded. "I know," Jonathan answered. "I'm blessed to have another chance to make things right," he added.

"I have no plan to take you away from your other father, Jonathan. I know you would like to spend time with the last remaining member of your family. Still, it would be a disservice to him and Amos if I don't tell you that we need men like you who can speak Greek fluently and travel well for a short trip to Antioch," Barnabas said.

"Antioch?" Jonathan looked at Barnabas, confused.

"Yes, Antioch in Syria," Barnabas explained, his voice taking on the measured cadence he used when teaching.

"There are people there waiting to hear the teachings, Greeks and Jews alike. They need guidance and structure." His eyes brightened with the energy that always accompanied his sense of purpose. "The community there reminds me of saplings that have taken root but need proper tending to grow straight and true. I've been asked to go to help them establish deeper foundations in the teachings of Christ."

"Dan and I must return to Caesarea first and discuss what else needs to be done regarding my father's last instructions. Then, I can ask Dan for his opinion about traveling with you to Antioch for a few months. I promise to send word to you once I have decided on this matter," Jonathan said to Barnabas.

Barnabas laughed and hugged Jonathan. "I said those very words when they invited me to Jerusalem," he confessed. "Now, here I am, having sold everything I own!"

The journey back to Caesarea took five days, each mile marked by a deepening bond between Jonathan and Dan. As their wagon rolled through familiar landscapes, the rocky hills giving way to fertile plains, then to coastal lowlands, they shared comfortable silences punctuated by quiet conversations about the teachings they had absorbed in Jerusalem.

At night, when they stopped at caravanserais or made camp beneath the stars, other travelers would sometimes join them. Dan, despite his weakness, would often answer their questions about the journey or share simple stories that left them thoughtful and reflective.

Jonathan watched with growing admiration as his surrogate father touched others who were seeking faith with the gentleness of a master potter, never forcing but gently guiding, so that their faith would find the strength to hold its form.

As they neared the outskirts of Caesarea, Dan turned to Jonathan, his eyes bright despite his lingering weakness. "You see it differently now, don't you?" he asked softly.

"What?" Jonathan replied.

"*Everything,*" Dan said, with that gentle smile that had comforted Jonathan throughout his childhood.

"The vision you see hidden unfolds precisely in its own time, Nathan. Whether in clay, in wood, or people. We can neither hurry nor stall it. It serves a reason; its own time and its purpose."

Jonathan nodded, understanding flowing between them deeper than words.

The coastal road brought the familiar scent of the sea, and Jonathan found himself eager rather than anxious about returning home. This time, he wasn't searching for answers; he was bringing them back with him, along with a deeper understanding of both his fathers' journeys.

~

Jacob was so ecstatic to see Dan that he ran down the road when he saw him descending from the wagon. Dan was caught off guard when Jacob rushed and hugged him tightly. Jonathan saw himself in Jacob when he arrived a month ago, hugging Dan just as tightly upon seeing him.

In that instant, Jonathan realized that Jacob shared his feelings for Dan.

Jacob loved Dan like a father, too.

While Jacob helped Dan settle in, Jonathan stood for a moment in the courtyard, his father's journal entry weighing heavily on his thoughts. The familiar path to the studio beckoned him, the same path he'd walked countless times as a boy, usually with reluctance and fear. Now, with everything he'd learned in Jerusalem still fresh in his mind, each step felt purposeful. The worn stones welcomed him home, warm beneath his step, as he crossed the sun-warmed courtyard, the fading glow of dusk casting a soft light.

Pushing open the wooden door, he was enveloped by the studio's unchanging scents, clay dust, glaze minerals, ash from the kiln, and the faint mustiness of damp earth. Dust motes swirled in the fading afternoon light, filtering through the small window and casting a golden glow over the pottery wheel at the center of the room. Time hung in the space, waiting for him to step in and close a long-unfinished circle. His father's last message waited beneath that pottery wheel, and Jonathan finally felt ready to receive it.

Jonathan carefully lifted the stone wheel, his father's legacy, and placed it on the worktable his father had used. The weight felt familiar in his hands, dense yet balanced, like a well-crafted bow stave before the first cut reveals its potential. He ran his fingers along its edge, feeling the tiny abrasions where countless clay pieces had been shaped.

Jonathan stared at the wheel, remembering how he had hated it with a vengeance growing up, seeing it as a competitor for his father's attention rather than an instrument of creation. After learning about his father's journey, which began with the wheel his father had inherited from his mother, Jonathan finally saw it for what it was, their family heirloom, as precious in its way as the finest yew he had ever shaped into a bow.

He promised himself he would treasure the wheel like his father did, recognizing now how it had quietly shaped him even as he resisted.

Everything in his journey - from Crete to Jerusalem, from confusion to understanding - had led to this moment. *What final message had his father left beneath this wheel that had shaped both their lives?*

He lifted the stone tile and found something wrapped in cloth inside the small hole beneath it.

He carefully unwrapped the cloth and saw the fourth pottery piece his father had finished. It was a clay figurine, something his father had never done before.

Two young boys walked side by side, arms entwined, one carrying a rope over his shoulder, with its weight tied to a stone wheel behind him. It was beautiful and poignant. Jonathan didn't need to open the letter bundled with the clay piece; he already knew who this was meant for.

Tears gathered, blurring his vision. His father perfectly captured the innocence, anticipation, sense of adventure, and bond of friendship he shared with his lifelong friend.

Their adventure led to him when he needed help the most.

He looked at the bottom of the statue. It read, "Treasure."

Jonathan finally let go of all the emotions he had been keeping so close to his chest and cried.

That night, Jonathan opened his father's journal to its final entry. It had been a month since he had arrived in Caesarea from Crete.

The truth he discovered in his search had shattered his old perceptions, just as surely as a potter breaks down clay to reshape it. Trust had built itself slowly, like his father carefully centering clay on the wheel. And now, transformation— the final firing that makes the clay permanent in its new form—had completed its work in him.

He was no longer the same person.

Like the clay figures of the two boys frozen in eternal friendship, he had been permanently transformed by his father's story, a potter's story. From the first piece about truth in Capernaum, to trust safeguarded in Cana, to the transformation his father underwent in Jerusalem, and finally to this fourth piece about treasure, here in Caesarea, his father's journey has become his own.

His father and Dan did not pursue wealth when they left Capernaum. They found purpose... or was it the other way around, that purpose found them? What they already had was of greater value, and it sustained them throughout their journey.

His father shaped his story through clay, turning the wheel Jonathan once resented into the very thing that reshaped him.

Jonathan had been transformed. Fired in the kiln of experience, glazed with understanding, made whole in ways his father must have prayed for every day.

The fourth piece wasn't merely about treasure; it was about understanding what was truly priceless.

Purpose.

Later that night, as the household settled into sleep around him, Jonathan stood in the courtyard, the figurine of the two boys cradled in his hands. Above him, the same stars that had witnessed his father and Dan's journey from Capernaum now looked down on him, their light a reminder of constancy amid change.

Tomorrow would bring decisions about Barnabas's invitation and his path forward.

But tonight, with the fourth piece, treasure, still warming his palm, Jonathan felt a certainty he had never known before.

Whatever choice he made, he would no longer be running from his past or chasing an elusive future. For the first time, he stood fully in the present, grateful for every step of the journey that had brought him here, each misstep, each discovery, each loss, and each gift.

All of it would lead to his purpose, whatever that might be.

23

JOURNAL ENTRY 5

PURPOSE

My son,

The clay clings more stubbornly now. It finds the cracks in my skin, settles deep into my joints, grinding against the aches that come with changing weather. Perhaps it knows these are my final pieces, the last moments I have to shape something meaningful for you.

As I write this, the evening light spills through the studio window, catching dust motes that never settle. The wheel stands silent, but even in stillness, it calls to me. The scent of damp clay and wood ash lingers, as familiar as my own breath.

Dan tells me to rest more. But there is still so much I need to say.

I have spent my life learning the secrets of clay.

I learned how it resists the wheel at first but yields when properly centered. I learned how it needs both strength and gentleness to take shape, how the slightest pressure can either form or destroy it. I learned how fire transforms it, how glazes melt and settle, revealing colors hidden within.

Only now do I see that the clay has taught me about life. About you. About us.

You will return to Caesarea when you are ready. I accept that I may not be here to see it. But I have learned that absence does not mean an end; the space between hands and clay is necessary for creation.

I know you will grow into a man any father would be proud to have, not because of your skills, but because of the heart that guides them.

I tried to give you everything I thought you needed. I focused on being a provider when you needed a father. I measured success by the number of coins gained, the number of vessels crafted, and the status of those who purchased them. I see that now. It's like a flaw in the clay, spotted too late to correct. A wisdom learned after the wheel had stopped turning.

Son, I was fortunate to learn this truth before it was too late. Passion alone is like raw clay—malleable, full of promise, yet without shape. Potential is nothing unless it is guided, molded, and given direction. Only then does it become something significant.

Only then does it find its purpose.

Your passion will lead you to success. But purpose? Purpose will lead you to joy.

They are not the same. But when they work together, like clay and water, one giving substance, the other giving flow, they create something lasting.

You will know purpose has found you when you look back and see that every mistake, triumph, and lesson has prepared you for what lies ahead.

Like a potter preparing clay, each step is necessary for what it will become. If you are fortunate enough to have passion and purpose merge, like a vessel emerging exactly as envisioned, consider it grace.

I found grace in being your father.

But I realized it later than I should have.

We are artisans. We have an undeniable need to create something from nothing. Some of us, like me, fail to see that every vessel we shape is a prayer, a quiet praise for the One who gave us the ability to create.

The Lord taught me this, though I met him only a handful of times. He saw value in vessels others would discard and in people others would overlook.

I wish I had understood sooner that the same was true of fatherhood.

Being your father was not about shaping you to my design but about recognizing the form already waiting within you.

I leave these pages blank for you, my son. Untouched, like fresh clay waiting for its shape.

My hand has done its work. Imperfect as it may be.

It is time for you to write your own story.

To discover what the Master Potter has seen in you since the beginning.

I know it will be beautiful.

Your father, Amos

The Last Fish Sigil of Amos

Marked at the end of his journal entry.
His final sign.

24

BEGINNINGS

DAN WAS SITTING IN HIS FAVORITE SPOT IN THE COURTYARD, SMILING and sipping something hot from his cup. The morning sun dappled through the olive branches above, casting shifting patterns across the worn stone bench where he sat. The air carried the earthy scent of steeping herbs and the tender sweetness of new blossoms, while the distant cries of market vendors drifted over the courtyard walls.

"You're smiling, Dan! Please share!" Jonathan said, giving Dan a loving pat and sitting opposite him.

"A trader was able to secure something I've been looking for over the last several weeks," Dan said. "The trader came while we were in Jerusalem, and Jacob received and kept the item."

"What is it?" Jonathan asked.

"Take a look," Dan said, handing Jonathan a bag. Jonathan opened the bag, his eyes widening in surprise. He took the item from the bag and marveled at it with the wonder of a child who had just received a new toy.

"An antelope horn!" Jonathan exclaimed.

"I knew you'd like to have one, as I have heard about the wonders it can do for composite bows, the kind you make, right? Does it truly add strength and flexibility to the bow?" Dan asked like a young apprentice open to learning something new.

"Oh, Dan, yes! It does! Horns are naturally elastic. They can bend and return to their original size without breaking. Andreas taught us to use the antelope horn in the belly of the bow, where it could provide the most benefit. The horn helps the bow withstand significant compression when the bowstring is drawn. The greater the compression the bow can handle, the more powerful the draw becomes," Jonathan explained enthusiastically.

"Can any type of horn achieve the same effect?" Dan asked.

"Other animal horns, like those from deer, could be used," Jonathan replied. "But the results wouldn't be as excellent or deadly as with antelope horns."

"So, the ability to bend and accept… what do you call it… Compression… also translates to strength?" Dan pondered.

Jonathan nodded. *"The greater the ability to bend, the greater the strength,"* Jonathan added.

"That's an interesting point," Dan said, his eyes closing in that familiar way Jonathan remembered from childhood lessons. "So many believe strength is the ability to withstand pressure without changing. I never knew it could also mean absorbing it and, in the process, converting it to power." His voice softened to the tone he always used when sharing wisdom rather than mere information. His voice became almost inaudible, like a very soft whisper.

That may be why the meek will inherit the earth. Not the brittle who break, nor the rigid who refuse to bend, but those who can yield without losing their essence. Dan pondered quietly.

"This must have cost you a fortune!" Jonathan said.

"The trader was more than willing to exchange the horn for a small pottery piece made by your father," Dan replied, looking at Jonathan. "We still have some left. It's your father who bought the horn for you, Jonathan. I was just the one who made the exchange on behalf of your father," Dan explained. "You like the horn, right?" Dan asked.

"I love it!" Jonathan answered, clutching the antelope horn. "Thank you so much for this!" Then, remembering his gift to share, he added, "Father prepared not only one but two gifts today. He asked me to give these to you."

Jonathan gave Dan the fourth piece of pottery he had unearthed under the pottery wheel the night before.

Dan stared at the cloth-wrapped item Jonathan had placed before him; his eyes were welling up with tears, and his expression was one of visible surprise.

"How did..."

"Father wrote about it in his journal. He said that if he could finish a fourth piece after truth, trust, and transformation, it would be hidden underneath the pottery wheel. When we arrived from Jerusalem last night, I checked if he had finished his fourth piece before I went to bed. He did.

"Go ahead, Dan. Unwrap it!" Jonathan prodded Dan.

Dan reached out and removed the cloth wrapped around the piece. He saw the last clay work his best friend made before he died, a figurine of two young boys walking arm in arm, with one boy holding a rope tied to a pottery wheel slung across his back.

Dan was speechless as he lovingly traced his old fingers over the piece... wondering how his friend had found the time to do such detailed, beautiful work. He thought it must have taken Amos weeks to finish. And Amos worked on it so discreetly that he never noticed anything unusual!

Dan turned the piece slowly, his fingers trembling as they traced the familiar craftsmanship, the care, the quiet devotion. At the bottom, he saw it, the Aramaic letters, Amos's final word: Treasure.

Then he saw the tiny note in Amos's handwriting.

Dan opened the note, read what was written inside, folded it, and began to sob.

Jonathan stood up, wrapped his arms around his surrogate father, and hugged him tightly.

My dearest friend, we embarked on an adventure in pursuit of glory and wealth, unaware that I was already cherished and embraced for who I am, and that I possessed something of far greater value than what I sought, your friendship.

We had quite a journey. Thank you for everything. - Amos

Treasure

It showed two young boys walking side by side, arm in arm, with one boy visibly holding a rope slung over his shoulder. The rope was tied to a stone wheel behind his back.

As Jonathan left Dan with the figurine, his father's final gift, connecting their shared past, he felt a clarity that had eluded him since his return to Caesarea. One path forward seemed suddenly blindingly clear. He wouldn't pursue commissions from Janus, despite the prestige and security they would bring. Some journeys, no matter how promising, needed to wait until their time was right.

The decision settled in him like a weight had been lifted.

Jonathan went to the *Praefectus Castrorum's* office later that afternoon. It was fortunate that Janus was in his office and could spare a few minutes for Jonathan, despite having dropped by without notice.

Jonathan was ushered into Janus's office and waited for the *Praefectus*, who was in another room speaking to another person.

Jonathan stared at the large map hanging on the wall, its parchment surface yellowed at the edges from exposure to light. The room itself was austere yet imposing, with bare stone floors partially covered by a richly colored Parthian carpet, and walls adorned only with military standards and campaign maps. The subtle scent of oiled leather and parchment hung in the air, overlaid with the faint aroma of the ink used to mark troop movements across provinces.

He could identify Judea and Galilee, see the regions of Galatia and Asia, and see the islands of Cyprus and Crete. Tiny red wax markers indicated land and sea transport routes, the vast network of Roman power spreading like veins across the known world.

"Hello, Jonathan," Janus greeted.

Jonathan rose from his seat and replied with a nod, "*Praefectus.*" He remained standing.

"Thank you so much for agreeing to see me on such short notice," Jonathan continued. "My apologies for stopping by unannounced."

"It's all right, Jonathan. I have been looking forward to seeing you again. What can I do for you?" Janus asked.

"*Praefectus,* I am not ready to be a supplier of bows for the Caesarea garrison, and neither am I prepared to accept any bow-making commissions at this time. My father's death has changed the plans I made in Crete. I need more time to reflect on the best way to begin that will bring honor to my father's legacy."

"When you finally decide on the path you wish to pursue, would you let me know?" Janus asked.

"Yes, *Praefectus.* I will. You will be one of the first to know," Jonathan assured the Roman official. "I would also like to inform you that your slave has once again saved my life when we met in Jerusalem."

"He what?" Janus exclaimed, surprised at what Jonathan had just said. "He hadn't told me about this."

"He covered me with his own body when I got caught in a melee between local protesters and a group of soldiers. We were both seriously hurt, but he managed to get me out of the crowd to safety," Jonathan explained.

"Samir is a good man," Janus said, deep in thought.

"He is *Praefectus.* I doubt I would even be alive without his help," Jonathan added.

"Thank you for telling me this. I will see to it that Samir is adequately rewarded for his efforts," Janus said, his mind already assessing possibilities. *A man who risks himself for others demonstrates qualities Rome values.* "I just sent him to Tiberias, along with several soldiers, yesterday. Two horses have been injured and require urgent care. Samir's reputation extends beyond this garrison. He is becoming increasingly sought after for his expertise on animals under duress. I instructed him to remain there until the two horses are well. That will take two weeks or more."

Jonathan nodded. "I am sure he will continue to make you proud, *Praefectus*. Please tell Samir how grateful I am. Thank you for your time and generosity." Janus nodded at Jonathan, then excused himself and left the room.

Though disappointed at missing the chance to see Samir, Jonathan knew there would be other opportunities.

As he stepped out into the afternoon sun, the bustling streets of Caesarea beckoned, offering a different kind of comfort, the familiar rhythm of the city he now truly called home.

The afternoon stretched before him like an uncharted sea. From the antelope horn that morning to his father's final gift to Dan to this meeting that closed one possible future, each moment felt like another piece fitting into place. Yet, unlike the precise measurements of his bows or the careful shaping of clay, this pattern was still forming.

Stepping out of the cool shade of the official building into the warmth of the late midday sun, he was drawn again into Caesarea's vibrant life. The streets bustled with the sights and sounds of trade.

The sweet, buttery scent from a baker's stall made Jonathan pause. Memories rushed in. He remembered himself, Benjamin, and Caleb as three boys turning warm bread into a contest of laughter and rivalry. A smile played at his lips as he recalled those carefree moments, the lingering warmth of fresh pastries. But just as nostalgia took hold, his attention shifted to a small figure standing nearby, which pulled him back to the present.

A boy in tattered clothes stood pressed against the stall's wooden frame, his eyes fixed longingly on the golden-brown pastries. Without hesitation, Jonathan selected two pieces of freshly baked sweet bread and extended them toward the child. The boy's initial surprise melted into a shy smile as he accepted the unexpected gift. Then he darted away, clutching the treats like they might disappear.

As Jonathan handed a *shekel* to the vendor, whose knowing smile mirrored his own, Dan's earlier words about his father echoed in his mind. Now he understood why his father had died content, not because of the wealth he had amassed, but because of the generosity with which he had given it away. True riches, his father had found, were measured not in accumulation but in the act of giving.

In that moment, surrounded by the warmth of fresh bread and the lingering joy of anonymous kindness, Jonathan felt truly rich.

This simple act reminded him of the morning's gifts. Jonathan also considered this meeting with Janus as another gift, as it freed him from obligations that might have tied him to a path he wasn't ready to walk.

Drawn by the pull of the sea, where ships came and went like the tides of his journey, Jonathan found himself at the docks, his favorite part of the city and his preferred spot in any place he visited. He needed the sea's vast perspective, as he had so many times before.

Sitting on a bench weathered smooth by salt and countless travelers, he watched ships sailing into the distance. The familiar smells of salt, tar, and fish surrounded him, while the rhythmic slap of water against stone pilings created a meditative backdrop to his thoughts. Gulls wheeled overhead, their cries carried on the steady breeze that tousled his hair and cooled his face after the heat of the city streets.

To Jonathan, each departing ship carried a profound truth: every journey teaches, every challenge strengthens, and every ending births a new beginning. The wisdom gained from weathering one storm makes the next one less daunting. The key is living each moment fully aware that it shapes all that follows, welcoming the happiness that comes in its wake.

Since arriving in Judea, Jonathan had asked everyone he respected about happiness. Each person he asked offered wisdom about something that couldn't be grasped, only experienced.

Levi's words echoed clearest: "The key to finding happiness is not to seek it, but to welcome it." He had pointed to Jonathan's chest. *"The door that leads to happiness opens from the inside, Jonathan. Open the door!"*

Standing at the harbor's edge, Jonathan felt the weight of his transformation over the past month.

So much had changed within him, like clay reshaped on his father's wheel. His heart ached with the desire to share these changes with Amos, to tell him how each revelation and challenge had molded him into someone new, someone who finally understood the lessons he had tried to teach him all along.

Jonathan would have given anything to spend a few days with his father and learn as much as he could from him before he passed away.

Though he might be someone else's missing son, in his heart, Jonathan knew he would always be Amos's son. A potter's son.

Jonathan stared at a ship crossing the face of the setting sun, feeling the same peace that had found him in Jerusalem's chaos. Dan was right, peace wasn't the absence of conflict but the acceptance that everything followed a divine plan, even when that plan remained hidden from view. Like grain patterns in wood that only reveal themselves after proper sanding, or clay that requires fire to show its true colors, life's purpose often remains concealed until the right moment.

The connections were undeniable: He could have apprenticed anywhere, but landed in Crete with Andreas and Marcus, who knew Janus. Janus could have found his stallion's savior anywhere, but found Samir in the slave mines. Samir and Raqmu could have followed any wagon, but chose the one he was in. Amos could have left an orphan in an institution, but didn't. Each choice, each moment, had led to this.

It was as if an invisible hand had written Jonathan's story, timing everything precisely to reveal that there was no such thing as coincidence, but simply one divine plan.

The interconnected nature of his journey now seemed clear. Each decision created ripples that shaped everything that followed. While a divine plan existed, people remained free to choose, to do right or wrong, to forgive or seek vengeance, to love or withhold love. It wasn't fate alone, but a dance between divine purpose and human choice that had brought him to this moment.

Everything felt connected now: the pottery wheel that had once symbolized obligation, the bow that promised glory, and this moment of perfect uncertainty were all like patterns in wet clay waiting to take their final form.

There had to be a purpose behind it.

Jonathan wanted to know and live that purpose, the one for which all these people and circumstances had shaped him.

His father had discovered his purpose. Would he find out his?

His eyes brimmed as the realization settled deep within him. While his purpose remained unknown, he felt profound comfort in knowing that it would be revealed at the right time, not a day early or a day late.

Jonathan closed his eyes and heaved a deep sigh.

Would joining Barnabas in Antioch be the right choice? Jonathan wondered. *Or would reopening the pottery studio with Dan's guidance be the better choice? Should he pursue building his bow-making studio and becoming a master bowyer?*

Which option would bring honor to his father's legacy?

Which one would lead him closer to realizing his purpose?

Joseph had given him something to ponder when he asked for his opinion a few days before they left Jerusalem.

"Passion wants you to follow it, while purpose demands that you live by it. They're two different things, often calling in two different directions. We can only follow one and hope that somewhere down our chosen path, we also find the other waiting."

Joseph spoke with the quiet certainty of a man who had long lived this truth.

Purpose doesn't need to be found. The wise know they don't have to seek it but respond to it. They can wait and respond while tending to and growing their gifts.

It doesn't need to be found...

Like happiness, he just has to open the door.

As he turned from the harbor to head back home, Jonathan smiled. *It opens from the inside,* he said to himself, and his heart felt lighter than it had in years.

Home waited, not merely a place but the person - Dan, who would be there, ready to listen, to guide. The invitation to plant seeds in a distant land weighed on him. Barnabas's words still lingered in his thoughts.

Dan would help him decide and chart the path ahead, whatever it might hold.

25

TYCHE OF ANTIOCH

A cold wind swept across the deck, sending a tremor through the top of the bow strapped to Jonathan's back. He reached behind to unfasten the leather bindings, bringing the weapon forward to hold in his hands.

His bow felt lighter than before. His repairs had not only restored it but also enhanced it. He had carefully incorporated pieces of the antelope horn Dan had given him into the belly of the bow, strengthening its core. The tips now bore delicate horn inlays, each beautifully engraved with his father's new two-fish sigil, a tribute that connected his craft to Amos's legacy.

His father would have appreciated the craftsmanship. Jonathan traced the newly added two-fish sigil with his thumb with quiet reverence.

Another gust of wind threatened to unwrap the cloth around his neck. Jonathan braced the bow between his knees to free his hands, then tightened the fabric against the growing chill.

Jonathan vividly remembered the conversation he had with Dan about the cloth, the *sudra*.

Dan handed it to him the night they had both decided that Jonathan would accompany Barnabas to Antioch. Dan was initially having second thoughts about letting Jonathan leave barely a few weeks after he had arrived, but when he heard 'Antioch', Dan stood still and remained quiet for a while, which surprised Jonathan. Dan left the room and returned a few moments later with a *sudra*.

"This is yours," Dan said, his hands shaking as he handed Jonathan the cloth. "You were covered with this when Amos found you," Dan said. "Amos snatched it from the wagon to wrap you in as I pulled and pushed him to run."

Jonathan now examined the *sudra* more thoroughly and marveled at the fading woman embroidered on the cloth, wearing a crown that resembled the battlements of a tower. How odd and how beautiful at the same time. *Where could this possibly come from?*

"Antioch," Dan whispered as if hearing his thoughts. Jonathan was stunned.

"Your father was able to meet a merchant who traded in Syria a few months before he passed away. The merchant wanted to buy a small pottery piece for his wife. Amos saw the coin the merchant had accidentally dropped from his pocket while searching for something. Amos asked to examine the coin closely and inquired about its origin. The merchant answered, 'Syria.' That was when your father showed him the *sudra*, and the merchant confirmed that it was the Tyche of Antioch. It is even found in their coins," Dan added.

"Antioch," Jonathan whispered, surprised but not so surprised at the same time that events were leading him to where he should be next.

"When you told me about the invitation you received from Barnabas, my heart ached. It would be painful to see you go again, but I don't think your father would say no either if he heard 'Antioch.'

"You are called to go. I realize this now after much thought and prayer.

"I remembered keeping this safe. It is yours, Nathan. You have to take this *sudra* with you." Dan lightly touched his son's head as if giving him a blessing.

The touch was all it took for Jonathan to turn and tightly embrace the man who had loved him as his own the day his father found him, and would continue to do so long after his father was gone.

EVENTS UNFOLDED FASTER THAN JONATHAN'S HEART COULD MANAGE. He needed space, not just for the journey ahead, but for the one within.

Amusingly, the solace he once sought at the docks, he now also found in his father's pottery studio, the place he had avoided as a child. Yet here he was, stepping into the space where his father had found passion and purpose, seeking clarity amidst the chaos. In mere hours, he would be boarding a ship to Antioch, leaving behind the familiar in pursuit of something unknown.

Before the sun fully rose, before Dan or Jacob stirred, Jonathan sat in his father's chair, staring at his most treasured possession, the pottery wheel. It had been the center of his father's life story. Now, it was the center of his own.

Our story is written in clay, Jonathan mused. A slight smile briefly crossed his lips, contrasting sharply with his sad blue eyes.

His fingers gently traced the rough stone surface, trying to remember all the breathtaking clay pieces his father had created—not for fame or fortune, but for the kind of future his father wanted to secure for him. The same wheel, where the pieces of Truth, Trust, Transformation, and Treasure were shaped—pieces that now bound them together more tightly than ever.

He stood up and picked up the Truth box he had placed beside him to put on top of one of his father's shelves. *It should be here. It should never be separated from the wheel,* Jonathan told himself, so that he would never forget where and how their story began.

He and Dan ate breakfast in the courtyard while the light was not yet bright and the night had not entirely gone. *It's the story of my life, Jonathan said to himself. I am never anywhere but always somewhere in between, as if being prepared in a kiln fire for what lies ahead of me.*

Dan was quiet throughout breakfast, looking intently at him, as if imprinting his face on his memory. "I won't be long," Jonathan assured Dan in response to his unspoken questions. "I will just see how I can help Barnabas help the community, and I will be back even before you miss me." He smiled at his second father, who smiled meekly back.

"Amos and I always knew there was something special about you. This is why we did everything we could to help you be prepared for whatever might come. You will always have everything you need, Nathan. Trust. You believe this, right?" Dan asked.

Jonathan nodded and placed his hand on top of his father's hand to assure him that he would be back. Dan looked at Jonathan, tears brimming in his eyes.

~

THE SUN GAVE THE DOCKS A WONDERFUL GLOW, BATHING EVERYTHING in a soft golden sheen like his father's highly coveted pottery pieces. Jonathan smiled, thinking his father was giving him a great send-off, assuring him that everything would be all right.

A colder gust of wind blew once more, freeing some hair strands from his ponytail. The strands immediately covered his eyes. Jonathan swiped back the hair strands, then deftly pulled a leather string from his pocket and tied his long hair back into a ponytail in one sweeping motion.

Now, a month after returning to Caesarea, Jonathan once again stood on a ship's deck. But this time, he wasn't fleeing home; he was sailing toward what might be his purpose, or the path that would lead him there.

He gazed back at Caesarea's skyline, now illuminated with countless tiny flames as evening settled and the sun started its descent into the sea. The sky wore a tapestry of purple, orange, and yellow hues, the same beautiful canvas he had witnessed with Dan, Caleb, and Hannah when Benjamin married Priscilla just days before.

The wedding had been joyous, bringing their circle of friends together as Benjamin pledged himself to a woman who promised to cherish him through all seasons of life. Ezra had beamed with fatherly pride throughout the celebration.

Benjamin and Caleb wasted no time teasing him about his turn to marry coming next. This prompted Dan to look at Jonathan with a broad smile and eyes that seemed to ask if he was ready. Jonathan shook his head and said that the time would come when the moment was right.

For now, Jonathan needed to listen more carefully than ever before. He had heard his passion calling to him years ago and had followed that calling to Crete. Now, he waited to discern if purpose would reveal itself next. He had learned from his father's journal that passion and purpose might walk different paths, and he was prepared for that possibility.

Barnabas joined him at the railing as the ship pulled further from shore. The older man noticed the cloth around Jonathan's neck and studied it with evident surprise.

"That image..." Barnabas said, his voice taking on the warm, instructive tone he used when sharing something significant, "I've seen that same crowned head on the coins of Antioch. It's the Tyche of Antioch, the protective deity of the city we're sailing toward.

"I thought you had never been there!"

"I haven't," Jonathan replied with a smile, his fingers touching the embroidered figure.

"Then how do you come to have such a cloth?" Barnabas asked, curiosity brightening his eyes.

"It's a long story. I'll share it with you during our journey," Jonathan promised.

Such connections no longer surprised him: one truth leading naturally to another, one path unfolding into the next. The cloth that had once wrapped him as an infant now pointed toward his immediate future in Antioch. Jonathan had learned to trust these revelations, these signposts that appeared at precisely the right moment.

Jonathan watched as the ship ahead of them slipped beyond the edge of the world, swallowed not by oblivion but by distance. It had not vanished, only passed beyond sight.

He understood now: the journey was not meant to break him but to refine him. The fire that once seemed a force of ruin was, in truth, the kiln: a trial meant to reveal and strengthen his true form, to shape rather than consume.

The ship carved through the darkening waters, steady in its course. Jonathan closed his eyes, breathing deeply, understanding now what had always been whispered in the winds that carried him forward.

Not an ending.

Not an answer.

A promise: Trust.

26

AMOS

AMOS LOVINGLY WRAPPED HIS LAST CLAY PIECE IN A VIVID RED CLOTH. After weeks of covertly working in his studio, he had finally completed it, always cautious of Dan's presence. It reminded him of sneaking around as a boy in Capernaum.

Amos chuckled softly as he positioned the tile and carefully slid the pottery wheel back into place.

He knew Dan would be astonished and immediately wonder how he had crafted such a detailed piece without his knowledge. Amos stifled another laugh, picturing the expression on his friend's face when the clay piece was revealed.

Amos settled into his chair, the worn wood creaking beneath him like an old friend. He had finished all his plans, including the final entry in his journal. On those pages, he had documented everything Jonathan needed, all the details he had consciously withheld from his son.

His last entry had turned out to be the hardest; it was his farewell. Amos sighed, feeling the familiar tightness in his chest intensify.

Deep inside his heart, Amos hoped he would still be alive when Jonathan came home, that he might personally hand Dan the fourth clay piece he had just finished. But he couldn't gamble on hope alone.

The physician's words echoed in his mind: his heart was failing him. Amos couldn't afford to leave things to chance. He had to be ready if fate didn't align with his wishes. In his own words, he owed his son the truth, whatever comfort writing that truth might provide.

Amos closed his eyes and sighed again. It had been almost five years. He could imagine how Jonathan must have grown by now, taller, stronger, and his hands were likely calloused from working in whatever medium or trade he had chosen.

A tear rolled down his cheek, catching in the creases that time and worry had etched into his skin. He wiped it away with the back of his hand, feeling the rough texture of clay dust still embedded in his fingertips.

He missed his son with an ache that no amount of searching had eased, despite scouring Judea and Galilee, following every lead, and traveling at the mere mention of a sighting.

He had finally come to enjoy his journeys with Dan across Judea and Galilee; the open road that had once felt so foreign was now almost a comfort. His body, however, had begun to rebel against each trip. While his backaches had gradually disappeared, they were quickly replaced by unfamiliar chest pains that stole his breath when he climbed hills or walked too quickly.

After a discreet visit to a physician in Ramah, he had learned the truth that his body had been trying to tell him: his heart wasn't as strong as it should be. The chest pains, shortness of breath, and diminishing strength for his usual activities were all silent harbingers of limited time.

He had kept this knowledge from Dan, who was fighting a different battle with illness. Dan had been steadily losing weight, though he tried to hide it with looser tunics and excuses about the heat.

They couldn't both be sick; Jonathan would need someone to welcome him home, to stand beside him as he confronted the darkest truths about his past.

One of them must be home when Jonathan returns. The thought that his son might come home to an empty house had kept Amos awake many nights, staring at the shadows on his ceiling.

Today, he had finally completed everything for Jonathan and Dan. All preparations were in place, even if his heart failed to beat until his son's return. Amos heaved a deep sigh and closed his eyes, his hand unconsciously moving to his chest.

He would give everything to be able to embrace Jonathan one more time. Everything.

"Amos?" Dan called as he stepped inside the studio.

"I'm here," Amos answered even before he opened his eyes.

"Would you like to join me in the courtyard for warm bread and a refreshing drink?" Dan invited.

"I'd love to, my friend," Amos replied.

"What have you been doing here? You've been quiet for several hours, and I haven't heard the wheel spinning," Dan asked.

"I just wrote the last entry in my journal for Jonathan," Amos murmured, his voice heavy with emotion.

"The *last?*" Dan asked, unsure he had heard it correctly.

"Yes, the last," Amos responded. "It's done," he added.

Dan smiled and nodded at his old friend. He understood the immense courage it took for Amos to write everything down for Jonathan, to lay bare his thoughts with unwavering honesty. "I'm certain Jonathan will cherish and value what you have to say," Dan replied softly.

"*Would he?*" Amos asked. "Or would he *hate* me for not telling him sooner?"

"Amos, we never taught Jonathan to hate," Dan responded quietly, feeling a familiar deep ache in his chest. "You and I both know we raised him well. I truly believe he has grown into a fine young man who thinks independently and understands that we have always had his best interests at heart."

Amos nodded in agreement.

"Now, the delicious bread Jacob prepared will soon get cold. You'd better get off that chair and join me in the courtyard, or I'll eat all the warm bread myself!" Dan laughed.

"I will follow in a little while, Dan," Amos said.

"Don't take too long, or I swear you'll have no bread!" Dan laughed as he walked out of the studio.

Amos smiled, imagining Dan trying to eat everything by himself, and chuckled.

Suddenly, an overwhelming weariness washed over him. Was it because he had finally completed everything as planned?

He exhaled slowly, feeling the effort it required.

He would join Dan soon. The warm bread did sound tempting. He just needed to rest for a moment, just a few minutes more, he told himself.

Is this what it feels like when the clay knows it's ready for the kiln?

A faint smile touched his lips at the thought. He drew another breath, feeling how deeply it had to reach.

Amos closed his eyes, the breath within him settling, slowing, becoming still. His hands met, callused fingers pressing together, clay forever etched into his skin. The weight of years, of love, of quiet work, rested in his chest. He bowed his head.

"It's finished," he whispered.

And in that quiet surrender, in one single deep breath,

Amos let go.

And started his next journey...

Home.

ABOUT THE AUTHOR

In Isoebella's world of stories, science fiction and fantasy illuminate paths to the extraordinary, while the Bible and historical tales of faith and hope lay the foundation of her spiritual journey.

When she isn't lost in a good book, Isoebella finds joy in creating with her hands, transforming simple materials into meaningful pieces. This love for handmade art naturally wove itself into The Potter's Story, where the act of creation becomes a gateway to grace.

For those who know her, it comes as no surprise that she chose to write Biblical historical fiction. The Potter's Story lived in her imagination for years, embodying everything she loved: craft, history, and faith. *"Purpose kept calling, and I kept failing to respond."* These words haunted her for seven years before she finally gave them to Amos in the story. His confession became her truth, too, purpose patiently knocking while she pretended not to be home.

At sixty, Isoebella finally answered that persistent call.

A graduate of English Literature, Isoebella lives with her husband and their two adopted companions, a stray dog and a stray cat who taught her that, like Jonathan in The Potter's Story, sometimes the best families are the ones we find along the way.

facebook.com/thepottersstory
instagram.com/isoebella

PRODUCTION NOTES

TOOLS OF THE CRAFT

This work emerged through a harmonious blend of traditional research, digital innovation, and the gracious collaboration of friends, beta readers, and ARC reviewers. Each one paused their demanding lives to help shepherd this story into your hands. In a world that rushes at the speed of light, time is a sacred offering. Those who gifted theirs have my deepest gratitude.

Cover Note. The cover is an original composition designed to reflect both the intimate heart of the story and the broader journey it represents. One visual element, the two traveling youths with their infant companion, was generated using AI-assisted tools, then meticulously refined and integrated into the final design. All remaining components, from layout and textures to symbolic overlays, were thoughtfully crafted by the author.

Judea-Galilee Map. The map featured in this book was conceived and designed by the author. It draws upon extensive research into first-century Judea and the intricate Roman trade networks that once linked its cities. While fictionalized, the geography honors a commitment to historical authenticity and cultural reverence.

Fonts and Licensing Note. Each typeface was selected for its aesthetic alignment and full commercial licensing, ensuring both beauty and integrity are upheld in equal measure.

Interior Images. The interior visuals, from character portraits to the rendered vessels shaped by Amos's hands, were created using AI-assisted tools to deepen the emotional and spiritual resonance of the story. For the printed edition, these images were digitally traced and graphically rendered by the author to meet the book's black-and-white printing requirements.

Every vessel, every brushstroke, every worn footpath within these pages was formed in service of the story's sacred purpose: to illuminate truth, to inspire the courage to trust the Divine, and to witness transformation unfold for His glory.

Truth. Trust. Transformation.

May you find and live your purpose.

Thank you for receiving this work with open hearts.

Isoebella

Made in the USA
Las Vegas, NV
04 September 2025

27370824R00163